SHORTS

Shorts

The Macallan/ Scotland on Sunday Short Story Collection

Selected by Robert Alan Jamieson

Polygon
Edinburgh

© The Contributors, 1998

Polygon
22 George Square, Edinburgh

Typeset in Galliard by Hewer Text Ltd, Edinburgh,
and printed and bound in Great Britain by
Caledonian International Ltd, Glasgow

A CIP record for this book is
available from the British Library

ISBN 0 7486 6245 6

The Publisher acknowledges subsidy from

THE SCOTTISH ARTS COUNCIL

towards the publication of this volume.

CONTENTS

Contents

FOREWORD

The 29 stories gathered in this collection have one thing in common: they were all submitted as entries to *The Macallan/Scotland on Sunday Short Story Competition* of 1998, along with over 2000 others. The success of 'The Macallan' can be measured by the ever increasing number of stories received. In the year of its inception – 1991 – there were over 700, and that seemed a lot then. But it has changed in another important way. In 1991 only the winner received a prize, albeit a big one. This year, besides runners-up prizes, 29 writers have the reward of inclusion in this volume for the first time, through a selection process conducted separately from the work of the competition judges – though all of the short-listed six were already posted for inclusion before that short-list was decided.

The task of selecting '20 or so' from '2000 or so' – roughly one in a hundred – was obviously daunting. Ultimately, no matter how objective we think we are, we bring 'our selves' to the reading of a story, as was surely reflected in the selection of the short-list, when five judges were each asked to nominate their top six stories – 20 different stories were mentioned in these dispatches, which must indicate the general quality of entry as well as personal preference. In justification of the contents, all that can be said is that those published seemed to shine out more strongly than others. They seemed to succeed on their own chosen terms, to intrigue, or amuse, or charm, or shock, in ways that seemed integral to the narrative, 'built-in' so to speak, rather than 'built-on'.

What is most striking about these stories is the sheer variety. From the burlesque of futuristic birth which is Jules Horne's 'agnus dei' to the mordant satire on Auld Scotia that is Jackie Kay's 'The Oldest Woman in Scotland', there is a broad range of theme, location and style which transcends the parameters of any literary competition. Despite the requirement that stories be less than 3000 words long, these 'shorts' suggest that common restriction has necessitated even greater invention and originality, with the consequence that it is impossible to be sweeping in any analysis.

There are stories which seem to depend more on a single incident, like Jacqueline Ley's 'Travelling to Gretna' or David Nicol's 'Leading Out'; others, such as Tom Bryan's 'Teething Pains' or Gordon Legge's 'About Perfection', rely more on character studied over time. Some, like Ruth Thomas' 'Cave Paintings', Lydia Robb's 'Spirits' or Morag MacInnes' 'The Brown Jug', evoke dislocation into other geographies and/or histories; others, like Mark Fleming's 'Snowmen' with its trippy Embra street-slang or Linda Cracknell's 'Life Drawing' with female narrator reclaiming her body-image, seem unmistakably here and now.

In certain stories, like Andrew Byrd's prose-poem 'Ishmael', the language and the ciphers of literature are brought to the forefront; others, such as Elizabeth Reeder's 'Crosswords' or Michel Faber's 'The Eyes of the Soul', use language more as a transparent medium for persuasive ideas about the relationships between people and their world. Some, like Alexander McCall Smith's 'Marriage' or Bill Duncan's 'Boys, Girls, Games', pack in enough material to furnish a goodly-sized novella; others, such as Kathryn Heyman's 'No Name' with its dynamic punch-line projection from girl to doll, are 'short short stories', more anecdotal in essence, but none the less resonant for that. In some it is a particular device that is memorable, as with the dice-game in Morgan Downie's 'The War'; in Alison MacLeod's 'Make Thick My Blood', the overall mood is so powerful that it lingers in the mind long after reading, despite the brevity of the narrative.

The contrasts continue: Cynthia Rogerson's gentle tale of unexpected conception, 'To Begin', and Frank Kuppner's droll dialogue on the supernatural, 'The Warning', both document the lead-up to a moment of realisation; Raymond Soltysek's 'The Practicality of Magnolia' and Dilys Rose's 'The Dead Woman and The Lover' begin from the cold fact of knowledge and show its effect through subtle dénouement. Alison Grove's tale of entrapment 'Accomplice' and Fiona MacInnes' brutal 'Outsiders' have that all too terrifying touch of everyday truth; Ron Butlin's 'What Colours Mean', Brian McCabe's 'An Invisible Man' and Regi Claire's 'In Memoriam' all tilt reality slightly before dramatising the psyche undone by suppressed emotion, while the surreal 'Like It's Never Been Told This Way Before' by John Pacione quite literally 'brings home' the whole horror of war as it impacts upon a single disturbed – and disturbing – family.

But as you'll realise when you've read the book, these contrasts only serve to show that every single contribution resists any simple catch-phrase description. There is no argument to this collection, other than unity-in-diversity – what you have is a subjective selection of 29 stories from over 2000, ranging 'Dubliners-fashion' from birth through childhood into adolescence, travel, work and play, documenting adult relationships and loss, ending with old age and death – or in the case of Scotland's 'oldest woman', the refusal to countenance mortality, even if it means rattling about like the only shortbread left in the tin.

Foreword

The Scottish tradition in the short story is a long one, far too extensive to summarise briefly. In recent years it has been particularly vibrant, partly thanks to the work of some who have contributed to this volume; but there are just as many writers included whose names are not yet known. If it is true that Scottish writing has never been more widely read than at present, maybe it is a fair proposition, based on the evidence of all these stories, that its popularity isn't due to any one dominant school but to the fact that so many people are writing about so many different things, in so many different voices. With such variety and skill around, the 'tradition' seems sure to grow, for in each of these assorted tales there's something remarkable to admire, to savour – a spirited collection of 'Macallan shorts'.

Robert Alan Jamieson

AGNUS DEI

JULES HORNE

When I was born, the moon sat high and full over the Cheviots, and the clouds slid apart for Aries to preside as I landed bloodily in the wet grass. That was not an honour accorded my twin, who I'm told was last seen stripped of skin and eyeless in the window of a shop in Melrose. Poor lamb.

It's like this. There's Fate. And there's Destiny. Though to the unfussy mind they mean much the same thing, there's a universe of difference between them. Somewhere between the infinite expansion of the galaxy and the infinite division of sub-atoms, a butterfly stamps its foot, a crow splats the pavement, a sticky willy hitches a lift on a cardigan – and the course of history changes forever.

For example: the crow splats the passing eye of Mr Wright, and as he's cursing the gods and smearing blindly with his Kleenex, Miss Wright walks past unnoticed and bumps three days later into Mr Wrong. Up in the gods, they're rewriting the timetables, issuing corrections. 'Wrong sort of butterfly, crow-splats on the line,' they announce, apologetically. 'Fate,' muses Mr Wright, years later, as he rolls dejectedly off his own unresponsive Miss Wrong.

My sister had a Fate. Dead, curt, cold, brutally monosyllabic and spitting with plosive finality. Whereas I was to have a Destiny. A dactyl, a saraband. Meaningful, wonderful, spiritual

1

and steeped in Romance. Why? Search me. Though – god knows – they've already searched through all my cunt and cavities, with all the blunt depravities they could dream of for my woolly self.

Now, my childhood was ordinary enough. The first few months were happy, and my sister and I would try out our twig-thin legs on the humps and hillocks of the farm. We were free as birds and bees then, and our mother stood near, cropping tufts of clover, her udder swinging full with the milk we grew fat on.

We were three months old when we found out about the Big End. Parental opinion is divided on this – to know or not to know? – but my mother believed that knowledge was power, and she was determined that when we stood in the killing pens we would be stunned by the guns and not by the sudden existential angst that this was it and it was all too late.

'One day they'll come', she said, 'and they'll pick you out. Sheep, goats. Goats, sheep. I can never work out how they decide. And they'll shove you into lorries, and bang the door – just pray you're not for export. It's pretty foul in there – you can't count on everyone to be calm in a crisis.'

'What happens?' we asked, shivering deliciously, not believing a word.

'Blood,' she said. 'The great pie in the sky. Hung, drawn, quartered, filleted, skilleted, minced, braised and minted. Messy.'

We shuddered, and huddled into her flank for the night. In the morning she was hard and cold, and ice furred the corners of her eyes. So she never knew what happened to her twin daughters, or that the prophesy was fulfilled.

Back to the lab and the future: there were twenty-nine identical eggs, ready for posting into the moist folds of our twenty-nine Blackface slots. Along with the others, my sister and I presented our twin cracks to the scientist, who with shaky gloved hands prised first her and then my lips open and inserted (a) Fate and (b) Destiny. Because as he prodded towards her uterus, down at his leather-patched elbow, down under the white coat on the fuzz of his Pringle's cardi, the tiny hook of a stray sticky willy caught the fibre of another, long-dead sheep and infinitessimally nudged his hand a fraction to the left. The egg bounced on the sponge of her womb and landed on the scar tissue of a previous miscarriage, where it died a few minutes later. But when he rammed my own damp depths, the metal syringe deposited the egg smoothly in a hollow, where it thrived and multiplied.

She – mince. Me – the virgin mother of the lamb of god.

What the scientist didn't know was that, far from being a father, a creator, a god in his own small white-tiled universe, he was in fact a puppet, pulled by the very same strings that made the crow shite in full flight into his myopic eye. But then, he wasn't there at the Annunciation.

Oh yes – I knew my destiny long before the holy lambkin was even a twinkle in the scientist's eye. I was told. I wasn't asked, mind. I might as well have had a label on my slit – 'insert here'. Insert daughter. You'd think that, being a scientist, he'd know his Latin. The very root of surrogacy is the word 'to ask'.

One night the farmer had hung chains of lanterns around the windows, and the house shook with music and laughter and the throb of arriving cars. The dog was in the house that night, curled beside a dead tree heavy with stars.

It may have been the music. It may have been the warm stench of roasted hen-flesh that crept out of the porch and into our nostrils. But something was in the wintry air that night and my mother couldn't sleep.

'Come on,' she said, briskly nudging us awake. 'We're going for a walk.' We squeezed out of the pen, leaving lumps of wool on the wire, and followed her up the hill.

There are places all the darker for the nearness of the light. All around was deep ditch-black, and as we climbed, we saw the sky grow acid from the glow of the town far beyond the rise.

When we were younger, we often wondered at the strange behaviour of stars. They would appear suddenly in the distance, and move smoothly down a hill, vanish into its side and burst out somewhere else entirely. As they grew closer they would split into twins. Then we'd hear the growing burr of an engine, and a Ford Escort would speed past at the foot of the brae.

Here, at the top of the hill, overlooking the distant farmhouse, we saw a new star. This one appeared in the usual way, growing larger and brighter until we had to turn away. But this time there was no discernible engine. And no twin. And it seemed to be right beside us. Star-shadows stretched along the ground behind us, tying dark giants to our feet. And down below, like coughs of smoke from a chimney, the rest of the flock were climbing up towards us, in single file, picked out by the blinkless brilliance of the angel. For angel it was. And it spoke.

'Be not afraid!'

I ask you. The message was so at odds with the thundering messenger that we paid little attention. Our legs quavered moistly as our terror plopped to the grass.

'I bring you good tidings of great joy!' it said. Silence. Who were we to argue? We waited.

'Unto you a child is born. But the child shall know no father nor mother, for its father shall be God.'

The word rang out across the valley, tattering in the wind. Still we waited. The angel seemed frustrated at the lack of feedback, and sent a flourish of lightning down towards the farmhouse. We murmured appreciatively. And waited.

'That's it,' said the angel. 'Show's over. Must dash.'

'Wait!' came the shout from behind – my mother, ever practical. 'To whom are you speaking?' she asked, judging that formal speech was best for this type of occasion. My sister and I stood at the front, trembling equally in the angel glare, identical, indistinguishable, unmarked lambs for Fate to doom and Destiny to groom however they chose.

Sadly for my sister and her casseroled future, a butterfly stamped its foot. It happened two years ago, in the suburbs of Tashkent, where the sun hammered down on a dusty market. It didn't make much impact at the time, but it set off a chain reaction in the swirls and eddies of the planetary winds which, by the time it reached the Cheviots, was enough to flick a mote of grit into my right eye. I blinked, momentarily distracted, twitched a leg, skidded in the soft droppings at my feet and slid spectacularly towards the booming light.

'Behold,' said the angel. 'The favoured one.'

And so it came to pass.

My daughter slithers from my sticky tube to a hail of flashing bulbs. I beam with surrogate parental pride at the lamb of god, blinking my blood from her eyes. Born of no father, born of no mother, despite her rent-free tenancy of my womb. She looks nothing like me, with her mild white face. So who does she look like? Not like her father or mother – for she has neither, poor lamb.

No, she looks like herself. In fact, she is herself. She is exactly the same Finn Dorset ewe that was born six years ago, now born again, risen from the dead, revived from one tit-cell taken from a laboratory fridge. The same ewe eaten by Mr Wright, the scientist, at a barbecue in 1993, where a burr hitched a lift on his cardi and a crow laid a clutch of freckled eggs.

Hello, Dolly. Nice to have you back.

NO NAME

KATHRYN HEYMAN

S helly is sitting in the brown and squeaky chair. She looks
at her hands. Just dumb, that's all. Stupid and ugly and
dumb. There is a brown-orange desk that the white-coat man
sits behind, pointing to lines on paper. He is the same white-
coat man who made Shelly look at the pictures on the wall and
tell what she saw. And now, because she got the pictures
wrong, Daddy has to go away, and she has to go with the
white-coat to another big cold room. Daddy kneels down and
puts his arms around her shoulders: 'Just for two days, hey
Flower?' Shelly looks down at the new shoes which used to be
new sister Lisa's and nods dumbly. Just dumb, that's all.
Stupid and ugly and dumb. The new room is better. Bigger,
and full of high shiny beds. As big shiny exciting as the double
bunks in what used to be the boys' room. Then there is that
bubble inside again, the same one as before, when they said
Mummy and the boys had to go away. Shelly closes her eyes
and tries to pop the stupid bubble.

And then there is a Nurse Green, who comes to take Shelly
to a soft blue room where toys and television and tumbling
faces blur. Shelly's eyes are wide on the Nurse Green – neat
and beautiful with a brown movie-star bun in her hair, and
softwarm hands. Even though it is four o'clock, Shelly is not
allowed to watch *Blue Peter*. They say, because of her eyes.

See, tomorrow, Shelly will have a long long sleep and when she wakes up her eyes will look straight ahead like new sister Lisa's and nobody will call her Clarence the cross-eyed lion any more, and she will smash the thick ugly glasses. And then she will be beautiful. All the people will look right at her, right at her face and go 'Oh, Shelly is so beautiful and smart, isn't she?' and Shelly will just smile and not even talk or play with them. She will just say 'thank you very much, how kind' like a grown-up.

Anyway, Daddy is coming tonight, and Shelly is having ice-cream for dinner. For dinner, not sweets. Green milk for sweets.

After the toy room, a new Nurse Green comes. This Nurse Green is the same, except her movie-star hair-bun is golden golden blonde, and her hands are cold. Her voice is like the click-click of Auntie Jacquie's heels on the outside tiles at night. The new Nurse Green's voice is cold like her hands: 'Come along, time for pyjamas, then dinner and we'll have no noise until Visitors.'

Shelly looks up and tries to touch her hand: 'My Daddy's coming.'

There is no response, except the hands of this not-nice Nurse Green, pulling back the stiff white sheets.

'And I'm having ice-cream for tea. For proper tea. Green milk for sweets.'

'Get in.' The cold hands point to the bed and Shelly climbs up the little ladder to the cold sheets, and waits.

When Daddy comes, he's holding something behind his tall back. He sits on the little black chair beside the bed and brings the surprise out. 'Company. She was lonely.'

She is made of raffia and pink, with long plaited legs and a sparkling pink-gold-blue dress. Inside the raffia head is a white cork ball, Shelly can see it when she slides the raffia strands away. Daddy says 'What's her name then?' and Shelly holds her close, because she doesn't need a name. Daddy hugs her hard before he leaves, and there's a whisper in her ear: 'A special doll for my most special, only special girl'. Shelly hugs and hugs the no-name raffia doll all through the long blue night, watching shining trolleys playing catch with tumbling night lights. And tomorrow, Shelly will be beautiful.

The tomorrow white bed is different. Longer. Skinnier. Colder. Harder. Shelly has a wool blanket over her knees. There are three Nurse Greens in this room, and one of them doesn't even have a hair-bun. The white-coat man is different, and there is an astronaut machine that he is tapping and turning knobs on. The no-bun Nurse Green is a smile lady, saying 'Now then, down over your pretty nose, and let's see if you can count to ten like none of the boys can and be the best little girl.'

Shelly takes a deep deep breath, and she will be the best ever little girl, and all the Nurse Greens will say she is good, and she will be the only special one, and Daddy will, and Daddy will, something, she can't remember what.

There's a patch on her Clarence the Lion eye when she wakes back in the long and bed-filled room. The patch is blue, and Daddy is beside her, saying 'What a wonderful patch, just like Long John Silver.'

And then there is the bustling together of dressing gowns and nursery case and special hospital bag, and no-name raffia doll, and the holding tight to Daddy's hand – and out and out through doors and doors and doors. Shelly sucks her breath in and remembers 'I didn't say good-bye to the Nurse Green.' Daddy says he'll wait and Shelly runs back and back through doors and doors and doors with feet not stopping and head turning, looking, looking for the Nurse Green. Then into the soft blue toy room, and there is the other Nurse Green, the cold-hands, click-click voice Nurse Green. 'Run along now

Shelly, Daddy's waiting and it's time for you to go. Go on, shoo.'

Shelly rubs her nose and breathes a deep breath and stares at the Nurse Green's hairbun. She opens her mouth wide wide wide: 'I saw poobum written on a telegraph pole. In paint.' She sees the Nurse Green begin to wobble as she runs back and back to Daddy's waiting hand. And then they are suddenly in a big, square, echoing room, with stairs running around the walls. The stairs run in a square, so in a square they walk.

Daddy goes all puff-chested and clever on happy days. Today he says: 'I am so magic, I reckon if we walk this same square six times, hey presto! We'll be outside.' Shelly and Daddy are both giggling on the counting squares, then, hey presto! – they are outside in the cool and wind with cars parked along the street. Shelly is yelling at the street 'Hey presto! Hey prestofestobesto!' Her hand is pulled tight and Daddy stops her walking. He kneels down and puts his hands on her shoulder in the Mummy's-going-away way. 'Your Auntie Jacquie and your new sister are in the car love. They're happy as Larry to be having you home.'

Shelly looks down at Daddy's black shoes. Her throat is tight again like before, with the mumps. She nods at his feet, says 'Yes, Daddy.'

Shelly can see them both smiling in the car, as they walk along the little street. Both of them waving, and new sister Lisa jumping up and down in the back seat. No-name raffia doll is pink and warm and comforting in Shelly's hand. She is Shelly's own, only Shelly's, and no one else can share her. She is the special doll for the most special girl. She grips the no-name doll tighter in her hand, and the bubble begins to float away. When Daddy opens the scratched back door, she climbs in over the front seat and even kisses Auntie Jacquie. 'Hello Auntie Jacquie. I had ice-cream for dinner *and* lunch.'

There is a glint, a hint of blue calling the corner of Shelly's eye as she wriggles to her back seat. And then the bubble again – colder and larger and harder than before. There's an eye-patch blue no-name raffia doll snug in the arms of new sister Lisa. And Lisa, new sister Lisa, smiling with the special doll for the most special girl.

There is a loud silence all the long drive home with Lisa, dozing against the vinyl, her eye-patch no-name snug in her arms. And Shelly, tucked in the back car corner, poking finger holes in the white cork head of the stupid, dumb, plaited and ugly no-name raffia doll.

TEETHING PAINS

TOM BRYAN

I remember the Holy Water, the monkey and the jet beads. The Holy Water is gone and the monkey is dead but I have the beads.

Two blocks and seventy years separated us – down a cavern of tenements, up a short flight of steps from the pavement, then into a door peeling in great green blisters. I was sent to take messages to my great aunt: baking soda for cleaning Devlin's false teeth (her husband was always just *Devlin* – I never knew his Christian name), sugar for Devlin's tea, but best of all – spices for Devlin's curry, for there wasn't much curry being eaten in those days.

The door opened to a long dark hall, with several more doors, all green, all peeling like dead skin. There was a coat rack on the right and at the same height, an ornamental font of Holy Water. Next to the font was a plaster Holy Virgin. She was lime green. Hung on the coat rack was a green and white Hibs scarf which said CHAMPIONS 1902–1903.

Bella snorted: 'Devlin's scarf *nae* mine. Dinnae cross yerself. Ye're nae ane o *them*.' (I didn't yet know who *they* were.)

Bella, as big across as tall, face ruddy, huge forearms the colour of corned beef but the one thing you always noticed: her eyes, like deep dark sloes; eyes which somehow didn't belong with the rest of her face, as they glistened like dark

13

beads. But I never got beyond that door or into the sitting room, where I imagined Devlin sat in an unravelling cardigan, in soiled baffies with the toes missing.

I was too young to know why she married *ane o them*, but my own aunt told me later.

'Like Bella, Devlin was born out in India, in the jute trade. He came back to Leith, but planned to go back to the trade and Bella married him because she was desperate to go back *tae the Ghats*, as she called it. Devlin got steady work at the warehouse so he never went back. They couldn't have children for some medical reason.'

Bella showed me a certificate once, with huge red seals on it like flattened roses. Her mother grew up in Bengal and was married at fourteen to a lad from Her Majesty's 44th, who himself wasn't much older than that. It was all on the certificate, including her own name, **Isabella Reidpath**.

Bella's father died at sixteen from a sniper's bullet, and the young widow boarded a ship with her child. Bella's mother had more than gone native, speaking Bengali to her daughter and the girl's first words in Leith were not Scots ones either. Bella pulled her hair back native fashion and walked down Lorne Street barefoot; when teased or upset, she always cried aloud in Bengali.

Devlin's family lived just up the street but with the jute industry in a slump and with the betting shops and his beloved Hibernian Football Club just around the corner, Devlin gradually forgot about India. Meanwhile, Bella's adult life became more of a sullen nightmare as her Indian dream retreated further down the grey streets until it melted back into the tenements, in the cold autumn rain.

'Oh, aye, Bella likes her curry so she does. Just you run along with this wee poke.'

Wee poke in the cold rain. I can still smell it: cardamom, cinnamon, coriander, cumin, turmeric. I skipped to those names:

> Curry powder, curry powder,
> Cardamom, cardamom,
> Yer mammies greetin, aye greetin,
> intae a poke o cinnamon.

Despite Bella's bitterness at Devlin, her curry was the one thing they still shared. I remember thinking, there is a song behind those black eyes:

> Farewell Ichalkaranji, Dharwad, The Ghats,
> dark Brahmaputra and the turquoise sea,
> the sugar sand of Goa, Ethiopia, Egypt,
> whispering Sudan and Araby.
>
> Great whales diving, porpoises singing,
> up from Suez, up from Suez,
> oh dark birds winging.

Devlin died, and my visits were few (for it had only been Devlin who needed sugar for his tea) but there were always the spices, and 'odd wee bits for the monkey'.

The *monkey*. Where did it come from? Did she always have it, even pre-Devlin? Some say Devlin kept it exiled ben the hoose, others say she bought it to replace 'that other ape' – Devlin himself.

One frosty day I went to the door and saw the beast above the coat rack. Devlin's font was gone now but the monkey was chewing a filthy and tattered Hibs scarf. The monkey had big bright coppery eyes, bigger than an old penny. It stood only a foot high and was tailless. It was brown above and silver grey underneath. The creature's nose was huge, as were its rounded ears. Its long fingers were wrapped around the coat rack. A few words in an Indian tongue and it retreated, dragging Devlin's old scarf into the sitting room. The monkey smelled of something like piss or the spray of an old tomcat.

I didn't really like that monkey so it was a good thing Bella never asked me in and never offered me a biscuit or tea or juice so I was always able to hurry away. Up to the Macdonald Road library to look up *monkey* in the books. I found it. A 'Slender Loris', native of Southern India or Tibet, belonged to the swamps and forests there. *Loris Tardigradus*, nocturnal, slow-moving, feeding on insects and small lizards. Nicknamed the 'urine-washing' monkey because it helped define its territory by trailing its urine scent everywhere it went. (Not exactly Devlin's *holy* water.)

My aunt told me *I* was the lucky one, if the monkey was called off when I went there. It seems Bella taught the beast to piss on command. One Bengali word and the monkey would piss on the socks, shoes, or stockings of the offending visitor: any friend of Devlin's, Hibs supporters, salesmen, ministers and any *o them*. Bella had few visitors.

The *beads*. When Devlin was alive, Bella always wore them. They matched her eyes exactly and I always thought they were some kind of prayer beads. She worried them, rubbed them. I know about them now: Albert Prince of Saxe-Coburg-Gotha died in 1861, and as the Empire went daft with mourning, jet beads became all the rage. This shiny lignite fossil – found in graves in Palaeolithic times and much loved in the Bronze Age as a talisman – polished beautifully, what's more, the beads were English to the core since the best jet deposits were from the Upper Lias of Whitby; a big industry as long as the stubborn Queen mourned for her man. In time the craze ended and the jet veins closed (Spain took over the jet trade) but at the height of an Empire in mourning, the young child Bella began cutting teeth somewhere off black Africa on board ship and her teenage mother offered the sloe-eyed child black beads to chew on, to ease the pain from one world to another one, and the girl left tiny teeth marks, like a fossil imprint; those rough ridges would be fingered by that same hand nearly ninety years later.

But when Devlin died, the monkey was given the beads, and one of my last visits to the door found me crawling around the dark hall, looking for beads scattered when the monkey had chewed through the rawhide string holding them together. I found them all, under the gaze of the beast who now only had one filthy corner of Devlin's Hibs scarf left, the bit that said 1902.

I wasn't there at the very end. I was told it was a February day, pelting with a cold rain, when my aunt went over with some curry spices. She chapped on the door. No reply. She went back over in the evening with her man. The house was dark, although a fire should have been on in the grate, visible from the street. They finally forced the door.

They called out. No reply. They went into the sitting room. No fire. No one there. They walked down the hall. Opened each door. Scullery dark, tea cup still full of tea. Then to the last door, the bedroom. The room was dark. They lit the gaslight.

The old woman was propped up in bed. Her bed was covered with statues of elephant gods and of blue deities with many arms. Bella's dark eyes were closed. Her long hair had been brushed out but plaited, Indian fashion. She wore a native silk dressing gown, which hung limp on her wasted frame. And among all the gods and dervishes on her bed, in the centre, was the monkey, stuffed and mounted like a museum piece, a tiny rag of green and white clutched in its fingers.

And on Bella's neck were the jet beads, her toothless mouth clamped firmly around them.

BOYS, GIRLS, GAMES

BILL DUNCAN

That's how the game started. Dark winter nights, no-where tae go amongst the vertical streets but stand in the wind tunnel between the multis. We'd lean intae the wind, three o us: me, Pete an John, held up by the howl o the gale ragin through the narrow corridor o concrete. The idea was tae wait till it really screamed an lean wi yer head as far in front o yer feet as possible an stay like that for as long as you could. A couple o times we managed tae stand like wrecked, broken puppets in the eye o the wind for ages. Once, when the three o us were suspended like that, I fought through the wind an stood in front o the other two, who didnae know I was there. I stood there leanin backwards intae the force, starin at them leanin forward. It must have looked like some weird urban ballet, wi the piercin white spotlights o the multis, an the three o us frozen in absolute stillness while the night howled about us. That one time I leaned back, starin at them wi their eyes closed, long hair whippin in front o their young faces, tranced an ecstatic. I knew then they would never be as beautiful again an that we'd never be as happy.

Once or twice the wind dropped in the middle o the ballet an that wiz wild. A sudden wind drop an ye'd be fightin for yer balance, maybe takin a lurch forward an swoonin towards the pavement wi a great uncontrolled heave. Once Pete wiz standin there, tranced right in, freezin hands jammed intae the pockets o his Wrangler. By the time he realised the wind had dropped he wiz hurtlin face first towards the concrete. Another night there were some crosswinds an eddies flyin around in the tunnel an I'm leanin sideways, totally still, screamin. It wiz pure joy when the wind wiz so mad ye could howl like wolves or roar or bark, just dependin, an the wind wid drown ye out. This one time I'm in the trance, the wind vanishes an I hurtle sideways an batter ma head off the harlin. The side o yer head crunchin wi the sudden shock o jabby stones, rakin yer hand through yer long hair an there's big spots o blood growin on yer white Wrangler.

Tae the right o the tunnel, the vestibule wi the nameplates we wid gaze at: twenty-two floors, eight tenants per landing. One hundred an seventy-six spaces for nameplates; about a third o them permanent, another third changin every few months an the final third, the most interestin, permanently empty, but denotin flats occupied for years by people who didnae want you to know they lived there. Leftwards, the cellars. My key would open about one in three so sometimes you would be able to steal a bike or a cardboard box full o Christmas tree decorations an you could smash up all the coloured globes an fairy bulbs an set fire tae the tinsel on a summer evening. Best of all, though, we found a bottle o shellac an Pete knew what you could do wi it. He poured a trail o it round the concrete floor o the cellars, outside an back in again. One match fae the top pocket o his Wrangler an a big whoosh o flame hit the roof.

John wiz gifted too. That time he went out on a verandah on the twenty-second floor an hurtled down a Superball as hard as he could. A wee thing made out o dense, vulcanised rubber – reminded me o the material at the heart o a neutron star. We watched fae the playpark as it hit the ground an zoomed straight back up higher than the multi, disappearin from sight. The most unpopular girl fae second year wiz standin posin between two older lads over at the swings as Pete an me gazed up in the sky. Ye could just make out the wee speck gettin bigger an bigger an we totally froze in excitement when we saw it fifty feet above her head, hardly daring tae hope, but sure enough, the thing plummetted down, peltin right intae the centre o the crown o the stunned girl, hurtlin back up wi the momentum it gained fae the strike. The lassie just slumped stupidly between her two admirers while we swooned wi the joy o just havin witnessed perfection. In fact, the ball still had that much energy in it that it bounced half the height o the multi when it next struck the ground.

Around this time girls seemed tae be there more often an this led tae slightly better behaviour. Before all the excitement an confusion lassies were on the edge of our lives but soon they were occupyin a central role, clearin up some mysteries, but more often increasin them. A few years before this, girls were objects that intrigued and mystified. Though ye couldnae quite see what all the fuss was about, sometimes yer pal's mother would be smellin nice an dressed up wi maybe a tight black jersey on at the New Year an she'd give ye a big hug an a kiss an ye would feel kind o shivery an glowy at the same time wi strange stirrins ye didnae quite understand. Other times Pete would steal a *Club International* or *Escort* fae the top o his old man's wardrobe an the mysteries o woman would be partially revealed in the form o the awesome, poutin, sullen creatures simultaneously evokin fear an desire. Before that I had been secretly mystified after lookin at John's mum's medical encyclopaedias in the reproduction sections. I had been troubled at the cross-section an drawins o female reproductive organs, complete with labels, Latin terms an arrows. I tried tae memorise the information in case I ever had the misfortune tae have tae use it. But it wiz hard tae visualise, an even harder tae relate these sombre grey medieval-lookin engravins wi the girls we were about tae know.

That wiz just the first o women bein puzzlin an difficult tae understand an things have stayed that way ever since, right enough. Ye didnae consider that girls were probably as fascinated as you wi all the stuff about sex, but I remember bein shocked when I got off the school bus an walked down the road behind the two best lookin girls in second year; quiet, slow-movin, self-contained creatures. When we reached their street there wiz a couple o doags copulatin on the pavement. This led tae averted eyes an embarrassed increases in walkin pace fae everybody goin past except the two girls, who stopped an studied the spectacle wi cool, purposeful fascination, exchangin quiet comments an circlin the two animals which by now were thrustin faster an faster, tae appreciate fully what wiz goin on fae different angles, inclinin their heads tae obtain a variety o viewpoints.

Pete, who wiz the most fascinated by dirty stuff, would bring in the instructions fae his mother's Tampax an we huddled together readin an thinkin o all this applyin, no just to our mothers, but to Sheila an Irena an Helen, who were fast turnin intae mysteries. Pete wiz always fascinated by devices like that an it wasnae long before he was bringin in packets o condoms an showin ye them an makin ye look at the instructions even if ye werenae that interested, which ye probably were. Mind you, once or twice Pete's incredible ignorance o the things he wiz fascinated by gave us a laugh. Like the time when we were on our way tae a party that some girls we fancied from our class were goin tae. Pete sidled conspiratorially up tae me, produced a packet o Durex Gossamer an enquired as tae whether I was puttin mine on before I went or if I wiz just waitin till I got there. Later he admitted tae never havin used one in earnest, but spoiled it all by tryin tae salvage his credibility, claimin that he had masturbated whilst wearin one an that it worked. Pete wiz the first person who ever brought in real filthy pictures, which his big brother had acquired when in Denmark on a school cruise. Once he produced a photograph o a man, fat wi hair like Elvis, wi his penis in a woman's mouth. I wiz mystified because I couldnae see the point o doin a thing like that; it just seemed stupid. I always remember the man looked fed up an still had his socks on, an the woman looked a bit like my auntie. In the end all the fascination wi condoms didnae help Pete in any practical way, as he married at seventeen tae a girl he got pregnant. The last I saw o Pete wiz a couple o years ago. He wiz in a scheme pub playin for the darts team. He wiz fat an wearin a Rangers strip that said Gazza an I looked at him an he looked at me but nobody spoke.

It wiz John discovered the coffin recess. We never knew at first that the black space behind the two doors at the bottom o the brushed silver aluminium o the lift interior wiz for puttin bodies in. Well no bodies, coffins but it made sense when somebody explained it tae us. All five o the multis had one, of course, but the faraway one, for some reason, wiz never locked so that's where we went. At first it wiz just for the daftness o bein in there; you an yer two mates, stuffed intae the dark, box within a box, glidin up an down as people called the lift from all floors throughout the multi. You had tae be really quiet, obviously, so the folk in the lift wouldnae know ye were sittin there, a couple o feet away fae them. You could look out at them too, if you sat beside the keyhole, but you really only saw from their waist down tae their knee, unless it wiz a bairn, dependin on where they were standin. One night this man came in wi a woman an John wiz at the keyhole an told what they were doin on the way up tae floor twenty. I'm no sure if I believed him, but after that there wiz always a lot o shovin an arguin about who wiz sittin where, until we resolved the situation by organisin a proper rota for coffin recess positions.

Nobody ever saw anythin as excitin as that ever again, though. I only saw a drunk pissin an Pete says he saw the Insurance Man masturbatin.

Normally the coffin recess wiz more what ye would describe as an aural, rather than a visual experience. There wiz a lot tae listen tae right enough. Most folk never said anythin an most o the time, they were in wi other people they only ever saw in the lift, so it'd be pretty routine stuff; good mornins, an caulder the day an stuff like that. Sometimes a bit different, though. A couple o drunks once started arguin about the time o High Tide at Wormit an this led tae violent verbal abuse followed by actual blows, which continued tae echo down the corridor away into the distance as the lift descended. The commonest rows were between husbands an wives comin home after the pub – marriage is a joke an the joke's on me, if you smile wance mair at that bastard eh'll thump baith yer puses an so on.

More interestin was how people spent their times when they were on their own, or thought they were. A lift's a strange kind o space; public but seeminly private. Once the door shuts it's a bit like bein in the bathroom, though certain folk took that idea a bit far sometimes. Few people would remain silent; most would hum, sing, whistle or talk tae themselves aboot all manner o things. Once or twice I heard somebody quietly greetin an felt a bit rotten. Usually when folk on their own talked it wiz funnier, though, mutterin on about shower o bastards, or, her sittin there wi a pus like a burst settee, or whatever. The best times were when the lift went really quiet an just the click o the windin gear, the slide an thump o the doors an the glide o the cables. The passenger in the lift would maybe whistle a couple o bars o 'Magic Moments' an John would say somethin under his breath but no quite. He would talk in a slightly quivery, strangled voice on the edge o panic an say somethin like please, no more, or Jemima or simply heave a low moan or maybe clear his throat briskly an businesslike. He usually managed tae get it just right. Of course, ye couldnae see their reactions, but things would usually go dead quiet for a few seconds then the person would cough loudly an the hummers would hum louder an the whistlers would whistle no tune at all slightly more hysterically. Sometimes folk whose breeks ye recognised would get off at the fourth floor instead o the twenty-second where they lived an the lift would go up empty.

The game stopped when Pete had a rush o blood tae the head an opened the door when somebody wiz still in the lift. The woman looked down in horror as the doors slowly opened, followin a series o low moans between floors, tae see three fourteen-year-old boys squashed intae the coffin recess. There was nothin for it but tae bolt out an make a dash past her as soon as we could stop at a floor. Next day the coffin recess wiz locked an that wiz it.

After that there wiz years o patchouli, dope, girfriends, drugs an women but these were the best things: the wind tunnel, the ballet an the coffin recess. The last time I heard o John he wiz in the local paper: 'Kirriemuir Man Brandishes Hammer at Wife'. I didnae realise he had moved, or got married. Seeminly he felt bad about bein described as a 'Kirriemuir Man'. I heard he had a leg off soon afterwards then died. Pete had his name in the papers for wife batterin no long ago an more recently faced charges for the sale an distribution o obscene materials. I'm still teachin.

No thanks. I'll best be goin. It's gettin dark.

THE WAR

MORGAN DOWNIE

I t started with a dice throw, brief flicker of red against the moon, dim blue music twisting into the night air, a whisper among the rhythms of crickets and the distant call of quail. I heard them arguing, crept closer until I was near enough to see the wild gesturing of their arms and the twist of their faces. I settled down in the shadows and waited. After a while they seemed to come to some kind of agreement. I saw the trailerman pull something from his pocket, saw his wrist flick forward, snake quick. I saw the dice fall.

They crouched there in the dirt for a long second, then, as the trailerman stretched himself up on to his feet, I heard his voice, broken, cracked, the tearing metal sound of a bad engine.

'Duke Ellington' he said, smiling as the other lurched away, 'is one of the great American geniuses.' He blew smoke into the darkness. 'Yes, sir.' And the butt flew from his hand, arcing towards me like a shooting star.

I was still very young, my parents still poor, my father struggling to make a business out of autoparts. In those days he would return home late at night, throw himself into a chair, slumped and hollow-eyed, his skin tattooed with oilstains like dark, malevolent bruises. I used to fear those marks, think that somehow the sweet-smelling darkness would seep through his skin, enter him and consume him, which in its own way is in the end exactly what happened.

My mother worked as a waitress in a truckstop by the highway. She would lie up on the couch in front of the TV, footsore with exhaustion, her pink and white uniform stained with ketchup, egg-yolk and the sour comments of the drive-by traffic. She had pale-green eyes shot through with light, which, even when dulled by valium, shone as if on the verge of tears, lit by the monochrome glow of gameshows. She liked country music, loved to dance so much that when she eventually lost her leg I realised that she was crying not from pain, she was already inured to that, but for the loss of motion, the whirling and tossing of smoky old barn dances, the band sweating and smelling of whiskey, vapour memories in her landless passing.

The kids at the trailerpark were looked after mainly by the owner's wife, a fat emotive woman, with no children of her own but who did have a dog called Nimrod, an English spaniel that so befriended me that now, whenever England is mentioned, I immediately recollect the smell of dogs and the pale, enormous warmth of her breasts as she crushed us into them after we had hurt ourselves, all the while crying, 'Oh my darling, oh my poor darling'.

Her husband was a small, wiry man, a Greek I think, who wore Cuban heels and had a well-known taste for the town whores. I remember little about him except his intolerance of debt and his incessant demands for money. As kids we thought this was pretty funny and we would mimic him, swaggering around out of earshot demanding of each other in thick Greek accents. 'Choo got my focking money?' When, years later, I heard he had been killed in a knife fight up in Flagstaff I was left unsurprised.

The trailerman had one of those big old silver trailers with the dark windows and the words 'Airstream' or 'Land Yacht' written in fine hard letters upon them. Where he had arrived from we never knew and he never cared to say. We knew he was tough, he had scars to prove it. He said his parents had brought him across from Poland when he was our age, he told us his father owned a grocery cart, he told us folk tales of forest wolves and impaled counts, he never told us how he got the scars. We asked him if he would ever go back home, to Poland. He said, 'I have no home. My country is dead.'

He smoked constantly, Lucky Strikes, the cartons stacked like books along the walls, lighting each cigarette methodically, Ohio Blue tip flaring in his fist. I heard my first Elvis Presley song on his radio. He played the mouth harp. He was pretty good. Once a girl from the East came to record him. She sat cross-legged and earnest at the bottom of his stairs while we admired the shape of her breasts.

He had a son, this much we knew from the pictures we could see from the doorway of the trailer, the trailerman and another, younger version of himself, holding a giant bass, smiling in some far-off rain. His son was killed in Korea at a place called Inchon. He never spoke of him except very occasionally when he was drunk shouting, 'The Chinese, the Chinese never killed my boy. It was the goddam war that killed him, the war that took him away. Two days he was there, never fired a shot. Goddam war.' We would hear him careening around the inside of the trailer, the sound of breaking glass, enraged.

Korea was the war no one talked about. In our war games we stormed the world to fight the Nazis or the Japs, we knew who they were, goose-stepping kamikaze tinheads, but the Chinese, all we knew about them was that they wore pajamas and ate a bowl of rice and that China was cold. As for the Koreans, they were ghost people. Some of the kids' fathers were old enough to have fought in the Big War. Some kids said their fathers had fought with John Wayne. Others said that their fathers still woke up screaming. But at least they won. No one talked about Korea.

None of the parents seemed to mind these endless battles against the Nazis, who were always weak kids or girls, though occasionally we did fight the Russians, in which case a strong and exceptionally brave kid would play the Russian but only on the understanding that he was a good Russian, an ordinary Joe, and could beat all of us until inevitably being betrayed by the men upstairs. No one minded much at all except the trailerman. He would shout at us from his steps, cigarette clenched between his lips. 'You want to see the war? I'll show you the war.' And he would lift his shirt to show us his scars. 'You want some of this? You want some?'

Even as we got older we did not dare answer back but the trailerman seemed to have forgotten that it was our duty as boys to be fascinated by scars of all forms especially those inflicted by violence. To really see the scars however, to get to touch the lifeless dead flesh, you had to play The Game, and you had to play it with him.

The Game was popular and we often played it among ourselves but with the trailerman it took on a whole new dimension. He would sit up on his steps with his torn body and we would beg him to play but he would just sit back and say 'I've fought my battles'. Then he would hold the dice up in front of his face and growl. 'Now I'm the war and you, you've got to take your chances. Who's first?'

A single throw of the dice was easy. A one meant you were okay and you could fight again, a two, a three or a four was a flesh wound of your choice. Ketchup on the arm or leg or a berryjuice scar on the face. A five was a quick death, shot in the heart, and mostly disappointing. It was only when you threw a six that things got interesting. On a six you got a second throw. When you threw the second time a one meant you had lost an arm, a two a leg, a three and you were burned, the skin stripped off your body so that even your girl couldn't look at you and you coughed so bad you couldn't smoke. The most terrible wound happened if you threw another six. To be double-sixed was the worst, to be double-sixed was to be shot in the balls. This involved not only the indignity of being called 'no-balls' for the remainder of the day but also a further badge of shame as you had to walk around with your hands firmly in your pants pockets so that if someone was to ask what was wrong you were obliged to reply – 'I have no balls.'

A four or five and you died. In our games it was glorious. After overcoming insurmountable odds you hoisted the flag with your last breath and your buddies took your medals home to your tearstained mother while a marching band played the battle hymn of the republic.

With the trailerman it was different. He would wait a moment as if he was looking down inside himself, then he would fix you with his eyes.

'Little man,' he would say. 'Little man, you're in a mud hole in the woods. You're dirty and you're cold and you're alone. Someone's shot you, you never even saw who it was, they just shot you, in the throat and in the belly. If you look down you know you'll see your guts, but you don't look down because you're afraid. And the pain, the pain.'

He let his voice drop and we instinctively clutched our stomachs.

'Up ahead you can hear your squad shooting, shooting wild, but the enemy, there's too many of them, no matter how many they kill they keep on coming, they're in the ground, in the trees, dressed in black, faceless. You hear your buddies screaming, you hear them dying, but there's nothing you can do. You want to shout for help but your voice has gone. You don't shoot because you're afraid they'll find you. And you're afraid, afraid like you've never imagined. You want your mother but she's not there and you realise as it gets real quiet that this is where you're going to die, in a mud hole thousands of miles from home and it's some other boy's bones they'll put in your coffin. You lie back and you feel yourself crying because deep down you knew it always had to be this way but still you went and now the war has taken you, kept you all to itself in the dirt and blood and endless silence.'

A kid could have nightmares for days after this, but he would always be back, to touch the scars, dreaming of our own and the test that would make us men. We could not realise how soon we would all get our chance.

The last day I saw him I found him hitching up the trailer to his truck. My family too would soon leave, my father finally starting to turn a tiny profit, but I had imagined that what would be left behind would remain, unchanging.

'What are you doing?' I asked as if the evidence of my eyes was not enough.

'Leaving,' he said without turning.

I stood stupefied in adolescent silence.

'What's the matter?' he said. 'Cat got your tongue?'

'Weren't you going to tell me?'

He shook his head. 'I hadn't reckoned on it.'

'But where will you go?'

'Don't know,' he said. 'Hadn't thought about it.'

Words were stilled in my mouth. I was already thinking of the gap where the trailer had stood, always, the knowledge of certainty slipping through my fingers like dry sand.

He reached into his pocket. 'I'll tell you what,' he said. 'A roll of the dice. Odds I stay. Evens I go.'

I watched the familiar flick of the wrist, watched the dice fall.

And he smiled. 'Man's got to travel.'

He put his hand gently on my stunned shoulder before turning away, getting into the truck and driving out of my life.

I did not call out after him nor did I run down the track behind him, but I did return later that night to find the dice where it had fallen, the same dice that sits before me as I write this. It started as it had finished, with a roll of the dice, and there in the empty darkness I knew the long desert summer of my childhood was at an end, the stormclouds ahead already gathering.

LIKE IT'S NEVER BEEN TOLD THIS WAY BEFORE

JOHN PACIONE

All soldiers everywhere love one another. All soldiers everywhere walk hand in hand stealing kisses on one another's lips. They have hard lips, bullet lips, steel-cold lips. Sometimes they kiss me.

Isaac is now home on leave and he wants to be with my father. They walk together in the park, gazing into each other's eyes. Holding hands with my mother we stand watching them from the balcony of our house. We see my father and Isaac kiss beneath a tree. We mimic them. There's no way of telling that Isaac is a soldier because he's not wearing his uniform; nor is there any trace of a march in his walk. On leave he walks like a civilian. Shielding his eyes he stares up at the sky while, like a foal, my father nuzzles against his shoulder.

'Kasia . . .' my mother begins, but then can't complete her sentence. She does that often nowadays. I think it's because there aren't many more sentences left for her to say and the few which remain to her she hoards. So instead of speaking she begins combing my hair while I level my gun at the foal's heart.

Isaac's recently completed a tour. He finished the tour as captain. He says he saw very little action but we don't believe him, we know he saw action every day. He's brought with him pictures of this latest tour and these are filled with the action he saw.

'Maybe you shouldn't be looking at these,' my mother says.

'Yes I should,' I reply. 'I need to know what's happening.'

'Nothing's happening,' Isaac says. 'It's really all very mundane.'

'What's mundane?' asks Kim, my brother.

Isaac complains about the weather during his recent tour. It was always raining, he says, the streets were rivers of mud. However his photographs contradict him showing streets flooded with sunshine and roads baked dry by the heat. I see children just like me. They all seem to be biting their knuckles or turning on their heels, or turning to mothers who are never there.

I turn to mine.

'I need to see the truth,' I tell her.

Isaac and my father cuddle on the floor. My mother joins them there. I'm so happy to be out of the fighting, our soldier says, while, like a puppy, Kim buries his nose in Isaac's discarded uniform.

'Take me with you,' I beg Isaac when we are alone together in my room. 'I need to know what's there, what's really happening. All I hear are lies.'

He won't answer. Instead he admires the pictures on my wall. He says I have a very optimistic room; he can relax here and forget. He puts his feet on my desk and lights a cigarette. I open a window. We hear birdsong and Kim shouting and yipping at nothing.

Isaac lies to me.

'I was fighting in the town where my mother was born,' he says. 'And we tore that town apart, levelled it, you could say we returned it to nature, if nature is dust and rubble. On the enemy side were boys as young as Kim. They were very good

36

fighters but they couldn't hold their rifles, which were too long and too heavy for them and toppled them over. This made them very easy to shoot. Imagine, Kasia, a field filled with boys whose rifles have pitched forward, the bayonets caught in the earth; imagine row upon row of these standing targets, their uniforms so black they looked like crippled crows – until we blew them away. We blow everything away, Kasia, anything that's in our path, anything that doesn't make our path easy, we line it up and we blow it away.'

Isaac levelled his lips with the top of the desk and blew dust at me.

'Tell me a happy war story,' I say to him.

'Look at my tan,' he replies, baring his bronzed arms and chest.

'But you say it's always raining.'

'Only on the enemy.'

My mother finds us together. She sits on my bed. I have to move away from her, it's too obvious what she wants; her tongue is almost hanging from her head.

'I was admiring Kasia's room,' Isaac says.

'Yes,' my mother replies. 'Yes, it's . . . it's a . . .'

She's tongue-tied, she's stammering, she doesn't know what to say, but she wants to stay here – her eyes are saucers of lust. Mine too. And I know why. Death. Making death. There's no telling what Isaac has killed, but knowing that he has makes him more desirable. By making death and making victims he's made himself irresistible. Equally it's the thought that he will also make victims of us, of our entire house, that forces us to love our assassin – we simply can't get enough of him. We'll be empty, spent shells when he leaves, sleepwalkers.

From nearby Kim harangues an unknown enemy.

'You'll be enjoying not . . .' my mother begins, 'not having to . . .'

We wait for her to finish, but she can't, she doesn't have one.

'Yes,' says Isaac eventually.

His hair is as dark and as blue as his eyes, as glossy as a polished helmet. He's exploring a book shelf, running his fingers along the books' spines.

My mother begins fondling her cheek.

'She's a hungry reader,' she manages to say, 'hungry and greedy.'

'I hardly read at all,' I say.

'These are good books,' Isaac says. 'And this is a good room.' He sighs. 'I could stay here forever.'

'It's the best room in the house,' I tell him. 'It might even mend your soul.'

'Then I'll take it,' Isaac says, slamming his fist on the table, making the room crack.

Us girls were in the kitchen. Us girls were stretched out in the garden showing too much skin to the sun. Us girls were cooling our feet in the pond.

My father was working at a trestle table shaping wood. Kim was standing by him, his ankles crossed.

Isaac was lying on his stomach, his back covered in shavings, one of my books held open beneath his eyes.

My father went into the kitchen and brought out bottles of ice-cold beer. He crouched beside Isaac who looked up from his book. His eyes were very red, his face was moist. He'd been crying.

'It's a very sad story,' he said, smiling through his tears.

But I had read this story before and knew it was weak and puerile. I had giggled at it, not cried.

'You're soft,' I told him, running my fingers through his thick mane.

'He's a captain,' my mother said.

'He's a murderer,' said Kim, 'a haloed, hallowed murderer.'

'It means I look at you differently,' Isaac explained.

'I know how you look at me,' I said, forcing his face down and rubbing his nose in the grass.

My father's beer fizzled and foamed. He poured some over my mother. She threw back her head and opened her mouth. Most of the beer went dribbling down her chin.

Then he picked me from Isaac's back and threw me at a tree. Isaac rolled over and sprang to his feet. He and my father clenched. They guzzled cold beer. Hand in hand they ran into the kitchen leaving us girls outside to soak up the sun and the silence.

We were where we didn't want to be. We weren't where the action was. We were waiting for our boys to return to the light.

I was in my bedroom with Kim, showing him some of Isaac's photographs, the worst ones. We were daring ourselves to look at them, and keep looking, until each photograph had nothing left to hide.

We felt sad.

'We're jelly,' said Kim, 'jelly waiting to happen.'

Isaac had written a poem on the back of each photograph. He'd written in pencil with a fine point and a tiny hand. On some he had squeezed in as many as thirty lines. I found the poems beautiful but that was because he had used only simple, beautiful words.

I heard my mother singing.

I heard some groaning.

I covered my brother's innocent ears.

He was taking photographs with the same camera that had taken all the horror. The camera didn't complain, we didn't complain. I wondered if when they were developed he would write poems on our backs.

It was my mother's turn to be snapped.

'Be yourself,' Isaac told her.

She posed, she preened.

'Be yourself,' Isaac begged.

'She is,' I said.

My father raised his fist to her. She rolled her eyes.

My father turned away in frustration.

Kim stamped on her foot.

Isaac was taking these pictures to use up a roll of film. I could only cross my legs and imagine the scenes of carnage filling the early part of the roll.

When it was Kim's turn we dressed him in a captain's uniform many sizes too large for him and placed a revolver in his hand. We had him turn the gun and place the barrel in his mouth. My mother tutted. We had a jar of blueberry jam whose contents we spooned across Kim's uniform. He'd been blown open and was succulent blue inside.

Isaac lay on his back.

We suspended Kim in the air – I was holding his legs, my father his arms. We spread him wide. Isaac took a photograph of that, excluding us from the frame so that it would appear as if Kim was flying.

When it was over my father did press-ups over Isaac's supine body while my mother walked briskly towards the kitchen, taking the soiled captain's jacket with her.

I lay on my stomach, rubbing my heels together, watching as my father made Isaac stand against a tree. A thick red rope was then tied around his middle until he couldn't move. He was wearing a white smock and nothing else. My father wore Isaac's powder-blue jacket. He also had a black scarf tied around his forehead. He was very handsome.

Isaac had been found guilty of going into another land and committing atrocities there. He had been shooting down everything that moved, until nothing moved. Then he began shooting that too. Now it was his turn to be shot.

My mother crouched beside me.

Kim covered his eyes, uncovered them, covered them again.

My mother took the photograph.

Then I was roped to the tree and it was my turn to experience the thrill of staring down the barrel of a gun whose every chamber was filled with a real bullet. I thought of our soon-to-be destroyed house, I thought of honeycombs and mindless bees. When my father pulled the trigger I would be stung and all my honey flow.

'Shoot,' I told him. 'If you're anything of a man, if you've not been sucked dry, do it, do it now.'

Isaac stroked my hair.

I closed my eyes. 'Please,' I begged. 'Please.'

A crack ripped through the garden, through my forehead and travelled to the back of my brain. I slumped forward.

'She's become another statistic,' I heard Kim say.

When I opened my eyes again I felt exhausted, completely drained. I had to go to my room and lie down.

Books aren't real, soldiers are real, and soldiering, carrying a gun is real, blowing a hole through a book is real and blowing a hole through a brain; destroying for money and comfort, destroying because you have to, because it's there inside you, compelling you, destroying because you're tired of the world as it is, because you want a better world, one that is born of destruction. Nothing from nothing. If I was fighting a war I would never take leave, because there is no leaving; Isaac has brought his war home with him and I resent him for that.

Isaac proposes to my father, my father proposes to Isaac, my mother storms out of the room. They drag her back and cover her with keys. They want the key to her heart, they say. I lie down. They open my head and open my eyes, they open my mouth and my legs. Kim is running everywhere squealing like a pig. I complain when I'm turned upside down and the world begins to spin.

'There are no clean edges,' Isaac says, holding a razor only inches from my eyes, 'there are no edges anywhere.'

He doesn't speak with conviction, he's speaking lines. I have the feeling that he doesn't kill with conviction either.

He turns off the lights and sits at the heart of the room, his face glowing like a lantern. We are all drawn to him, both for his light and for the heat from his body, because without him we are very cold; when he's not here we are four blocks of ice that could lie in the sun without melting. Only Isaac can melt us. It is the heat of all the death he carries which melts us. We want a taste of that too. Is that why my father is sucking Isaac's tongue? Is that why my mother has fallen asleep with her head buried in Isaac's thigh?

I feel warm too. It's sad that it takes war and death to keep us warm, but peace is evil.

My mother was asleep in my bed so I pushed her on to the floor. She fell on her back and sprawled there like something washed up by the sea. I had a shell I wanted to drop on her white stomach.

'Can I come back to bed?' she whimpered.

I propped myself up on an elbow. 'Only if you tell me what's happening in yours.'

My mother paced around the room.

She put a light on, blinding me.

She began picking through my books.

'What are they doing?' I asked.

She opened the curtains then sat on the window ledge. She put her feet on the ledge and wrapped her arms around her knees. She rested the side of her head against her forearm and stared at me.

'Put out the light,' I said, 'I'm trying to sleep.'

From another room Isaac or my father coughed.

My mother didn't take her eyes from me.

I turned the other way: 'Put out the light.'

I talked to the wall: 'What are they doing? Why aren't you with them?'

I heard her feet slide from the ledge.

'Why don't they need you?'

The house shivered.

'I need you,' I told her. 'Turn off the light and come back to bed.'

Somewhere in the house Isaac or my father laughed.

Quietly my bedroom door opened, quietly it closed. A small voice sighed. The light was turned off. My bed filled with all those who were kept from the soldiers' room.

I went there. They were sitting up in bed watching TV. I had the distinct impression that everything worth seeing had already happened and that this was the aftermath, the calm following the storm.

I dropped on to the bed and squeezed between them.

'Tell me what happened,' I said. 'Blow by blow.'

'Blow by blow?' said Isaac.

'Blow by blow.'

My father excused himself.

I snuggled up to Isaac. I licked the sweat from his back.

The sheets were cooler than a mountain stream.

Isaac sang to me with the clear voice of an angel.

My mother appeared and carried away the redundant TV.

Isaac had hung his cap from a hook above the bed and draped his uniform around a headless mannequin which stood guard by the door.

My family paced the corridor all night.

We were all deep in leave fever.

*　　*　　*

'I am the enemy,' Isaac said. 'Be good to me.'

He invaded our house and raped my family. Once upon a time we had been innocent but now we were tainted forever.

He was the occupying force. We gave him our bodies and souls. He went from bed to bed enjoying the spoils of war. If we did not cooperate he would destroy us, every one. We gave in to him because our instinct for survival was stronger than our instinct for death. We gave in without a fight. We laid open our borders and our territory disappeared. There was nothing now which was ours, we were ghosts in our own land. That is how war must be, surrendering, capitulating, absorbing. In the end we'll be forced into the sea, or into ovens.

A soldier who is too lazy to bury the dead, a soldier who eats his victims, a soldier who is no warrior, a soldier who is no narrator, a soldier who is a slave to technology and not a master of the killing craft.

'They came at us on horseback,' Isaac was saying. 'We came at them in jets. It was not an equal contest. Horses cannot swallow jets: jets swallow horses.'

A soldier who polishes buttons then pushes them, buttons which are mightier than the sword.

'You have to look good,' Isaac was saying. 'You must shine.'

The enemy ran into the jungle.

'We're not very good in jungles,' Isaac admitted. 'I wouldn't be the first to volunteer to go in after them. Let them stay in their jungle, give us the green fields.'

Where our garden is, that was once jungle, or forest. I wonder who lived in our jungle before it was cleared. And now the jungle's returned, a revenant jungle made of stone, wire and broken glass. I certainly don't go in there. Civilisation is not there. Sometimes at night the noise of this jungle carries to my bedroom. I hope it will spread and some day reclaim us. It's only two miles away, but it could be 2000 years. Our borders are being devoured. I swear that the noise of the jungle is diminishing as it closes in on us. If we don't move out soon its silence will swallow us whole. We have Isaac to keep the jungle at bay, living, sprawling Isaac.

There is no hope for us, all the glamour is on his side.

We send him out to destroy and bring home the glamour.

We're all going to be quite dowdy again once his leave is over.

He slaps me until my cheeks are scarlet. He inserts his gun and then his lens. His eyes are fish dead. He's seen too much and done too much and all too soon. He can never have a family of his own, but he can have us. He's home on leave to pass on all his poison. We have a great appetite for poison, we can glut on it for days. He feeds that appetite. He's telling lies. He turns me over and pokes at me to see if I'm still living. He has stories of capturing hills and magic moments. He has lost count of the children he has already made. I guess I could be his, Kim too. He browbeats me. He says that when I grow up I must become a doctor or a good wife. He shows me a book of anatomy and then, again, the pictures where anatomy has been taken apart, beyond the repair of any doctor. He's very good with his hands, doesn't need to be told where to touch. He has healing hands. Carrying a long, curved knife he enters villages which have already been destroyed and decapitates corpses – he told me this, showed me the proof, slid his fingers around my neck, had my corpse in his arms. When I look in his eyes I believe I can see everything he has seen. It doesn't spoil me. We talk about blood lust. I don't love him, he's my father's. He rolls on top of me. I'm crushed. I feel tiny. He is tender. With his beautiful, clear voice he sings us to sleep, the logs crackling in the fire, the flames tangled in his hair.

For the last three days of his leave he went out alone early in the afternoon returning late the following morning. He never told us where he went or what he had been doing. My father moped, my mother became annoyingly busy.

One afternoon I followed him. His destination was a hotel, a good hotel, much grander than our house. I didn't discover whom he was seeing there, if he was seeing anyone. He wasn't in the hotel bar. I waited for almost an hour but he didn't reappear.

On his last day with us, when I was alone with him, I asked him why he went to the hotel.

He denied having been there. 'You followed the wrong man,' he said.

'I didn't. It was you.'

He leaned forward. 'Room 515,' he whispered, 'but only when I've gone.'

When he departed I did return to the hotel and visit room 515. There were two maids inside and they were making a bed. When the bed was ready I was told to lie on it and close my eyes.

When I next reopen them Isaac's leave will have returned.

SNOWMEN

MARK FLEMING

I was hypnotised, watching them all die. I stared at the snowdrops melting on his nose, his shivery lips; the bits sticking out the balaclava. His breathing was dead harsh, steam snorting through the hole in the black wool. He looked evil, like an Ulster paramilitary murderer. Like Darth Vader.

'So where's your light sabres and Death Stars the night? I mean . . . What d'you get up to when you're not making orphans?'

The mask twitched to life, eyes bulging white. Suddenly he giggled. 'Happy B Day, Kylie! That's you official, eh.'

'What?'

'Sixteen, eh. You're legit.'

'What d'you mean, like?'

'*You're sixteen, you're beautiful and you're mines!*'

While our tongues wrestled I blinked my eyelids like a strobe. Our teeth kept clicking together; I imagined the sparks we could make and my fingers squeezed pizza bases with his arse. Then the booby trap exploded.

Everything was still slightly trippy so the chainsaw coughing freaked me out. When I touched the deck again I burled round. There was this snowman with a hunchback, with skin like a walnut. The snow plastered to its head and shoulders glowed blue with light reflected off the giant Bingo sign above the bus shelter. Plus there was a smell like Moscow Mule puke.

Bex crept outside. I stayed put and stared at this snowman, imagined he lived by the canal, came out to scare folk waiting for the last bus.

My boyfriend's voice was muffled. Out the corner of my weepy eyes I saw his mouth pressed to the glass like those sucker fish that slither round aquariums. His lips made these noises: 'Late-night specials at the flicks? Quality. Best way to watch them, eh, Kylie? Wrecked. How nasty were they insect things, eh? I'd've joined the Starship Troopers, man. Sound visuals. I'm still seeing the Federation Fleet when I stare at these streetlights! What about they space cadets two rows in front doing poppers during the battles? While the grunts were getting sawn in half by giant bugs, man. Quality.'

But the snowman was exhaling drink. It was an alkie; one of those radges who got enjoyment from filling their guts with gallons of gassy poison like my upstairs neighbour James Kelly, who's Mum's age, who needs a new liver.

'Kylie. This bus shelter tastes fucking braw, man. Like a giant ice cube.'

I shook my head at them both; drunk snowman, stoned sucker fish. But Bex was right. It *was* official. Today was marked on my Brad Pitt calendar with a delicious 'X' that crept closer and closer all month. It had landed like the eighth on a coupon: Kylie Dalgleish had hit the big One Six.

Bex, my eight-week boyfriend, gave me Goldie's new CD plus a quarter acid. My gran's present was her trial for Murrayfield Royals when she tumbled on black ice going for her pension and since Mum was looking after her over at Craigentinny I wasn't just sixteen, I was sixteen with a free house *and* some horned-up cock. Snowflakes splatted on his Diesel hood, on the peak of his baseball cap under it. His whole body jolted like a human on an electric-chair.

Next the snowman coughed so loud his hat popped off. 'Penguins!' it burst out. 'They're all this weather's fit for, hen.'

'I could scran a whole shelf of them in Scotmid, mister.'

Crouching I grabbed this cosy tartan bonnet, but barfed at the dandruff. Half a Colombian shipment was inside.

'You should quit tabbing, mister. You almost make me want to stop.' I poked the cloth into his shaky hands. 'Hey. Usually see these on some London comic on telly doing a drunk Scot, eh. They think this side of Hadrian's Wall we *all* drink Buckfast and talk Weedjie like Rab C., eh.'

'What, hen?'

'Just saying. My mum says the English think we're all either paralytic or obsessed with what church our neighbours don't go to. And *these* caps're supposed to represent *us*, eh, but they end up in America, or Australia, or England, eh.'

'Thanks, hen.'

Sucking air in huge bongfuls his fluffy clouds reminded me of chemistry experiments. About-turning I stared into his ghost. Snow fell through it. There was this film about a man with X-ray sight who saw inside dying people, saw their leaks and lumps. The snowman's insides gargled. I imagined all those tubes in there, the burnt-out stomach like a kid's football that's burst and it's just lying there in the garden, all the signatures of the Scotland squad fading; there's one in my next door neighbour's from Munich 74, sits there with Billy Bremner's signature at the top.

The visuals were still healthy; not tripped-out hallucinations, just speedy wee bursts. Earlier there were flashes, like being gunged on Noel Edmund's House Party by multi-coloured lights instead of slime. Now the snowfall and all the lights made a twinkly 3D Xmas card.

Orbital at Glastonbury blazed out Bex's Walkman. Miming keyboards he plucked music out thin air, out the snow. His arms conducted an invisible orchestra; pointed at the orange streetlights; at a cabin light which turned a crane into a lighthouse. Beneath me the pavement quivered to his sounds.

'Look at the Capital city wearing its white coat, eh, Bex? And *check* the lights! There's *so* many. Like *Blade Runner* on your computer . . . Couldn't have picked a better night for this, babes!'

Clouds steamed the glass till I couldn't see his face, just a headless jacket, a musical mist above it. I skipped out the shelter. But he didn't look when I cuddled him. Bastard slapped my chin.

'Steady!'

Rummaging inside his jacket he clicked the tape off and hissed, 'I'll fucking steady you, Kylie Dalgleish!'

'The fuck's *your* problem?!'

'Giving jakeys the time of day, eh?! Think you're in that shan book we're having to read at English the now? Down and Outs in Paris and London?! First time I done trips I stood on Corstorphine Hill for hours, imagined I was riding on the back of a giant fucking tortoise! You turn into Mother Teresa!'

The huff meant time grew even more elastic. After hours and hours a 6 rumbled out the storm, guppies at its frosty windows.

'*Look*, Bex! A giant maroon sauna on wheels'.

'Mmm?!'

'It's steaming inside . . . Rows of gadges as fat as their wallets just spread over the seats. Imagine?! The young lassies doing them, giving them chat, but thinking inside what a hackit bastard you are, seen bigger shrimps in my fried rice!'

'What?!'

'Just imagine the background music, eh. Guitary as fuck. Mind that telly programme we thought was about computer games but it was actually the fucking Gulf War, eh?'

'What programme?'

'Firefights by camcorder! You saw matchstick people creeping out their trenches, then an Arnie voice saying "Take 'em out!" and you saw the tracers homing in while they legged it but once the smoke cleared the matchsticks were all flat!'

'What?! What the fuck're you on about, Kylie? I've *no* fucking idea what you're spraffing about!'

When the bus lurched off, faces clustered at the upstairs back window; all these fingers pressed to the glass to make 'Vs' at the snowman.

'Bairns! Wounded for my country when I was just a bairn.'

'Where?' I asked.

'Anzio, hen.'

'Your *what*? *Which* bit of you got wounded, mister snowman?'

It raised its left hand so I thought I should shake. When I squeezed the wool just crumpled up. The glove was half-empty. This really freaked me out. The snowman had half its fingers missing.

'Spent Christmas forty-four in Stalag Four B, hen. East Germany. The Ruskies were cordoned off. Camp within a camp, see. No huts, no shelter. Each night they went. Scores of them. You'd see them in the morning. Frozen in the snow, ken? Like snowmen, hundreds of them, that had all fell over . . .'

'What the fuck's he on about, Kylie?' Bex whispered in. 'Must be on acid and all! Heh heh!'

'Haven't a clue, Bex . . . He's telling me he spends all day drinking the Special Brew. Drink shite, talk shite.'

'Hey!?' growled the snowman. 'What age're youse?!'

Bex just shrugged. I snapped: 'Both sixteen, eh!'

'When I was in my teens, I seen sunsets that lasted for days. That was how we got the Germans to stop fighting. Made funeral pyres out whole cities.'

'I'd love to gouch at a sunset that lasted for days, eh,' Bex declared. 'Just climb up Arthur's Seat with a bar of hash, ten packs of Veras, chill . . .'

'Mmm. Healthy. Let's pray to God, Bex.'

'What for? A healthy sunset? The Lottery?'

'Nah! Something dead simpler. Dear God. Please send us a 34 part-route to Longstone.'

This sprinkling started. What looked like a thin lava stream cut through the snow to the kerb by the bus shelter. The snowman skulked into a corner, still slurring to itself while it pished.

'Somebody said the weather this weekend was going to be like Russia, ken? When the Ivans broke through they gates their Colonel was on a white horse! This weather . . . That shitey DLO heater . . .'

'Hey!' Bex pointed into the distance. 'God answered your prayers, sweetheart! Check it out! Part-route to Longstone!'

'*Beauty!* Look at her gliding along, eh, like a Spanish galleon . . . It's *glittering*. It looks so fucking *beautiful* . . .'

While fishing his pass out Bex nipped my arse. Climbing aboard we claimed the engine seats. The doors sighed shut. My head was bursting with the thought of him staying over, his first ever dirty stop-out. Bex had never even been allowed back since my mum smelled what she called *Marawhana* off his green Ralphie jacket.

And I'd waited for it. Not like some of my mates. Mandy and Charlene was shafting in 1st Year; Kimberley 2nd Year. Dana's another bammy cow dying to miss her reds. Every 4 weeks it's a hit and miss who the blood fairy's turning up for.

I clocked my coupon in the opposite window, pure beaming like a hostage meeting their family at the airport. Beyond, the snowman watched us pull away.

'He was Abraham Lincoln, eh, Bex? Pure stinking.'

'Not half.'

'Pishing at bus shelters in a blizzard. Minging.'

'Ken.'

'I'm stopping bevvying at thirty. That's a *definite*, Bex'.

He leaned his head on my shoulder, raised his lips. We kissed. He reeked of my Tommy Girl I squished over him when the lights went down. His tongue pure tasted of the Snickers choc-ices and grapefruit Hooches we arsed during the film.

Peeking I saw him sketching a drug helpline, his eight-ball yacks sweeping backwards and forwards. I sussed his Chevignon jeans, sizing him up. My voice dropped into that slapper bunny who used to advertise Caramel. 'I want you to taste me *inside*, too.'

Opposite the brewery a thirtysomething couple struggled on like they'd just hiked off the Cairngorms, bustled in to the seats right opposite where they sat in silence, puffing with cold, gawking at us. They looked the kind of people who come to brainwash you about Jesus when *Home and Away*'s just started.

I licked Bex's ear-lobe and hoops, murmured: 'You gagging for me?' A hand brushed his thigh, tip-toed to his crotch. He smacked my fingers.

'Shabby for old folks this time of year, eh, Kylie? Your gran and that . . . Pure shanner. Plus. Imagine being the poor bugger answers that Hotline, eh. Ears must be ringing. Bet half the Hotliners end up Mainliners themselves, eh? Heh, heh! That was a good yin, eh . . . Christ, Kylie, each time we hit a bump I get shivers like a live wire through my dick.'

'We'll hit Mum's cider to get us totally back down and straight, eh? We're such horny puppies. But we're being watched by these two Jehovah Witness robots who think we're dirty sinners, eh, who want us transformed into kebab meat in hell for having our wee bit nookie, for guzzling a teensy-weeny bit acid.'

My gloves slid up between his legs; as he pressed his thighs tight together I pushed harder. Bursting out laughing I gave him healthy mouth-to-ear, felt him squirm.

'School's pure getting the go-bye the morn, eh,' I went on. 'We'll be snowed in, in our wee love nest, eh?!'

Winking at his reflection I tugged his Raiders baseball cap right down over his face, ruffled his hair, heaved his hood up. Then I pinched his knee cause he pure *hates* that and when he tried to grab my wrists I jabbed him in the belly, making him jump so much he cracked his head off the window. This had me decked for ages, there was no way I could stop laughing. The old couple were staring like they'd seen cloven hooves under my Cats and this just made me a hundred times worse. He slapped at my hand so straight away I shoved it under his jacket, fighting into the folds of his Tommy Hilfiger sweater, digging under that to his CK Jeans sweatshirt, under that to his skinny ribs to claw my nails. Now he was wriggling into the corner, tears streaming down his cheeks, his face squealing with laughter but fuckall sound coming out his mouth, just this weird whistling noise. So I just shut my eyes and kept tickling, crushing against him to keep him trapped there till it felt as if we'd been this way for hours. We'd moved on one stop.

I stared into the blackness past all our reflections and decided that tonight was the night. On my sixteenth birthday I'd tell Darren Beck I loved him. That gave goosebumps fuck all to do with the cold. Even after such a short time I felt that close. I mind my dad once told me how he felt he was in love soon as he *saw* my mum, in a Human League bob, at some club called 'Valentino's'. We'll never split, though. Tonight I was definitely telling Bex. After I'd given him my virginity. If he didn't say it, too, we were *finished*.

I felt like passing out, like a hooked fish, trembling, gasping for air. His fingers gripped my shoulders numb but I couldn't speak. Our crazy heartbeats died, like sprinters after they've crossed the wire. And in my mum's Hampden-sized bed, we were all giggly moans and sighs; I felt as if we'd been sky-diving, had landed with a big, gorgeous bang. But before I remembered anything about love I was drifting off on sleepy seas.

Mum's bedside clock read 04.11. There was a hint of a stone but I was more shattered. The condom felt like his shrivelled cock had shed a layer of sticky skin.

'*Yeeeuch*', I hissed, flicking it from the duvet. I squeezed in till I felt his heart's tiny drum against my chest. As my mind wandered I struggled to hold on to this: would these feelings be so extreme when I woke? But I *knew* they would.

I dreamt we were amongst thousands of kids. We were all wearing khaki rags and shivering with cold. A huge barbed-wire fence enclosed us. A Russian horseman was leading an army to the gates. We all shared the same ecstasy when the gates crashed open.

I ran past the white horse. I kept on running, through white, white snow. Into the space.

CAVE PAINTINGS

RUTH THOMAS

C arlos Gonzalez was two years older than Linda. He drove a moped but he still wore childish shorts. In his first letter to her he had written '*Hallo Linda! I am pleased to be your pen-pal! I am fifteen and my eyes are blue, brown, green.*'

'He sounds as if he's got three eyes,' said Linda's father, when she read the letter out at home. Now she was in Spain, staying with him, and she realised that he was not pleased to be her pen-pal. The whole thing was embarrassing.

The Gonzalez' house, *Casita Bonita*, was the furthest out of town. It had a wishing well, a kidney-shaped swimming pool and palm trees. Mr Gonzalez worked for an insurance company, but he spent a lot of the day sitting at the side of the swimming pool wearing thick rubber flip-flops. He never swam. He had a dark tan and chest-hair. He would play a tape-recording of chirping crickets if the weather wasn't warm enough for the real thing. 'You swim,' he said to Linda, and she would like to have leapt into the pale, shining water, holding her breath, but the sight of his chest and his striped swimming trunks deterred her.

Mrs Gonzalez had a gold handbag. Everything about her was gold and sparkling. Her hair was dyed blonde and her perfume was the colour of amber. She was out working all day and when she came home in the evenings and saw Linda she sometimes made a strange noise with her mouth that sounded like disapproval.

'You're really lucky,' Linda said to her friend Trish after the first weekend, 'your family's really nice.' Trish had got a traditional Spanish mother with black hair. She made ratatouille and had *jamón serrano* hanging from hooks.

On her first Monday there, Mrs Gonzalez had knocked on her bedroom door, given her money and asked her to walk to the bakery to buy bread. 'Good for your Spanish,' she said. 'You know how to say *I would like bread please?*' and Linda had got dressed and walked down the lane, feeling jettisoned but almost exhilarated to get out of Casita Bonita. There was a wide view from the town, of navy-blue sky and beige mountains. Casita Bonita, from a distance, made her think of sugar cubes; she could imagine picking it up with tongs and dropping it into a cup of tea.

The bakery did not have any bread on the shelves, just a small framed picture of the Virgin Mary. The bread was kept in a large sack under the counter. 'Queria pan, por favor,' Linda said. The bread woman looked at her with small brown eyes. She went to the bread sack, took out a curiously-shaped loaf and thumped it on to the counter. 'Cien pesetas,' she said. There was a plate of biscuits at the back of the shop, under another Virgin Mary picture. Linda pointed at them. 'Cien,' said the woman. Linda gave her the money in small change. Then she walked out of the shop with the bread and biscuits. The biscuits were good – crumbly and tasting of cinnamon. People appeared from doorways and watched her as she ate. People stared a lot, she had noticed – the men playing dominoes in the bars; the women washing the pavements, the women dressed in black. 'Hola,' she said, but the women just stood there with their arms folded across their big stomachs. She took another biscuit out of the bag and turned up the lane that led back to the Gonzalez' house. She walked slowly, sliding her sandals in the dust.

Casita Bonita was white and cool. It was like an igloo. When she got back she let herself in through the kitchen door, walked through the house and out again into the garden, where Mr and Mrs Gonzalez were sitting, silent, on plastic chairs. The garden was the beautiful thing about the house. She had never seen anything so colourful. There were roses and lilies and olive trees and a peach tree. She approached the table and Mrs Gonzalez poured her some coffee. She pulled pieces of bread off the loaf Linda had bought, and put them on a plate. 'Linda, why not pick olives?' Mr Gonzalez said almost as soon as Linda had sat down. Mrs Gonzalez put her sunglasses on and smiled a thin smile. 'OK,' said Linda. She wasn't learning much Spanish. She got up from her chair, walked up to the top of the garden and sat on a tree-stump. There were little lizards sitting on the tiled roof, blinking, sunning themselves, and when she looked up she could see the Gonzalez' neighbours sitting like bigger lizards on their terraces, reading and sunbathing. Carlos had gone out some-where on his moped; she could hear the noise it made, the echo of it in the lanes, ricocheting against the white walls of the houses.

When she walked back down the steps Mr Gonzalez had gone, but Mrs Gonzalez was still sitting there, reading a book. Linda had picked a handful of olives from the tree, and she put them on the table. Mrs Gonzalez looked at them. 'Very green,' she said, and she made the disapproving noise with her mouth. She put her book down.

'Linda,' she said, 'In Spanish, Linda means "nice". Do you know that?'

'Yes,' said Linda, 'my teacher told me.'

'And you are a nice girl, Linda,' said Mrs Gonzalez. 'You are very English,' she said. 'I'm Scottish,' said Linda. Mrs Gonzalez put her head on one side, like a big bird. Then she leaned across the table and patted Linda's arm. The sun had created prickly heat bumps already, on the backs of Linda's hands. 'Oh look,' said Mrs Gonzalez. Her voice caught. 'Oh no,' she said, dramatically, and she picked up her tube of sun tan cream and squirted inches of it on to Linda's hands. 'Pay attention of the sun, Linda,' she said. 'Yes,' said Linda. 'Now I must go,' said Mrs Gonzalez. She stood up and adjusted her bikini. There was a zig-zag pattern impressed into her thighs.

Linda was meant to walk to school with Carlos, but he seemed to spend all day skiving with his friends. Some of them had thin moustaches. They went up into the mountains with their mopeds, and threw sticks at tourists as they walked past. After Mrs Gonzalez had left, Linda walked back into the house and lay on the leather couch, behind the venetian blinds. Mrs Gonzalez kept a little caged bird in the sitting room. She called it Chico. It looked like a sparrow. Linda felt like opening the cage door and letting it escape. She got up from the couch, walked towards the cage and put her fingers against the bars. The sparrow came and pecked at her fingernail for a while, then it flew away again. Linda went into the kitchen and opened the fridge door. It was full of things that she had never seen before; strange cheeses and vegetables and milk that wobbled about in plastic bags. She took a four-pack of crème caramel from the top shelf and snapped off a carton. She peeled back the lid, up-ended the carton on to a saucer and watched the dessert slide slowly down the plastic. It was a perfect castle-shape. She found a teaspoon and ate the crème caramel slowly, cutting little curves into its sides so that it resembled the mountains around the town. She left the caramel sauce until last. Mr Gonzalez came into the kitchen as she was putting the final spoonful of it into her mouth.

'What are you doing?' he asked in Spanish. She couldn't think of the Spanish for 'I am eating,' so she just smiled. 'Hola,' she said. That was all she could think of. Mr Gonzalez looked at her. He didn't smile. He walked out of the kitchen and into the living room. He started to move things around loudly in there, as if he had mislaid something.

When she got to Carlos' school she couldn't see anyone she knew so she walked back up the lane, past the bakery and the women standing in doorways, and into the town. There was a little cafe in the square. During the daytime it was full of old men in hats playing dominoes. The old men turned in their seats and stared as she walked in. Then they turned back to the dominoes. There were tupperware boxes standing on the counter. They were full of dried-up tapas – olives and chorizo and a kind of potato mayonnaise. Linda asked the barman for a coffee and he looked at her as if she amused him, and gave her a tiny cup of espresso. After a while, he walked away and started throwing pastry into a pan of oil.

Linda sat at a table next to the domino players. She took some postcards out of her bag and looked at them. They were views of the town; one of the church, one of two old men with walking sticks, and one of the mountains. They looked like the kind of postcards she received at home, that said nothing about anything. She turned one of them over. 'View of the stunning 16th-century church of the Virgin Mary'.

> *Dear Mum and Dad*
> *It's hot here. The Gonzalez' have a swimming pool*
> *and an olive tree. I am sitting in a cafe next to some*
> *old men playing dominoes.*

The door opened. There was a tiny breeze, and in walked Trish with her penfriend, whose name Linda had forgotten. They were both wearing suede trousers.

'Linda,' said Trish, 'what are you doing?'

'I'm writing postcards,' said Linda.

'But shouldn't you be with Carlos?'

'Yes I should,' she said. She felt angry suddenly, and sad. 'I should,' she said, 'but Carlos is on his moped in the mountains.'

'Oh,' said Trish.

Trish's penfriend put her hands in her pockets and looked at her.

'We thought we'd get a coffee before school,' Trish said.

'I thought you didn't like coffee,' Linda said. Trish ignored her.

They went to the bar and Trish's penfriend asked the barman for two coffees with milk. She said something else to the barman and he winked and gave her a little bowl of sweets, wrapped in coloured paper. Then she and Trish walked back to Linda's table.

'Do you want some of mine?' Trish asked Linda when the barman brought the coffee over. 'I could pour it into your cup.'

'No thanks,' said Linda. 'I've had plenty.'

Trish looked at Linda's tiny espresso cup and didn't reply.

'So, Linda,' said Trish's penfriend, 'What have you been doing at the weekend?'

Linda gripped the tablecloth and tried to think of something interesting to tell them.

'I went swimming,' she said, 'And I looked at the church of the Virgin Mary.' She couldn't think of anything else. 'How about you?' she said.

'We went to Ronda and got these trousers. You should go, Linda,' said Trish. 'They're really cheap. You should get a pair. And we went to Alcatraz. And we looked at a cave yesterday. It's got stone-age paintings in it.'

'It is not far,' said Trish's penfriend.

'It's just in the mountains up there,' said Trish, pointing through the window, 'but you have to make an appointment with a man.'

'Right,' said Linda. Mr Gonzalez had asked Carlos to take her to the cave on Saturday, but Carlos had just shrugged and said something Linda didn't understand.

Trish's penfriend drank some coffee. 'Linda,' she said, 'do you know that in Spanish, Linda means "nice"?'

'Yes,' said Linda, 'people have told me.' She unwrapped a sweet and sucked it for a while, until it was a sharp diamond in her mouth.

Her bedroom was at the far end of Casita Bonita. When she had arrived from the airport, Mrs Gonzalez had taken her to see it straight away. She told her she had papered the walls herself. The paper was the colour of apricots, and there were pictures of flowers on the walls. There was also a picture of Mr Gonzalez, taken several years earlier, when he was thinner and better looking. He was sitting at a table drinking beer.

Mrs Gonzalez told her she should have a siesta at lunchtime, and Linda had tried to sleep, lying on top of the duvet, but she had kept sneezing. She wondered if she was allergic to the Gonzalez' pillows. When she came back from school, she would sit by the swimming pool if Mr Gonzalez wasn't there, but if he was she went to her room. There was a fan in the corner, and she would switch it on to try to dispel whatever it was that was making her sneeze. At around eight o'clock, Mrs Gonzalez came back from work. Linda would hear her throw her bag and keys on the kitchen table, sigh, walk into her dressing room and shut the door. She would spend about twenty minutes in there, then she would emerge in different clothes: crisply casual things with motifs and bits of fake jewellery sewn on to them. She would begin to cook dinner while Carlos and Mr Gonzalez sat by the swimming pool. Every so often, Carlos would throw something into the water – an olive stone or a leaf – and Mr Gonzalez would shout at him.

Linda walked into the kitchen when Mrs Gonzalez got home. She stood at the sink, flexing her toes inside her trainers.

'Can I help you?' she asked.

'No,' said Mrs Gonzalez.

She walked lightly over the kitchen tiles in a pair of gold mules. She gathered things together – vegetables, ham from plastic packets, a bottle of Coca-cola.

'I am making tortilla,' she said. She cracked four eggs into a bowl and started to whisk them together. She looked through the window.

'Carlos is not a nice boy,' she said.

Linda leaned against the cool marble worktop. Mrs Gonzalez stopped whisking the eggs and looked at her. 'Too much sun today,' she said. 'You are very pink. Very English.'

'I'm Scottish,' said Linda.

When the tortillas were ready they put plates on the table and Mrs Gonzalez called to Carlos and her husband. 'My husband is angry,' she said, closing the window.

Carlos and Mr Gonzalez came in, sat at the table, folded their arms and said nothing. Carlos had wet hair, and Mrs Gonzalez tapped him on the head with a wooden spoon and said something to him in a sharp voice. Carlos shrugged. He didn't eat any of the tortilla. He sat with his elbows on the table and made small comments. Occasionally he picked up the mayonnaise jar and dipped breadsticks into it. Mr and Mrs Gonzalez ignored him. They cut up slices of tortilla and broke off pieces of bread from the loaf Linda had bought. From time to time, Mrs Gonzalez would get up from the table and feed pieces of ham to Chico the bird.

On Saturday, when everyone else was at the beach or visiting the Alhambra, Mrs Gonzalez decided that they would stay at home and have four o'clock tea. 'You do this in Britain?' she said to Linda. 'Tea at four o'clock?'

'Not really,' said Linda. 'Not any more.'

Mrs Gonzalez said it again: 'Tea at four o'clock,' as if she wanted to confirm something, some belief. 'You have cakes and sandwiches,' she said.

'No', said Linda, 'we don't have four o'clock tea. We aren't often at home then.'

Carlos sat in the armchair behind them and sniggered – from where she was standing she could just see the edges of his big, beige knees. Mrs Gonzalez sighed. Before the shops shut she went out and bought cakes at the bakery – chocolate eclairs and strawberry tarts and more of the cinnamon biscuits. She opened the packet of Earl Grey tea that Linda had given her, and made ham sandwiches with very white, crustless bread. This time Linda didn't offer to help. She just sat and watched her buttering bread. It was a still day; the air in the kitchen hung.

Mrs Gonzalez placed the cake stand on the table. She put some orange blossom in a vase and placed it on a crocheted doily. At four o'clock they sat down. Mr Gonzalez cleared his throat and rubbed his hands together. He was still wearing his T-shirt and swimming trunks, but Mrs Gonzalez had changed into a red dress and high-heeled shoes.

Just as she was pouring the tea, Carlos suddenly got up from his chair and went into his room. He came back with a video camera. He sat down again and began to film them all. 'Carlos!' said Mrs Gonzalez, but he didn't reply. He sat opposite Linda and pointed the camera at her. She didn't look up. She pretended not to notice him. She talked to Mrs Gonzalez with all her concentration, twirling a strand of hair around her finger, holding her head in an unnatural position to make it as annoying as possible for Carlos. She thought of his first letter to her: *Hallo! I am pleased to be your pen-pal! My eyes are brown, blue, green.* When she had received the letter, she had imagined somebody nice.

'Now, Linda,' said Mrs Gonzalez. She smiled and offered Linda a strawberry tart. 'They are little,' she said, 'have two.' She filled her cup from a very ornate teapot, and glanced across the table at her husband. Mr Gonzalez was just sitting there, with a linen napkin tucked into the top of his T-shirt. He was glaring at his son, who had finished filming the tea-party and was now playing the picture back. From where she was sitting, Linda could see them all, tiny and upside-down on a little screen. Even from that distance she knew that she didn't want to look any closer. The sound-track had Mrs Gonzalez' loud voice, Linda's inane, ungrammatical mum-blings, and shrieks from Chico in the background.

'That is enough, Carlos,' Mr Gonzalez said, but Carlos didn't look up. He continued to play the film.

'That is enough,' said Mr Gonzalez, and he suddenly burst up from his chair like some big, dark wave, projected himself across to Carlos' side of the table and grabbed the video camera. He opened the back of the camera, pulled the film out and strode, swearing, through the back door with it. Carlos sat with his mouth open and his hands still in a camera-holding position. Then he started to shout in a hoarse, cracked voice. Tears came into his eyes. We all watched from the table as Mr Gonzalez reached the edge of the swimming pool and hurled Carlos' film into the water.

After that, Carlos changed. He became quiet. On Sunday, while Mr Gonzalez was out, he opened the door to Chico's cage and let the bird fly away. He stopped going out on his moped; he just went into the garage and stood looking at it.

He didn't speak to his parents, but suddenly he started to talk to Linda, about three days before she was due to leave. He took her for walks. On her last day in Andalusia, he took her to see the cave paintings. Not because his father asked; he just took her there. He knew a way in. The cave was massive inside, like a cathedral, and as cool as a well. After they had been in there a while, the lack of oxygen made it difficult to breathe. Carlos said that people would never have been able to live in the cave; nobody really knew what they had used the cave for. There were just these paintings. They walked further in and it took a few moments for their eyes to become accustomed to the dark, but when they were, they saw pictures on the walls; drawings of horses, fish, people. There was one of a deer and one of a seal with a fish, upside-down, inside its belly.

'These are twenty thousand years old,' Carlos whispered. They were older than anything Linda could imagine. Looking at them, it was hard to believe in things like swimming pools and four o'clock tea. It was hard to believe that these things mattered.

LEADING OUT

DAVID NICOL

A listair came up to Fawhope at the end of April. His big
idea was to go to Spain for the summer. That's why he
tried his hand at the tree planting. Though the wages were not
enormous, there was no rent to pay, nor electricity. It would
be money in the bank until June.

A big dopey creature, he was always the first to lend a hand,
even though he never had much idea what was going on. If he
jumped in right up to his neck he never knew till it was too
late. That was his downcome.

The second day he was up on the hill with the squad, Steven
came by to tell them a van was on its way.

He said, We have to lead out some trees.

Andrew and Jim grumbled a bit. They had been working for
a while and were well into the rhythm of planting. But Brian
was pleased. The hourly rate for unloading trees and carting
them up the hill would earn him more than the piece rates they
got for planting them. For Alistair too, he explained, Leading
out is better.

They walked over the burn to unload the trees from the van.
These were one-year-old spruce, which they counted in
bundles of fifty, digging them into a seuch near the shale
quarry. The track was too rough for the van to drive any
further. Even the track to the quarry from the farm at

Fawcleuch was too rough for some vehicles. While the van could make it, and wreck its suspension no doubt, Steven always parked his car at the bottom, and hiked up. Likewise they had their caravan parked in the shale quarry. It was their home for the season.

So Brian put the kettle on, while Steven went to hire Fawcleuch's tractor and trailer. When he returned, the planters were standing in the spring sunshine, swirling tea dregs in their mugs.

They threw forty thousand trees on board the trailer. Steven was counting as Andrew caught them on top. He stacked the bundles, taking care to keep the roots covered, until the trailer resembled a small mobile burial mound. Then they all clambered on top, as Steven fired the engine to tow them round the horseshoe track.

The scent of spruce was sharp in their nostrils, as they sprawled on the bed of soft needles. Underneath them the trailer would bounce and swing over ruts and potholes. Then, going round the saddle, they saw the howe spread out below them. Faw Burn flowed out at Fawcleuch, the farm small as a match box with its plumes of smoke. The loch lay still, and skimmering blue against the brown hills in slanting spring sunshine.

But on the far side of the howe there was no sweeping view of the loch, and the weakening sun was obscured by a bank of low cloud drifting in from the west.

The trailer plowtered about in wet clay. Up here the partly excavated track was more like a mire than a road. Diggers and bulldozers had gouged deep caterpillar ruts in the sodden subsoil. The ruts held water which ran down the furrows off the brae. Less than a mile from the head of the howe, the drainage seuch spewed a pool of liquid clay over the etched surface. This was dammed in on three sides by huge mounds of soft boulder clay.

Steven cut the engine.

That's as far as we go, he shouted through the cabin window.

Jim was counting out the bundles by the time he got round.

Throw them down gently, he said, They're starting tae bud now.

Nae bother Steenie, cried Andrew.

He continued throwing them down gently, with an ironic wink to Alistair.

While they were stacking the trees in a furrow, Steven unhitched the trailer and backed the tractor behind it. He had to reverse down the track as far as the saddle, then turn it round and reverse again up to the trailer. Rain spattered the windshield as he turned.

Jim started in as foreman, ordering the planters about as a blast of hail swept down the howe. Brian jumped into the furrow, piling the trees in from the top downwards. Alistair slaistered about at their back busily, while Andrew spaded soil between the trees and the edge of the seuch.

The rain was dinging down hard and icy on their bare heads when Steven came back. Andrew was cutting turves for Jim to pack round the exposed trees at the end, filling the gaps with earth.

The next problem was to turn the trailer round and hitch it on to the tractor. Throwing on his cagoule, Steven perused the droukit planters. Having worked flat out, their breath came in warm clouds against the cold air.

Now three pairs of hands gripped the tow bar. Two shoulders were pressed to the trailer's rear. Their muscles strained, their feet slorked and scraped. But the wheels had settled deep in the clay.

No wey man, cried Jim at last, throwing up his hands. It's tae heavy.

Five meenits, said Andrew, slipping his pipe from his

pocket. But it was turning to sleet, and beneath his jacket the tobacco was damp.

He kicked a boulder moodily.

Ye havena got a rope there, Stevie? said Jim.

He was really half joking, but the manager's eyes lit up.

Ay, in the cab.

Typical, said Andrew as Steven reached through the door of the tractor, They never learn common sense at the Uni.

Jim rubbed his hands together.

We'll be back ben the caravan in a jiffy, he encouraged them.

Ay, said Brian, But mind and put it in the timesheet.

Ye're nae joking. At least we'll be peyed for staunding about in the rain. We'll put in a hail dey for it.

Never mind, said Steven, I'll see ye get paid.

He was as drenched as any of them by the time they hitched up the trailer. He looked at his watch and said, Four o'clock. We'll be back at the quarry by half past. But I'll make sure ye get paid until six.

Was that eight o'clock ye said?

That was Drew, chancing it.

Six.

We could be earning twice as much planting wi tither squad up at the Law.

Seeven I think he said, put in Jim.

Seven then, said the manager, shaking his head.

The planters were swinging over the trailer board as he climbed into the cab.

The empty trailer shoogled and jumped over the ruts, hitting unseen boulders beneath the surface water. Each bump transmitted a shock straight up their spines. Brian began to chitter from cold. They had not gone far before he jumped off the trailer.

Walking through mud was better than rattling about like a

pea in a whistle, and the movement brought warm blood into damp flesh.

Jim and Andrew followed soon after. They trauchled along the edge of the track, flyting at Alistair.

C'mon ye fat pudden! cried Brian.

Mind, ye'll wrack your back staunding there, Andrew advised him helpfully.

Why daes he nae jump aff? Jim was wondering.

From where they saw him, Alistair seemed to be thrown in the air like a plastic duck on a fairground waterspout. Andrew raised his spade and pretended to take potshots at him.

Ken what it is, Jim? he said, He doesna like exercise. The walking's tae much for him.

But Brian noticed Alistair's face was changing. Gone was his placid expression, to be replaced by an anxious frown.

Haud on, he said to his companions.

Alistair had one foot on the board at the back of the trailer. But the more often he tried to jump over, the more he felt himself thwarted, and the greater his panic.

C'mon on! cried Andrew, laughing as Alistair fell backward again.

His knuckles were white where they gripped the side of the trailer, and his eyes were wide open. He was staring pleadingly at Brian.

Wheesht Drew, he said. The puir bugger's feart.

Jim turned to Brian as they walked.

He should jump, he said.

He daurna, said Brian, I'll get Steenie tae stap.

Brian tried running. His wellies were sucked in by the clay so that he almost ran right out of them. Then he took to the side of the track, where he tended to slide on the wet grass.

He had just caught up with the trailer, when the inside wheel suddenly sank in a puddle, where it struck a submerged boulder. Brian jouked aside to avoid the spray. Alistair was hurled off the tail as the trailer pivoted upward. He fell sprawled in the track, while the trailer, coming loose from its coupling, buried its tow bar in the clay.

Andrew and Jim were the first to reach him. But Alistair slapped away their outstretched hands and slithered to his feet, while Brian came running.

The eedjit! he hissed.

They made a grim huddle between the grey earth and a lowering sky, when Steven reluctantly jumped from the warm tractor cab and strode over.

What happened?

He scanned their smeared faces.

Alistair?

Just winded, he gasped.

His face was deathly pale.

Is he alright?

Ay, said Andrew. He alwise luiks like a drouned rat.

No bones broken any way.

Luck alone had spared Alistair worse.

Jim was livid.

Ye should hae watched where ye're gaen, he rounded on Steven.

I thought ye were all off, he said. I never saw it. Thon puddle, eh?

There was no blaming anyone really. It was just one of those freak accidents. Alistair stoatered about. As soon as he had gotten his breath back, he used it to turn the air blue with curses. Then he took off his jacket and tried wringing it out. But his shirt and trousers were pasted to his shivering body.

I should maybe run hame, he said.

The caravan was actually quite near; if you run down the brae to the burn and up the other side you would reach it before anyone was half way round the track.

I'll be fine once I get out o the wet.

Nae bruising at all? said Brian.

Just a bit shaken.

Shaken, said Andrew, not stirred. Come on Steenie, let's get your tractor back up and we're away. It's nae the right kind o weather tae hang about in.

Brian signalled, as Steven brought the tractor back up to the trailer. Then Jim turned from the tow bar.

Drew? he said. Our resident strongman.

Andrew flexed his biceps.

Nae contest.

Jim was in his bantering mood. Encouraged by Andrew, who would always rise to a challenge, he must wring some fun from this miserable circumstance.

What about Brian? he said, Brawn-ower-brain Brian. For a shot at the championship? The warld class trailer lifting. Heavyweight. Roll up now. And dinna be blate. Competitors ready.

But Alistair was the first to go forward. Maybe he was eager to show he was useful for something. Or perhaps he was impatient to get back to the dry caravan. Maybe it was his way to overcome the embarrassment of being thrown off the trailer. If he hadn't yet learnt the skilly parts of tree-planting, he could at least win through by brute strength.

The bucking bronco kid! Andrew announced him.

Quit foutering about, said Alistair. Let's get on the road.

Stooping, he grabbed the end of the tow bar in his hands and flexed his back.

Hauld on, cried Jim. It's only a joke, man!

But Alistair had committed himself.

He might have managed under better conditions. As it was he had the bar lifted up to the height of his thigh, when the full weight of it slipped from his grasp.

He leapt backwards, screaming, as the head of the tow bar dropped with a sickening crunch on his foot.

Within minutes his ankle swelled up till it was taut as a football. It would be a long painful journey to take him back round by the track. So they took turns at carrying or oxtering him straight down the brae to the farm.

Fawcleuch met them coming through his neep park.

He offered to help but the manager said, No thanks.

He had his car parked right there, and Alistair would be better off if he drove him straight to the clinic in town.

The next time Steven was up at Fawhope he had told the squad that an X-ray showed a crack in Alistair's ankle. The following day he got the bus back to Edinburgh with a stookie on his foot. Steven would make sure he got paid in cash for the work he had done.

That was the last they heard of Alistair. After they led him off the hill, his bunk stayed empty for the rest of the season.

When the planters had finished at Fawhope they moved on to clear bracken and gorse at the Law. The few belongings he'd brought up were submerged in the caravan's junk. But nobody found out if he made it to Spain. Nobody ever heard how his foot mended.

TO BEGIN

CYNTHIA ROGERSON

There was the sun, the dripping heat and there was the metallic taste in Sheena's mouth. Now she knew what caused it, it was not repulsive, but a harbinger of hope and change. A quicksilver flash that could save her.

Earlier, when she was offering flyers to the passing current of strangers, she hadn't known and the urge to spit had become so strong, she'd fled up the stairs to the toilet. Instead of spitting, she'd vomited. Sour, the enamel scoured off her teeth. But her stomach felt relieved, and she picked up her pink flyers from the floor and went back to work.

PARISIAN FASHIONS
CUT RATE PRICES
1067 SPADINA, 3rd Floor

Paris was three thousand miles away, her boss was Turkish, she was Scottish. She'd not met many Canadians since coming to Toronto. There seemed to be a home for everyone, except perhaps coastal dwellers, of which Sheena was one. The lake could not quite answer her need for the sea. She sometimes dreamt she was home on Skye, with the Atlantic out her window, wild and familiar. Awake, a kind of claustrophobia threatened. Too much land between her and the open sea.

Some women put out their hands automatically when she gestured with her fanned-out sheets. Others looked through her, made her feel insubstantial. She was wearing one of Sammy's outfits, Modelling, he'd called it. A long white linen skirt and a tight turquoise sleeveless blouse. Probably he thought it improved her chances of delivering his flyers. Better than her jeans and T-shirts.

An odd job, but no odder than most of the jobs she'd had. It was money and enabled her to live in foreign countries. Living, as opposed to visiting, felt genuine. And somehow, someday, it would all be useful.

That was the theory. At the moment, empty-stomached and light-headed, Sheena felt as purposeless as a wind-borne seed over the ocean. Random, unconnected.

She thought about the appointment she'd made at the clinic for that afternoon. The skirt band felt tight, and if she didn't pace a little, her bare feet in sandals ached. She trawled the pavement, keeping a light smile on her face. She didn't bother with the men, though mostly they sought eye contact, while she sought women's eyes.

She hadn't told Daniel. Why worry him if there was no cause?

Anyway, he was probably thinking about Natasha, the beautiful Russian woman they shared a house with, along with seven others. Daniel and herself were the only couple.

They had a big bed but no place to put their clothes, so they kept them in folded stacks on the floor and a chair. The kitchen and bathroom were like all communal rooms. If you wanted a dish or pan, you had to wash it first. No one bothered with the bathroom. Somedays there was toilet paper, most days not. She had begun to keep a roll in their room.

Natasha had very dark and large eyes. She wore black and hennaed her short hair red. Definitely Sheena's superior, style wise. Natasha told Daniel he looked like John Lennon. She giggled and said John Lennon was her favourite Beatle, even if he was dead. Daniel said it was just the glasses, but smiled.

Sheena had felt surprised someone like Natasha thought Daniel was worth a flirt. Was there something she'd missed, had she finally hit on it by accident? He was new to her, she was still looking at him. Was he the one?

At one o'clock, she took the remaining flyers back up the stairs.

'Here you go, Sammy. Get any customers?'

'Three lady. Two come in and leave. One, she try red dress. End up buying two. One for daughter. What you think? Hot enough today. You want Coke?'

Sammy was short and fat, with smooth olive skin that glistened. She had no idea what he thought of her. Maybe he didn't judge her at all, had no curiosity. She wondered if he'd heard her retching. She hadn't thought of that before.

'Thanks Sammy. Boiling out there, I can hardly breathe. I think I might be getting a bug. My stomach.'

'Oh, you no want sick. Tell it go away. Bug, fly out window.' He smiled, gold teeth glittering.

How did he stay so happy? He was like a placid Buddha, sitting up here in his empty shop, waiting for women to waft up the stairs on the hot air. And what did the women think, being alone with him, peeling off their clothes in the tiny cubicle to try on his dresses? It wasn't even a real shop, just a converted apartment. This part of Spadina was a smoggy noisy neighbourhood far from the cafes and art galleries. So who were these ladies, who were both brave and wealthy, for Sammy's prices were not cheap?

Maybe they were all illicit – herself, the customers, Sammy. Frauds aping the lives of normal citizens. Travellers who knew life was just a series of accidental events. Maybe that was why, despite everything, she felt so comfortable with fat happy Sammy.

'Hey bug, listen to Sammy and bug off. There, I feel much better now.'

'You go change, I get ice for Coke.'

'Nice skirt, Sammy.'

'You want? For you, forty-five dollars. That half price. Direct from France, cost two hundred.'

'Sorry. How about a fiver?'

'Get away. You make big joke.'

The lady at the clinic asked if she wanted to wait or not. She could phone back later. No, she wanted to wait. She read the brochures on the table. Alternatives to motherhood abounded, even after birth. Trips across the border to New York were advertised. Different laws. When was a bundle of cells a human being? Several pamphlets claimed to know.

There was no air conditioning and a slight breeze of exhaust fumes strained through the window screens. While watching a fly that must have come in with someone through the door, the metallic taste resurged and she closed her eyes to concentrate on her equilibrium. Everything in her was clouded, slow, stupid. Her name was called and she was ushered into a small room.

'I'm sorry,' said the nurse, assuming from her ringless finger it was bad news.

Sheena left the clinic and re-entered the summer day. A long day, one which had seen her step lightly over boundaries. From Sheena the lost wanderer to Sheena the bearer of important being. Untethered kite to rooted tree. On the bus down Bloor, she crossed her hands over her belly and half smiled. Around her, in the air and through the earth, she could feel a kind of sense emerging where there had been nothing but arbitrariness before. Endless options narrowed down to one, an unstoppable momentum with a unique set of routines and limits. A baby. A relief.

'But how can we, there's no money, you know,' said Daniel later, kindly not reminding her how little time they'd known each other, how perhaps she was not his choice of mother for his offspring. How much he disliked having to think about people in new ways.

She remembered when she'd first arrived. Long days of not speaking to anyone, reading novels. Walking the streets or sitting in cafes drinking cappuccinos and eating pastries black with poppy seeds. Scanning *The Star* for jobs. It had been freezing. She had been cold, pierced with loneliness and boredom. When had her adventures started feeling like this, when had freedom started feeling like dislocation? She couldn't remember.

She'd met Daniel and lunged for him, to stop floating away. In the beginning, she'd watch the clock, waiting for him to come home from work. Ten minutes late seemed hours. Later, urgency melted into a softer rhythm, but there was still a sense of coming to when she saw him. As if she was dream-walking through her days.

They did not know each other, would never know each other. Their conversations were clumsy words tossed on the wind from one island to another, arriving battered and foreign. Only the clear and solid fact of their pull towards each other survived. This did not seem to require articulation or even thought.

I know this kind of news is supposed to come at a different time, she wanted to tell him. After much thought and choosing and public celebrations and mortgages and yellow-painted tiny bedrooms with teddy bear borders. All safe and right.

I know. But.

She wanted to ask, does it really matter so much how it

starts? The proper timing and reasons, these might be only social niceties. Has a child ever been born who cared about anything but love and warmth and food?

'Not now,' he repeated softly, reaching out to touch her tears.

'I need to begin,' said Sheena at last, looking at him. 'This is my beginning.'

Then Daniel did a remarkable thing. He smiled, he smiled because he couldn't help it. The pleasure was that sudden. He laid his hand across her belly, and she covered with it with both of her own.

And all the rest of her life, whenever she wondered how anything had come to happen, she traced events back to this moment. Her tears, his smile, their hands.

ABOUT PERFECTION

GORDON LEGGE

All his working days, near enough twenty year now with Allied Biscuits, Ramsey Buchanan had had women for colleagues and bosses. Not that that was ever a problem, mind. Indeed, what with its longstanding dependence on team-work, and, more specifically, its sit-down breaks, the work was ideally suited for the bachelor Ramsey to indulge in a playful degree of flirting and teasing. Also, when things weren't going so well, and Ramsey had been binned or whatever, as happened every now and again, it was good to have that feminine reassurance at hand. 'Ach,' he would be told, 'she doesn't know what she's missing, Ramsey, son. Lovely young lad like yourself.'

Just what Ramsey was wanting to hear. Sometimes he would even get a comforting cuddle.

But then this new start appeared. Trainee management. And – surprise, surprise – it was a bloke. Some young fellow. A total straight with the big new car, the bought house and the bidie-in fiancée. Now, thing was, Ramsey didn't take to having this young fellow around. No, there was an undeniable awkwardness; an awkwardness which came to a head one morning when Ramsey was going on about what he called 'the latest bit of intrigue'.

'Aye,' said Ramsey, 'wonder if she'll be the one, eh? Awfy quiet lass, mind. Not really a lot to say for herself.'

'Away,' said Madge, rinsing out her mug, 'you never know unless you try.'

'True,' said Ramsey, 'true. Just see what happens, eh.' Then Ramsey did his usual. First, he gave Madge a silent, studied grin, then he cast a slow, sideways glance. Finally, he leant forward and whispered, 'Aye, now there's a thought.'

Ramsey was forever saying 'now there's a thought', and it was forever accompanied by the grin and glance routine. It always got a laugh.

But on this occasion, the new fellow, the young fellow, he wasn't having it. No, he just turned round to Ramsey and said, 'Nah, trouble with the likes of you, right, you playboy types, is you'll never find yourself a woman. Want to know why? Cause you've got this daft idea – perfection. Now there's a thought for *you*, eh.'

The young fellow laughed. The women all laughed. Even Ramsey laughed – but then, horror of horrors, he started thinking.

'Are you all right, Ramsey, son?' said Madge.

'Aye,' said Ramsey, 'aye. Fine.'

But all afternoon, Ramsey's head was buzzing. See, as he'd tried to explain, when he went on about lassies he wasn't sure of, he went on about their faults. It was supposed to be funny, harmless, a kind of entertainment. And when he went on about lassies whom he did like, and who invariably binned him; well, it didn't take a lot of effort to find fault with them and all. And that, too, was supposed to be funny, harmless; this time, a kind of defence mechanism. Nothing to do with perfection, nothing at all.

'I know, Ramsey, son,' said Madge. 'I understand. Don't take it too seriously. Fellow was just . . .'

But Ramsey kept on about it, and the more he went on about it, the more he repeated himself, and the more he tied himself in knots.

'You're all right, Ramsey, son,' said Madge. 'Watch and no get yourself in a state now.'

Then, of all things, Ramsey started thinking maybe the young fellow was right. Maybe Ramsey was looking for perfection all the time. Now there was a thought. After all, that was twenty year now he'd been out actively chasing lassies. Twenty year with nothing to show for it. Twenty year looking for perfection? Well, surely, if you spent that long hunting for something and you couldn't find it, the only logical conclusion was – it didn't exist!

Ramsey made a decision. It would be a new Ramsey from now on. More tolerant, less picky. To start with, after tea, he gave Celia a call, the lass he'd met at the weekend, the 'awfy quiet' lass, the lass with 'not really a lot to say for herself'.

'Hello, Celia? Hiya, it's Ramsey, Ramsey Buchanan. Just wondering how you were doing, what you were up to.'

'Fine. Fine.'

'Fancy doing something, going out or that?'

Celia took a couple of seconds before answering. 'Nah, don't think so. Don't really go out. Just staying in, watching some telly. Come round if you want. I'm getting a pizza later on.'

'Great,' said Ramsey. 'You want me to pick up a couple of videos?'

'No,' said Celia, 'telly. Just watch telly.'

And that, believe it or not, is what they ended up doing. Admittedly, snuggled up on the sofa, it was all quite easy and everything, but it was just telly. True, Celia'd mentioned on the Saturday as how she liked her telly, but Ramsey assumed it was just for the sake of having something to say, some mutual thing you'd have in common, like the weather or school or whatever. He hadn't expected her to talk about nothing else.

Come nine o'clock, Celia phoned for her pizza, and Ramsey uncorked the £12.99 bottle of wine he'd shelled out for. After she'd necked a couple of glasses of vino, Celia told Ramsey all about herself: she worked in a shoe-shop ('Like Al Bundy!'); she watched telly; and, eh, that was it. The only reason she was out at the weekend was cause it was the day after pay day, the only time she ever went out, out for a meal and a drink with her colleagues.

Even though he wasn't really into it, over the next couple of months, Ramsey persevered with Celia. Every three or four days, he'd head round with his bottle of wine and they'd sit and watch the box. On those evenings when he didn't go round, Celia would phone and keep him up to date with all the programmes he'd missed.

This was no good. If only there was a wee bit get up and go about her. Not before time, Ramsey decided to give Celia the heave-ho; and, no, he told himself, it wasn't cause she wasn't perfect, it was cause she was boring. Anyway, in boyfriend/ girlfriend terms, they weren't really going out, just watching telly, with some strictly pre-watershed kissing and cuddling come the end of the night.

It was during her favourite programme – *Crimewatch* – that Ramsey broke the news. 'Eh,' he said, 'I'm not really looking for a relationship just now. Just be friends, aye?'

'Okay,' said Celia. Then she got excited. 'Wonder what it would be like seeing somebody you knew on this, eh?' She looked at Ramsey then added, spookily, 'Now, there's a thought.'

Meanwhile, back at the work, Ramsey filled in his breaks by trying to join in with the newly established crossword crowd. This was a group instigated by the young fellow, the management trainee. Trouble was Ramsey had no time for crosswords. But, it had to be said, the women were giving it a go. Soon, they were so competent and pleased with themselves they started bringing in broadsheets, and tackling the more convoluted puzzles. Changed days indeed. Ramsey contented himself by flicking through the year-old pile of gossip mags – and trying not to find fault with all the glamorous models, actresses and socialites.

Ramsey was quiet these days. Gone was the flirting and teasing. Gone, too, were the tales of his love-life. He never mentioned Celia. No way was anybody going to accuse him of looking for perfection. To think, too, the work had always been his salvation. Ramsey had met these women hundreds of times, been with them for years, and he'd always thought they loved him; well, maybe not loved him exactly, but at least really liked him. That was what kept him going, knowing that if a bit of intrigue hung around long enough, stuck in there, worked at it, then they, too, would get to see the real Ramsey.

Now that notion was shot to pieces and all. Perfection, thinking of everything in terms of perfection. How stupid could he have been?

Back on the love-life front, Ramsey started knocking about with Sally-Anne Sturgess. A notorious party animal, Sally-Anne was the sort who measured the quality of her nights out by the number of acquaintances she bumped into, the amount of money flying around, and the hour she eventually got to her bed. On their first date, Sally-Anne spent most of her time yapping away with other folk, leaving Ramsey to part with the best part of £150, buying drinks for strangers, and ferrying them round in taxis. Come one o'clock in the morning, they all piled on to a pre-booked minibus, bound for some mysterious party out the west coast. On the way, the minibus stopped off at a cash machine, where, and with a quite uncalled for degree of euphoria, Sally-Anne brandished her printed statement, passed it round, and declared herself to be totally skint. Everybody cheered. They were totally skint and all; all these unemployed musicians, part-time theatre folk and

apprentice hairdressers – the very folk who made the baking of
biscuits seem like a public service. Ramsey paid for the minibus. It was the back of noon the following day when they
finally got to bed. Somewhere near Helensburgh, Ramsey
later discovered.

It was the same the next night. And the night after that.
Before the weekend was out, Ramsey's wages were gone.
Before the month was out, Ramsey's savings had joined them.
Ramsey was brassic. He got a bank loan, borrowed money off
mates, sold old records and unwanted CDs. The nights out
were draining, not only financially, but also on his energy.
Ramsey was looking frazzled. Every so often, Sally-Anne
would extricate herself from the luvvies. She'd come over,
give Ramsey a lengthy snog, then ask if he was all right.

'Course,' said Ramsey. 'Course, I'm all right. Having a
great time.'

But Ramsey was far from all right. After work one day, a mate
came round, looking for money that was owed.

Ramsey was sorry. He couldn't help the guy. See, as Ramsey
began to explain, he'd skipped a few bills, and, well, the paying
of bills had to come first.

'Aye?' said the guy. 'Well, not maybe about time you were
thinking of changing your name then? How about Norman,
Norman Nae-mates?'

With that, the guy stormed off. The first of many such calls.

Ramsey missed his mates, but what he really missed was the
work. Used to be that life revolved around the work: making
the women laugh, just talking to them. He didn't fancy any of
them or anything – they were all old or spoken for, anyway –
they were just his pals, his best pals. To think, too, it wasn't
that long since Ramsey used to go in early, clean the place up
and have a good blether with the women off the early bus.

Nowadays, more often than not, Ramsey was late, dishevelled, noticeably underweight and hardly saying a word.

And the women were hardly speaking to Ramsey. Comments were made about his weightloss. He would be asked if he was all right. Ramsey would take the huff. Then one day Madge said, 'Hear you're seeing Guaranteed Grief these days.'

'What?'

'That Sally-Anne Sturgess.'

'So,' snapped Ramsey, 'what's it to you, like? At least she's not perfect.'

Ramsey had had enough. He took off his white hat and his white coat.

Madge chased after him but it was too late. It was quarter to four on a Friday afternoon. Ramsey went to his locker, put his stuff away and clocked out, a good forty-five minutes before he was supposed to.

When he got home, Ramsey phoned Sally-Anne, but she was away. Away over to Holland, according to her mother.

'Holland?'

'Did she not say she was going?'

'No,' said Ramsey, 'she did not. Where did she get the money?'

'I beg your pardon.' Mrs Sturgess matched Ramsey's indignance. 'Paid for it herself. Been saving up. Saving up for ages.'

Sally-Anne's mother then asked if Ramsey was all right.

That done it. Just one too many folk had asked that. Ramsey hung up, went out and got ripped. Totally mortal. After, he went to a nightclub, but the bouncers wouldn't let him in.

'Away you go home to your bed, son. Sleep it off, eh.'

'But,' slurred Ramsey, 'I've got to get in. See, listen, listen, pal, I know you're only doing your job, but, look, this is important: I've got to find me the most imperfect specimen of womanhood, and I've got to . . .' Just then Ramsey spotted this lassie, this lassie getting out a taxi. 'You, hey you, are you imperfect? You totally imperfect? Imperfection personified? Then marry me, darling. Marry me! I love you!'

Just as the woman was about to assail him with the lethal combination of handbag and high-heels, the bouncers got hold of Ramsey and propelled him down the apparent safety of the alleyway. Ramsey crashed into a pile of rubber buckets. God, thought Ramsey, what a mess it all was. The only consolation was things just couldn't get any worse.

Or could they?

Ramsey heard this voice, this familiar voice, a lassie. 'That's him,' she said. 'That's the bastard.'

Ramsey tried to place the voice. Somebody he knew? Somebody off the telly? *Telly?*

Then he noticed these two guys heading towards him. Your classic things, with the photofit faces, the wardrobe build, the anonymous dark clothes, like something out of – *Crimewatch?*

'Celia?' said Ramsey. 'Celia, what's going on?'

'Nail him,' said Celia. 'Stiffen him. Said we were friends. Haven't seen him for months.'

The classic thugs laid in to Ramsey, booting him, picking him up, flinging him against the wall, then flinging him into the rubber buckets. Then, for good measure, they did it all again.

And again.

And again.

For all his injuries, Ramsey still managed to struggle to work on Monday morning. He hadn't reported the incident, hadn't been to hospital, hadn't done anything. Just stayed in bed all Saturday, all Sunday, suffering.

God knows what he looked like when he finally clocked in, but Ramsey wasn't bothered anymore. He was in debt up to his eyeballs, he'd no mates, and he'd bunked off work on Friday, for which he was probably due the order of the boot. Pain was the least of his problems.

To add insult to injury Ramsey could hear what could only be described as a party going on. *A party?* Ramsey went through the staff-room. Sure enough, streamers were hanging from the striplights, the Christmas hats were on. Everybody was clinking glasses – until, that was, they caught sight of Ramsey.

'By God,' said Madge, 'what happened to you, Ramsey, son?'

'Never mind me, what the hell's going on here?'

'Celebration,' said Madge. 'Danny's got the job. He's now a manager.'

Nervously, the young fellow raised his glass.

'What?' said Ramsey. '*You?*'

'Ramsey, son,' said Madge. 'Mind your tongue.'

'Why should I?' said Ramsey. 'If Mr High and Mighty here's in charge, that's one thing that's out the window, standards. No need for perfection, that's for sure.'

The new manager wasn't getting this. 'Sorry? Look, I know you and I don't get along too well, but, really, if we're going to be working together, then I think we should maybe clear the air, eh? Want to tell me what all this is about?'

'I'll tell you all right.' Ramsey told them all about it, the four-month nightmare, the perfection thing, Celia, Sally-Anne, everything.

'My God, Ramsey, son,' said Madge, 'but you've been seeing these lassies for ages. We thought this was serious, no just one of your flings. That's why everybody thought you were so miserable, you were in love, you were missing them.'

'What? I can't stand them. They were horrible to me.'

The young fellow had taken a whitey. 'And all because I said you were looking for perfection?'

'Aye,' said Ramsey. 'You! Let's get back to you, ya bastard.'

'But, but I was joking. Your colleagues all said you liked a joke. They said that whenever you were joking you always said "now there's a thought". I said "now there's a thought" after I said that to you. I did. Didn't I everybody, didn't I say that? It was a joke.'

The women all nodded or said, 'Aye.'

Ramsey put his head in his hands.

'Ramsey,' said Madge, 'you're a pillock. Typical bloody man. Can dish it out all right, but can you take it? Can you hell. Tried to tell you, but would you listen? Noh, noh, no you. For God's sake, could you no've said something?'

'No,' mumbled Ramsey, 'I didn't want you to think I was being critical, that I was looking for perfection all the time.'

'Ramsey, son,' said Madge, 'nothing wrong with you looking for perfection. I hope you find somebody perfect – *perfect for you*. But you've got to mind, your idea of perfection's no going to be the same as mine or anybody else's. Christ, I dread to think, if that was the case, and we all wanted the same thing, what would happen to the likes of you, me or anybody, anyway, eh? Especially the likes of you!'

Ramsey looked up.

'Ih?'

'Aye, you!'

They were all smiling. In fact, if anything, they looked as if they were holding back, waiting for something – some kind of prompt.

For the first time in ages, Ramsey seemed to understand what was going on. It was good to be back. He gave them the grin. He gave them the glance. Then he turned round to Madge. 'Aye,' whispered Ramsey, breaking into a laugh, 'now there's a thought.'

OUTSIDERS

FIONA MACINNES

N ow I may as well admit it. This really is true.
The main thing was he was always after money. And
even if you said you hadn't any on you, it didn't matter.
Whatever story you made up, he'd want you to get a loan off
of somebody or sell something.

So you'd borrow off somebody for a pint and you'd get
down to the hotel at opening time, with a hangover, when the
sun was shining and it was a bonny day, a Sunday, and play
snooker in the daylight. And the juke box would come on and
everybody would have a fag and you might as well too, getting
that first sickening feeling over with and then the day was set
and you might just as well go along with it.

Well, he said he'd shag me every day if I took him back to live
in the city with me. And he would say things like that to shock
me but I always just made out I wasn't shocked. I just listened
to him and showed no reaction and stored it up to unpick later
on. It was too much to puzzle out then you know.

Anyway he wanted to come away and live with me, and I'll
admit it to you that I was surprised and flattered that he saw
things in me. This was someone who could see the inner
person as it were. One thing was however, I said I wouldn't
wash his clothes. I had to keep him wondering a bit. He was a

kind of a savage you might say. He landed up there fish-gutting but really couldn't stick the wet and the stink and just kept hustling. He had some crazy scheme for making fish-skin knickers and becoming a millionaire, but you could take that with a good pinch of salt. He would say these sorts of things to test out how bourgeois you were.

I had this idea of a noble savage you could rescue and show off to the town folks so I thought, OK. I would just capture him and ask questions later.

I did have money, for I was a canteen worker at the camp and that was the way to keep him. He just didn't like to work. Unless the broo got on to him, and he would say he was looking for a job as an existentialist. He had these two words that he kept on saying and they really impressed me. One was 'existentialist' and the other was 'metaphysical' and I used to ask him what they meant, but I never understood the explanations. He probably meant for me not to understand and I usually felt pretty stupid but I kept that quiet.

I was the one with the education after all.

He said he was like 'The Outsider' in some book, so I read a book by Albert Camus. Can't remember any of it now, except I couldn't find any clues and thought I was probably missing something so just didn't let on. And anyway by that time he was past talking about Albert Camus and on to Aleister Crowley, so I read that too and I thought it was pretty weird.

I once found a plate of corned beef and beans shoved under the mattress. That really shocked me.

A lot of folk in the island didn't like him. He was an incomer for a start and a layabout that didn't want to work and dressed like a hippie and smoked roll up Golden Virginia and was likely on drugs.

He would tell people to fuck off and go away laughing. He

said he was illegitimate and had never seen his father and never went to school and ran away to London and was self taught and discovered books. It could have been all talk you know. I thought I could try out this theory I had on him, about homing in on the good and spinning it out like a web that would consume all the bad and thereby save a human soul. God's job really.

That's what appealed to me.

He thought he looked like James Dean and though he told me he'd been a rent boy in London I just didn't believe him. He'd get pissed drunk and sit with his fag in his hand and pontificate and hold court.

On these days he just looked like a bad cartoon.

He put fag burns in the duvet cover. He told me he read loads of books and sometimes he looked quite erudite. That's when he was in the mood for drinking Earl Grey tea. And he would sit in the afternoons crosslegged with round-rimmed spectacles on and the light slanting in the Georgian window panes, reading some book, telling me that was definitely it, he was seriously going to get into Buddhism. I could never read with someone watching me. It seemed phoney.

I had high hopes of this being the kind of relationship like you read about in *Cosmopolitan*, where the issues would be about equality and mutual respect. That's why I said from the outset I wouldn't do his washing. I was well aware that was a symbol of feminine submission.

My sister said that if he really wanted to be with me, I should make him get his own fare together.

But of course I couldn't chance it.

I had too much staked on it. I knew deep down he wouldn't come if I didn't ease the way. And I told myself it was a justifiable part of the rescue package. I'd told everybody I was bringing this guy south with me and we needed a place to live. They couldn't wait to meet him.

He was pissed in the bar when it was time to go and I had to drag him out of course. His girlfriend was pregnant, tearful and shouting at him, so I guess I was the easier option. I was getting briefly illuminated as the scarlet lady, so I just kept my head down and didn't gloat although really I was quietly warming to this new status. He was telling her there was nothing in it and he was going to work on a film script.

Pile of lies of course.

Then he met this guy on the boat. And I can say now this one was really scary and they sat in the bar and I bought whiskies for them. This scary guy was going to Glasgow to do a robbery and he was asking how you get hold of a shooter. And he was all for getting this shooter, really mad keen and drunk. And that worried me a bit but I drank the whisky too. You had to drink it neat. I made out it was fine and nothing fazed me.

That would impress him and he wouldn't be able to call me bourgeois. But I was having to keep a watching eye on things. You know how it is when your drunken self is being watched from inside by your sober self.

Anyway I was getting kind of mad because they drank so much money on the boat and I had thought we might have the chance just to be together and alone on the start of our journey. I could start the rehabilitation so to speak. So I was thinking, this can't carry on, and I knew he'd be at me to pay for everything, and call me a middle-class bourgeois that knew nothing. I hadn't really bargained for him getting pissed before we got on the boat.

And we were getting through it. I had sixty quid left and I rolled it up and hid it in the pocket of my rucksack. He might make me give it to that guy to buy a shooter or anything. He was that kind of really wild scary kind of boy that could just erupt into a fight in a split second. He had a scar on his face where the stubble grew through all squint. He told me it was a burn but I think somebody knifed him.

I waited for him to come and sleep down beside me in his sleeping bag on the floor of the lounge but god knows where he got to. He must have met somebody or fallen asleep in the bar talking about shooters and bank jobs. Maybe it was all talk, but I think he was capable of just about anything.

I fell asleep anyway, deciding I would make up a story.

I would tell him the money was done and we'd have to hitch-hike the rest of the way. He'd done lots of hitch-hiking, that's what he told me, so it would be fine. It's a thing you would do. Hitch-hike with your boyfriend.

It was all part of the official scenario.

So I told him we spent the last of my money in the bar and it was all gone. He was too drunk to remember and I said I was really sorry and pretended I didn't know what to do, so that I could let him be manly and take charge of the situation.

I made out I was vulnerable and said maybe we'd have to hitch-hike. He'd got remorseful from the drinking and was subdued, aquiesced and said we'd just have to do that. That was good. He was taking responsibility for me. I could indulge in a little weakness to let the good come through.

I knew he'd just about kill me if he found the money. I wouldn't have put it past him to empty out the whole rucksack and find it. It made me a bit scared. And if he knew I'd hidden it . . . I would just have to think up a story quick and pretend I never knew it was there and be really happy that this money had turned up and take him for a drink to celebrate and we'd get drunk in a bar but I'd be watching out the whole time and get him in a good mood and push him the way I wanted.

God.

In another mood he would definitely go crazy, but he was too knackered. We walked in silence for miles to the outskirts of the town. Long boring roads of grey concrete that seem nothing when you whizz through in a car. He lit a roll up from the dross in his tin. No fags. I tried to be helpful and found some loose change that I knew was there all along. He went into a shop and bought three singles. He was pissed off.

That was the kind of time he could lose his temper, and my false jollity jarred and seemed to announce the lie as plain as anything in everything I said. I almost felt sorry about the deceit but there was no going back. It was for his own good and I had to keep faith with the lie right the way through. Cold turkey. No money, nothing in the bank, no nothing.

Going with my plan now. He'd no escape. He was seeing he was trapped with me and the cold realisation was dawning. I was still hoping.

I lent him money all the time. It was OK when I was working but I'd given this cock and bull story to the personnel guy about having to leave at short notice; that down south there was a problem and I'd have to go and sort it out. I was sounding grown up and responsible, but just vague enough that he could never check up. I worked it out so that there was just enough acting to make it work and he gave me my pay up front and I left on fabricated but good terms. I was getting good at this. I had lied my way into getting the job in the first place. I said I was an islander and not an incomer. They only gave jobs to residents to stop the flood of itinerant hopefuls.

I pretty soon knew there was no way I'd ever get the money back. He would get me to borrow a car and we'd drive north and visit the archaeology.

I could drive.

And he'd take me past all these oddball friends who were incomers with uncomfortable names that sounded ill in the landscape, who bred goats or kept a pig and I'd sit there politely, an incomer too, while they drank tea. I would be glad nobody offered us a real drink so he would get abusive. It was OK for a bit but eventually I guess I realised he'd always be at me.

At me for money.

He reckoned he would get a job in the south and that would be fine. We would have a normal life and live together in a flat and I would go to college and he would mix his own spices to make curries. When we got south I got a job in a theatre cafe and gave away free meals to all my friends and watched him get drunker in the bar putting on his posh voice to all the producers and directors that came through. Then he would fall asleep with a lit fag in his hand and the management would get embarrassed and I would take him home and finish my shift early. Then he would wake up in the taxi and demand to be let out, and I would go home and sleep on the floor of some flat where we crashed, so tired I could sleep on the bare boards hardly caring anymore when he came home but still keeping faith that it was all fixable.

All it needed was a job or a proper flat or something.

And soon he started to find his way again in the city and I was getting too tired watching out for him and chasing him. And I was getting real good at lying about how much money I had or where it was, though he still went on about a saxophone he wanted and I had to keep asking this girl if she would sell hers for a tenner. Every time I saw her I had to ask and he'd ask me if I'd seen her and if I said 'no' he'd look mean and say 'you're lying'. And in my head I was saying 'I'm not going up town to look for this fucking girl to plague her about her bloody saxophone again. Piss off.' But I never let on what I was really thinking.

And then he found my post office savings book where I'd put the fifteen pounds I got when my grandfather died and never touched it like some sort of talisman. He made me go to the post office and cash it. I couldn't think up a story that time. He came with me and waited and I couldn't let on that this money was special in a stupid way and just had to act nonchalant. That was bad but I still thought it would come good.

And I hid till four in the morning in a wardrobe naked and terrified, wondering what to do and if anyone had heard in this flat full of hippies that we shared. There were some places I knew we just couldn't take, I was doing the landlord a favour turning them down. I knew he'd end up pissing on the floor or smashing things up when he got drunk and I'd have to do all the covering up.

In this flat with the hippies he got his hands round my throat and wrenched out my hoop earrings and I scrabbled on the floor like a blind woman for them. That was after he'd got hold of the mattress, drunk of course, and shaken me out of it like a floppy toy. Tipped over by some slight I had given and rolled me on the floor and kicked.

All in silence so that the others wouldn't hear.

In that dead silence. Before the 4 a.m. traffic starts on the main road and the buses start to grind round the corner swishing as the doors open and close. Lying on the polished sanded floor boards with the only visible mark, a busted lip.

And of course I did wash his clothes and he never shagged me.

I just sewed up the ripped mattress because I didn't want the landlady to see.

And the next day I got in a mini bus with ten hooting feminists and drove to a women's conference like nothing had ever happened, and they never knew, and my booted ribs ached, and if they had asked about my lip I would have lied. And when I got back he was really really sorry, so sorry he might have moved me if it had been before. He couldn't hardly remember a thing about it all and I wasn't going to tell anyone. Least of all let him know what an absolute sucker I was.

The dislocation from the affair was bland. Each party knew they had reached unspoken limits. He even assisted in off-loading me on to a drooling public school boy who was looking for some country girl to turn into Nora Joyce.

Eventually I discovered I had read the wrong *Outsider*. But it probably wouldn't have made any difference.

ISHMAEL

ANDREW BYRD

Out here on the periphery, on the torn fringes of inky black night, there are no stars. Out here there is just milk and perhaps a little honey. Not so out on the mountainous seas of the North. Not so where the *Pequod* rolls and yaws.

Is it time yet Cap'n?

No Ishmael, not time yet.

Shall I get below Cap'n?

Yes lad, get below.

Ah well. I've been staring at the wall. It's not a bad wall, hell it keeps the ceiling from crashing in, but it's blue and even jolly posters don't seem to cheer it up. I've tried throwing parties, but it stays at the edge of the room not saying anything. What can you do? The rest of the time I've been staring at these things and trying to arrange them into some meaningful order that might elicit an emotional response. I tell you, they're slippery. Like eels are slippery. Like ice is slippery. Like eels skating on thin ice are slippery. And when they get into groups they can also be very stubborn. Like Mendel was stubborn.

Rosa knew all about Mendel's stubbornness. She'd been a dancer at The Dipso Facto Revue Theatre for more years than she had a care to remember and all that time Mendel had been the musical director.

Quickly, move away to the side of the stage and let all the pretty dancing girls with the painted faces and weak ankles shuffle past in a bustle of sequins and try and catch the eye of the lonely brunette with the broken smile, worn like a scar upon her glowing face, bouncing along the wooden boards, satin shoes sullied in the rising dust from the unswept stage. All to the sound of the gasping, wheezing, farting band swaying in the pit to the rhythm of the conductor, the mercurial megalosaurus, the mellifluous Mephistopheles; Mendel.

You are not going to find too many partners in life dancing like that, are you girls! He shouts above the bang and crash of the moth-eaten orchestra and the bounce and thud of the hard-working, hoofing girls.

Fuck you Mendel! Rosa breathlessly retorts from the stage.

That's right, hold hard me hearties! A beaming Mendel continues whilst bringing the musicians beneath his baton to a break-neck climax. The girls culminate in a spastic finale and leave the stage to a clumsy chorus of erotic rhetoric from the sparsely occupied auditorium.

Our Master of Ceremonies approaches the front and centre of the stage, looking off to the wings and clapping;

How about those girls! A collection of coughs and other noisy bodily expulsions from the stalls is our M.C.'s answer. He continues, Well, would anyone like to say a few words?

Yeah, I'd like to say a few words. The M.C. peers out into the stalls with his hand shielding his eyes from the spotlights and can just make out in the dimness a tall handsome young man standing at the back of the theatre.

Yeah, sure kid. Go ahead.

Now Cap'n?

No, not yet Ishmael.

*　　*　　*

There were never any real dancing girls, nor stage to behold them on. Just the heavy heaving seas sloshing through the gunwales and the timbers creaking against the crashing waves. Throw away your seaside ways and your buckets and your spades and venture forth with your little greasy paws clutching at the fringes of your coat-tails and your sooty little nose pressed hard against the windowpanes, smudging the glass. And inside, those metaphysical dancing girls who will gently tap upon the booming atrium of your peripatetic heart.

And now Fate is coming towards him like a weight . . . a steamer . . . a whale, amidships he lies as the *Pequod* rolls and yaws, yaws and rolls.

Now Cap'n?

Not yet Ishmael.

Oh well, call me . . .

SPIRITS

LYDIA ROBB

S mall globules of blue-white translucent milk erupt from
one exposed nipple, trickle down the smooth black skin
of her breast and gather in a widening wet patch near the
baby's chin. He has stopped sucking momentarily. His mother
is drunk. Her neck tilts at a crooked angle and she cannot keep
her fingers from her scalp. The sight of her makes my skin
crawl.

There are nine of us in the back of the rusting Ford Transit –
four men, four women and the child. Ben sits in the front with
the Japanese driver. There is an overwhelming stench of body
odour mingled with the reek of alcohol. The eight Aboriginals
are drunk but then, that's what they're here for. The dispossessed. They come from a 'dry' community. Colonisation has
much to answer for.

We have come to a halt. I can't be certain when we left
Balgo Mission for Fitzroy Crossing. Perhaps it was the other
way round. I have a strange feeling of disorientation and every
muscle in my body aches with the jolting of this ancient
boneshaker. There seems to be some unwritten rule about
the seating arrangements. I am squashed into a corner. My
stool of repentance – shredded leather spiked with disen-
tangled rusty springs. After every stop, we reassemble in
exactly the same order as before.

'The Rabbit Flat Roadhouse' is in the middle of nowhere and has the reputation of being the most isolated pub in the Universe. The temperature is steadily rising and Ben, the driver and myself sit in the shade of a gum tree sharing a flask of chilled pineapple juice. A mosquito buzzes round my ear like escaping electricity. In my present state of lethargy, it takes some effort to swipe the predator away. It is too hot to do anything other than wish I was somewhere else. Anywhere.

The driver pulls himself into his seat and hits the high notes with the horn. It is some time before the clamour has any effect. The Aboriginals finally straggle through the doorway and slowly lurch towards us, the men protesting loudly, the women shrieking with laughter and playfully poking each other in the ribs. The baby's head lolls precariously over the edge of a makeshift sling knotted round its mother's neck.

We climb aboard and sit in the same sequence – the elderly granny with leathery pock-marked cheeks and crimped hair like silver wire-wool, the old auntie, followed by the mother and child. Finally, the stout sister-in-law eases her broad hips into her position next to the door. Her unsupported bosom juts like ripe fruits under the ruched red bodice of her seersucker dress.

The grandad sits opposite me. His eyes are closed and his head tilted at an angle. His greying moustache is curling right up into his flattened nostrils. Food stains jostle for space amongst the pointillist symbols on the front of his oversized T-shirt. His uncut, horny toenails curve yellow half-moons under the thick leather thongs of his sandals. His foot taps to some unsung rhythm in his head.

They are used to my silences. I mean, what the Hell can I say? And, when I do, there is bugger all in the way of response. I could be invisible. I dig a novel from my backpack, open a page at random and pretend to read. Focusing on the print is well nigh impossible as the old Ford bucks and jolts along rust-red roads.

Within a short time they are all asleep but for the granny, who sighs meditatively while sucking her gums. Her job, it seems, is to fix the baby on to its mother's breast. There are snuffling sounds such as a small marsupial would make as the child feeds. I can't help wondering if he too will become drunk from the effects of the alcohol in his mother's blood. As if he can read my thoughts, he turns, looks vaguely cross-eyed at me and gurgles through pale milky gums. Grandad opens his eyes. *Chook, chook chook*, he grins at the baby.

The old man in his wisdom knows many things. He suddenly grunts instructions in his slow pidgin English and the driver swings on to the verge in a shower of dust and gravel. North of the watering-hole, the land is scrub, sand and the odd stunted tree. Bush fires are a constant threat in this weather. The distance is a vast blue shimmering heat haze. We boil the billy-cans and drink the stewed tea, taking care to douse the last remnants of fire.

The mother has been tippling from a flat green bottle which she produces now and again from the folds of her skirt. She flirts quite openly with her brother-in-law. He is dressed in skin-tight jeans with a blue checked shirt unbuttoned to his navel. Now and again he slowly, and with obvious deliberation, scratches his genitals. She snickers loudly at this. He throws back his head and laughs like he's gone mad.

The baby starts to cry. She crouches down with her legs too wide apart and props the baby up in such a way that he can see what she is doing. She makes pictures in the sand with her index finger then, with the flat of her hand brushes her efforts away. The child is already learning to recognise his ancestral roots.

The stationary transit van has, in a short space of time, become an oven. Diesel fumes add their noxious smell to the stifling heat. Even with the windows down, the temperature is unbearable. We travel the remaining forty miles in silence. The motion of the vehicle has lulled the child to sleep. His black hair is stuck in a wet question-mark to his forehead.

The old grandad gives the signal. Sundown. Time to pitch camp for the night. I know the format by now and follow the women to their chosen site where we lay out our packs in the same arrangement as we sit in the van. Ben has warned me about the dangers of sleeping too near the road. Truckers, trying to keep awake on amphetamines, have been known to mount the verge and kill the odd hiker.

Ben and I have known each other since childhood. Good friends. Nothing more. It was on his suggestion that I am making this supposed trip of a lifetime.

Good on yer said my father.

Remember to brush your teeth said my mother *and watch out for poisonous snakes.*

Bottles and billies are filled at the fresh-water spring and a fire started. The scent of eucalyptus rises from the smouldering branches. Somewhere in the far distance, the low grumble of thunder and the first flicker of lightning on the horizon. You can feel the electricity in the air, crackling and rising on its hackles.

I am reminded of a story I heard from a guy in the outback about the head man of an Aboriginal tribe who was keeper to the God of Lightning. His first wife had died. After a period, too short according to ancestral practice, he remarried. One day while hunting with two other men on the land created by his forefathers, he ventured on to a 'sacred site'. A violent storm erupted.

I swear it was true said the guy narrating the story. *Zapped. Just like that,* he told me, snapping his thumb and forefinger together. *The Gods were angry you see.* He paused. *Weird. Can you believe it? The other two men were completely unscathed.*

The brother-in-law has not been idle, having shot and skinned a bush-turkey. He guts the bird, throws the entrails some distance away in order to attract the flies then places the bird on a makeshift spit, directly above the glowing embers. A couple of gutted marsupials are treated in the same fashion. The night is filled with the smells of woodsmoke and charred meat. When everything is cooked to his satisfaction, he uses his bare hands to tear the meat from the bones. The pieces are distributed, a larger portion for the menfolks.

Two of the women have cleaned and winnowed the seed. The husks have been ground between two large stones and water added to the coarse flour to form a paste. This is shaped into two flat loaves. The damper is placed in white-hot ash. It too is shared amongst us. I nod in appreciation, trying not to choke on the unpalatable lump stuck to the roof of my mouth.

When the food has been consumed, they start drinking again. The women are dark silhouettes noisily hunkered in a semicircle round the fire. The men stand on the perimeter gently swaying to the dirge-like rhythm of the didgeridoo. The noise intensifies to an ear-splitting pitch. I watch this surreal spectacle from a distance.

An ember explodes like a firecracker in a shower of sparks. The young mother is in a drunken stupor by now. She almost throws the child to the old auntie then slowly starts to unbutton her blouse. She advances towards the brother-in-law. His eyes are red-rimmed in the light from the fire. He laughs and starts throwing burning twigs at her. There are murmurs of protest and alarm when, within seconds, her skirt starts to smoulder. She is screaming hysterically and tearing off her clothes. The granny quickly wraps a blanket round her. The driver comes with a handful of aloes and applies the translucent juices from the leaves to rising blisters.

There seems to be no escape but I can't stand the racket any longer. I pick up my gear and, as discreetly as I can, make my move. I have walked little more than a hundred yards when there is a sudden drum-roll of thunder. Sheet lightning blinks on and off like a faulty light bulb. The land is flood-lit in one giant stage set. The Gods are angry.

Pointless thinking about home. I think about home. I picture my mother in the kitchen. Cooking smells. Corned beef hash. Apple pie with cloves. Her voice comes back to me.

Gnarled wattle roots have assumed the shape of snakes. King Browns, Taipans. Every one deadly. I can't believe it. My face is wet with tears and I'm trembling with fear. I am a long time in falling asleep.

A sixth sense is telling me I am being watched. I keep my eyes closed, conscious of the thud thudding in my chest. Jesus! Hands tugging roughly at my sleeves. In the fading flicker of lightning, four black faces, white teeth, dark sockets where the eyes should be.

The old granny is gibbering at my lack of understanding. Her bangles rattle in irritation. She repeats herself, more slowly, for a second time. Realisation. The evil spirits will get the one who is detached from the others. Two black hands are placed within mine and I am led back to our original sleeping area.

We settle down, the old granny, the auntie, the sister-in-law, the mother and child. A small shower of sparks bursts in a fusillade from the dying embers in the fire. They spiral lazily towards the heavens. Suddenly the night is filled with stars.

THE BROWN JUG

MORAG MACINNES

W a, na, mee, who is also Mrs Factor Thomas, arrives at Albany Fort late in the season. It's his fault she's late. He kept sending delaying messages with the Orkneys and French who ply up and down the river – the new quarters weren't to his satisfaction yet, the Honble. Coy. had issued a wad of pestilential Instructions which had to be attended to, the Home Indians had falling-down sickness and were dying like flies. To begin with she was happy enough to stay in Moose, where things were familiar. She kept herself busy, sewing, and trying copperplate out of *Mrs Chesham's Book for Good Girls*. There's a new school at Albany, with two teachers, and twelve children, boys and girls. She thinks she may be able to help there. If it's fitting, that is.

But it got lonely, sitting under the American clock. The rest of her family have been trapping all summer, of course; but her hands are too soft for that now. She uses bitter almond oil in Venice soap and lemon juice every night, and seems to see the skin lightening as the callouses disappear. He chose her because she was quite light.

It's late August when she lands at Factor Thomas' new Post, surrounded by casks of salt. He isn't there. There are no orders about her, obviously; only about which supplies to unload first. The men say there's a big Ball on, in honour of a party of

Norwesters camped down the road. She understands immediately; she has been a country wife long enough to know how
her man manages things. He will get his rivals drunk. Then
he'll send a party out to raid their fur cache while they sleep it
off. The North West Company isn't just a bunch of crazy
Frenchies any more; plenty of Scots have found their way in,
Highlanders mostly – and they'll promote an Indian, give him
fair share. They're a threat, Thomas says; you have to outwit
pirates, or they'll sink you.

A couple of boys conduct her to his quarters and leave her
to unpack. She has to cup a palm round the candle – the wind
is sharp already, cutting through the wadded planks. She can
hear fiddles, and stamping and heughing. Perhaps she should
dress up pretty the way he likes, and make her way across to
the party.

In the big trunk there's a Trafalgar blue turban trimmed
with green feathers, and a scoop-necked lilac chintz, soft and
flowing, caught just under the bosom. The beaded indispen-
sable for her wrist is nearly the same green as the feathers. It's
this year's fashion, he brought it back for her from Home. No
one on the Bay will have seen anything like it.

She pours water into the basin, carries it and her light into
the bedroom, and begins, as she's been taught, to soap the
hair in her armpits and scrub it with a rag. In the mirror, the
candle, doubled, flickers, casting erratic shadows on the mess
of bedsheets. She stops dead, arm raised, water running down
her brown wrist; and then turns. Yes, she was right. There is
something lying on the bed. But it's not a body; it's a
chemise. And on the pillow there's a pair of drawers, inside
out.

They're very delicately made, with lace insets. The new
fashion, from England, on the boat. Meant for her, surely. But
he's put them on someone else. And taken them off again.

*　　*　　*

The Ball is a laughable occasion, if like Edward Nicholson you have drunk in White's Hotel, conversed in Holland House, and tried an Irish jig under the eyes of the daughters of Atlas who decorate Castletown's magnificent drawing room. But it is of abiding interest as a curiosity.

The gentlemen and ladies – if one can so denominate a rabble of Baymen and halfbreed Crees – stand along each side of the Room, with a gap like a river separating them. As one musician keels over from exhaustion or drink, another leaps to take his place, buoyed up by cries of: 'The arbre seul, now . . . Mrs MacCallum's Fancy . . . allons, Jeemsie, bow up!' Some well-known virtuosi expect silence, and the company sways obediently, wrapped in enjoyment of a clean tenor or a frisky Shetland fiddle. Most, selfless, play for the dancers.

There is an air of restraint at the beginning. The river, it seems, will never be forded. But drink flows, pipe smoke thickens, and the native women begin their own kind of dance. Individually, they traverse little circles. They stamp out patterns around themselves. They weave around each other. Sometimes they hum, or shake, or nod, and the sleepy babies on their backs nod too, lulled by the jog-trot rhythm.

It is a private thing. Politely each traverses her own route through the crowd. Perplexed by these eddying currents, the banks of the river seem to swell and burst, and the new Servants, shiny little fish from Stromness, St Peter's thumb planted firm in the whorls of their curls, find themselves engulfed and gasping in a stream of muddy smelly blackness. Drowning in Indian.

The Hudson's Bay Company is exerting itself. Factor Thomas required the menu to be an eloquent demonstration of the virtues of English cuisine – none of your French messes here – and accordingly Cook Halcrow has toiled in a sweat for two days and nights, broiling and blending. Sixteen dishes have come and gone, all toasted with wine and French brandy (by the officers) and porter and British spirit (by the men). But Nicholson, as Molson's Canadian Representative, still retains his dignity. Business comes first. He will not indulge himself until he has made his deal and pocketed the Chief Factor's signature.

The other guests are roistering, hiccuping, slavering drunk; and Thomas has his girl on his knee and his hand up her skirt, in full view of the men. Nicholson is pained by this; but the dance is in its full frenzy, and no one seems to notice. Perhaps the Servants expect such conduct of their new master. Gossip – which any Representative worth his salt encourages, for information's sake – says he's ruined the Fort since he arrived, reinstating Sunday work and liquor rewards. It doesn't take much.

He is pondering whether to waltz up to one of the women and whirl her off – and whether he is afraid to make such a move or obscenely excited by the strangeness of it – when Mrs Factor Thomas enters, neat as a pin, all five foot of her. She passes very close by him, to get to the top of the room, and he notices that she is quivering, as if beset by some kind of shivery ague. The dyed owl feathers tremble; he smells lemons.

He has seen angry ladies before, in Dublin and London and Paris. When they shake thus, in his experience, they are about to make a scene. The ladies of his acquaintance do not, however, throw themselves upon their errant lovers armed with embroidery scissors. Not even those who are intimate with poets, or unhinged by melancholy.

Mrs Factor Thomas, ungovernable, strikes out blindly. She reminds the Representative of a cat tied for drowning, all spit and claw, and he is captivated. What a show of spirit! He liked what he saw of her while he dealt with the contract at Moose, but thought her a touch insipid. Now he cannot hold back an incredulous smile. That'll show the lecherous old devil, he thinks. She won't stand for it.

116

The music falters. A ragged silence rises around her screams. 'It's his country wife,' whisper the bateau crew from Moose. 'We took her up this very night. He never asked her to come. She just upped and done it. She's got no right.'

'But,' whispers Nicholson, 'she's *Mrs*. I was introduced. At Moose. A month ago. It is Mrs Factor Thomas, and her first name is Jane.'

'Only in the custom of the country, sir. *Wa, na, mee* Isbister, that's her right name.'

His girl has fallen off Thomas' knee and lies, half drunk, half stunned, showing a quantity of French lace. She looks twelve or so. Her skin is the colour of dumpling, almost English in its pallor. The country wife strikes out at her. In return, she pulls her clothes together sulkily and sticks out her tongue.

The Factor has drunk too much to be able to protect himself quickly, and suffers real damage as a result. His face and neck are bloody. His shirt gapes as he struggles to grab the flailing wrists, trying to take advantage of the half turn Wa, na, mee has made away from him.

'Hold her down!' he shouts; and the Chief Trader pins her arms behind her back, throws the scissors across the floor and forces her to kneel.

No one expects what comes next. It still isn't entirely clear who this exotic, green-feathered woman belongs to. She's not kin to anyone. She cowers at their feet, shouting and crying by turns.

'If you'll step back a pace, gentlemen,' Thomas says; and, swaying slightly, he braces himself on a chair, unbuttons his britches and pisses a copious, leisurely stream all over the lilac chintz. Nicholson can see the bones in her spine; the naked brown nape of her neck. She wears her hair like Empress Josephine, in the modern fashion.

Time stops. The Factor rests a foot, for balance, on her

rump, as he fishes for his linen handkerchief. He wipes himself, prick and then face, and throws the bloody scrap of white down beside her.

'Out,' he says.

In the pause that follows, he buttons up, shouts the fiddlers, calls for gin, persuades the girl into his lap again to dab his head with it – and calls boisterously for Molson's Canadian man.

'Here,' says Nicholson.

'Don't look so affrighted! It was just the brown jug, sir, needing to be set in its place. Now then, drink up! Let's have a toast to the Honourable Company . . . no, damme, we've had a barrel load of those. Let's drink to business, Mr Nicholson, and to the brave man that brings it to these barren shores. To the installer of the Molson Still – and a hundred gallon a year!'

'But . . .' says Nicholson, and knows he will go no further. The signature will nestle in his pocket; and he will have a fine frontier tale, suitable for passing the port to. He raises his glass. Behind him the dancers regroup, flowing round Mrs Factor Thomas, or *Wa, na, mee* Isbister, as she is also known, like water round a stone.

MARRIAGE

ALEXANDER MCCALL SMITH

There was a hotel in Swaziland, a small one, reached by a dusty white road along which somebody, years before, had planted a line of eucalyptus trees. The hotel stood on the brow of a hillside and the air was clear and sharp. From the front verandah the visitors who came up from Manzini for the weekend could look out to a distant range of hills that in the morning light seemed painted an impossible, attenuated blue, like the blue of a faded water-colour.

The hotel was owned by a Portuguese from Mozambique who had been dispossessed by the revolution. He thought only of return to his abandoned latifundium, and spent his time in endless discussions with fellow émigrés, dissecting every scrap of information, every item of news which might point to a change in their fortunes. The hotel provided him with somewhere to live, quite apart from the income it brought him, but he had no feeling for it. When the Swazi woman answered his advertisement for a manager he was delighted to find that here was somebody who had some appropriate experience and who seemed to know exactly how to run the business with no assistance from him.

She proved to be as good as her referees had promised. She gave the hotel her utter loyalty, as she had done with all her previous employers. She never took a holiday, rarely went to town – unless it was on some business connected with the hotel – and she was scrupulously honest. When he realised what sort of person he had employed, the Portuguese was content to hand everything over to her care. He now paid no attention to any details of the business and effectively moved to Manzini, where there were more Portuguese with whom he could sit about and contemplate the discomfort of the Mozambique Government and the ruinous guerrilla war into which it had been drawn.

She was thirty when she took the job and had done it for three years by the time she married. She had been too busy for marriage before that, but now she felt sufficiently secure in her job to make time in her life for a family. For her, it was not really a question of romance or passion, although there was never any question in her mind but that she would give to her marriage the same loyalty and commitment that she gave to her work. She merely wanted somebody who would be companionable and for whom she could make a comfortable life. She envisaged herself doing all the work, because it was in her nature to think in that way.

He was the owner of a store in Manzini. He met her when he came up to the hotel for a weekend meeting organised by the Chamber of Commerce, and his businessman's instinct told him that he would never find a more competent, reliable wife. He returned the following weekend and invited her to have dinner with him in the hotel. He noticed how she watched the waiters, and what they were doing, even while they had dinner together, and again his commercial instinct approved.

But he wanted more than a good business partner; he wanted a woman whom he could dominate. He was by nature a bully – not in any physical way – but in a more subtle, psychological sense. He wanted somebody whom he could own, who would do his bidding, who would make him feel in control.

She saw in him a man of some charm, who was probably not the sort to go running after other women. She could rely on him, and he would be there when needed. She could make a good home for him too, as he appeared to like the hotel, and might well be happy to live there. When he proposed to her, which he did quite soon, she accepted without hesitation, and they were married in the Anglican Church in Manzini, opposite the George Hotel, under the jacaranda trees.

He moved to the hotel, leaving the day to day running of the shop in Manzini to his father's cousin. Now he spent his days on the verandah of the hotel, reading the newspapers which were brought up to the hotel two days late. He did not listen to the radio, because it would spoil the papers for him, as a story or a film might be spoiled if the ending is revealed by one who already knows it. He played cards with his friends, who came up from Manzini to see him, and when they went he would instruct one of the waiters to play dominoes with him until it was time for his evening drink, which he took by himself or with the guests.

She had lunch with him, promptly at one, and she was never late. If she kept him waiting, he became sulky, and implied that the running of the hotel was more important to her than her husband. She denied this, of course, and made sure that she dropped whatever she was doing in order to be ready to join him at his table at the appointed time.

He was a perfectionist, she found. If his shirts were not ironed in precisely the way he liked, or if there were not enough hot water for his morning bath, he would look at her reproachfully, as if she had somehow failed him.

'I'm not a fussy person,' he said. 'It's just that I like things to be right. You should not forget who I am. I am related to King Sobhuza. I am the same family. Should I have to tell you that?'

She tried to meet his exacting standards but it seemed as if whatever she did, it was just not good enough. And she became aware of his jealousy, too. He did not like her to have her own friends, particularly if they were friends that she had known before they met. If any of these telephoned her, he would not pass on their messages, or would just say: 'Somebody phoned you. I forget who it was. I don't think it was important.'

The Portuguese watched this with amusement. He said to his friends, amidst the political gossip and nostalgia: 'That man has the best wife in the country, you know, the best. And he sits there and orders her about and moans and moans – you should just see it. And she never complains, you know. She puts up with it all.'

At times, when something happened which really aroused his ire, he would raise his voice against her, and imply that there had been other women who wanted to marry him and that she might find one day that he had gone back to one of them. They, he said, might not have proved barren.

These words, reserved for those occasions when he really wished to hurt and humiliate her, found their target. But she did not fight back, because she had been trained at home that it was a woman's role just to get on with it, and to put up with the difficulties that came one's way. If women started to complain, then nothing would get done. There was just no point. Men would never change; that's what they were like. But there was an anger within her which she made no attempt to still, and it burned with a hidden flame.

There was a political change in Mozambique, and the exiled Portuguese made their first, tentative trips back into the ruined empire they had sucked so dry. They came back with stories of deprivation and corruption and the streets full of the maimed victims of war. But there was a light in their eye, too, as they saw the prospect of return. Eventually, this proved to be possible, as the rhetoric of socialism was replaced by an acceptance that there was a role for the entrepreneur. People who knew how to run farms and businesses could come back and would find their property restored, if they wanted.

He took up the offer, and announced to her that he wanted to put the hotel on the market. She could buy the hotel, if she wished, at a slightly lower price, provided that she could raise the money from the banks. He would tell them, he said, what a good manager she was and this would help them to conclude that their money would be safe.

Her husband suggested that the hotel be put in his name, as he said this could protect it from creditors. She raised this possibility with her attorney in Manzini, who advised her to ignore the suggestion. She did so, telling her husband that banks had insisted on the hotel being in the name of the borrower, who was her. He did not contest the point, although he was displeased, and sulked for several days, ignoring the celebration which she had planned to mark her acquisition of the hotel.

He now began to introduce himself to the guests as the owner of the hotel. She did not contradict him, because it seemed to her to be unimportant. All that mattered from her point of view was that the hotel be well managed, which of course it was. The fact that she now owned the hotel, though, seemed to annoy him. He went to greater lengths to belittle her, as if he needed to assert the fact that although she was the owner, he was the husband, and that counted for more.

The hotel staff, whom she treated well, disliked him intensely, seeing him for the bully that he was. Some of them tried to annoy him by keeping him waiting, or doing something in a way of which they knew he disapproved. This did not have the desired effect, though, as he would blame her for their shortcomings and they did not like to see her suffering. So they humoured and indulged him, like a spoiled child, and he basked in their attention, which he took as no more than his due, as husband of the manageress and then owner.

Then one morning he woke up with his vision clouded in his right eye, and she drove him down to the doctor in Mbabane, who immediately referred him to an eye specialist over the border.

'You have had a hæmorrhage at the back of the eye,' said the doctor. 'Quite a bad one. Your blood pressure is way up. I'm very sorry. We'll try to bring the pressure down, but if there's further bleeding it could get worse.'

It did, and this time, it was in the other eye. There was no pain, no warning, just a sudden fading into total blackness. He panicked, shouting out and stumbling through the hotel in search of his wife. Again they made the trip over the border, but again they were given the bleak message that the damage had been done. After three futile days of waiting she drove him back in almost total silence. It seemed as if he were blaming her in some way for what had happened and that he must punish her. She brought him back to the hotel, leading him to his place on the verandah, where he sat with his face turned slightly upwards, as if awaiting a sign.

The staff talked about it in whispers, and crept out on to the verandah to look at him. He thought he heard somebody, and turned his head sharply, but could see nothing. The staff watched, and looked at one another, exchanging glances of sympathy, because this was a fate which they would wish on nobody, not even him.

She took him into lunch, leading him by the arm, and he fumbled clumsily with his chair, lacking the instincts which develop in those who have become accustomed to their blindness. Then he sat down, and turned his head to his wrist, as if trying to look at his watch.

'What time is it?' he said. 'You're late, aren't you?'

She said nothing for a moment, and he repeated his question in a tone of increasing irritation.

'It doesn't matter,' she said. 'It's only a few minutes after one.'

'It matters to me,' he said peevishly, putting on the expression that preceded a sulk. 'You know I like my lunch at one o'clock exactly. Exactly.'

His face was turned towards her, but he could not see what effect his words were having on her. She looked at him, as she was never able to do before, because his eyes had frightened her, and she had been unable to meet his stare. Now she saw nothing there; his eyes had emptied.

'In future,' she said quietly. 'We'll have lunch when I'm ready.'

His mouth twisted, and she saw the fury mount in his face, but it was a fury that was utterly trapped.

'Don't think that just because I'm . . . I'm . . . I can't see, that you can treat me . . .'

He stopped. He had heard the sound of a chair being pushed back. Suddenly he reached across, knocking over a heavy salt cellar as he did so, and grabbed at the place where her arm might be. But there was nothing. He got up and turned towards her chair, but became disorientated, and was not sure which direction he was facing. He reached for his stick, but could not find it, because it had fallen.

A waiter came to his side, and touched him on the arm, which made him start.

'I am here, sir. Here is your stick.'

He held on to the waiter and recovered himself.

'Take me to Mrs Dlamini. Take me to my wife.'

The waiter shook his head. 'She is in the office, sir.'

'Then take me there. Take me now.'

The waiter hesitated a moment. It was not easy to say this to him.

'She said you're to go to your room, sir. She said I should lead you there. She'll see you later, when she is less busy.'

He stood quite still. In his grip, the stick quivered slightly, picking up and magnifying the otherwise imperceptible shaking of his hands.

She finished her work in the office before she went outside and stood by a frangipani tree, looking out towards the hills. She felt light-headed, excited, as if something portentous had happened, as if life was about to change in some way, to get better.

TRAVELLING TO GRETNA

JACQUELINE LEY

S he rattled the tin. 'One barley sugar left. Do you want it?'
  'No thanks.'
'Sure?'
'I said, "No thanks," didn't I?'
She popped the sweet in her mouth and gazed out of the window. Her tongue was raw from eating them, but it was something to do as the grey landscape rolled by, a bland accompaniment to counting off the motorway exit signs, comparing the numbers with the map on her lap, shifting the dwindling lump around in her mouth until the last sliver slipped down and her hand reached for another.

They hadn't really said much since Preston. It was a bit of a strain really, sitting next to one another for hours on end like this, just the two of them.

'Shall I put the radio on?'

'If you like.' He glanced at her briefly, impatience simmering. 'You can sling that tin in the back now. There's no point clutching an empty tin all the way to Glasgow is there?'

She unscrewed the lid and ran her finger round the powder of sugar in the base of the tin, tracing a circle round and round, sucking her finger thoughtfully.

'For God's sake, Jean, you'll get that stuff all over the seats. Put the bloody thing down.'

She dropped the tin on the floor and watched him compress his lips in irritation, flicking his lights at a crawler in front of him in the fast lane. As the car pulled in and they flashed past, she swivelled her head to look, blinking her eyes like a camera shutter, taking an impression: an elderly man in a flat cap, head poked forward, gripping the wheel, a woman asleep in the passenger seat, jaw slightly agape.

Sleep was another option of course but not the way Gerry drove. Jean's right leg ached with the tension of pressing an imaginary brake pedal. Across each palm lay neat, twin rows of tiny indentations, self-inflicted stigmata where she kept clenching her fists and digging her nails in, every time the tailgate of a lorry loomed. That irritated him as well.

'For God's sake, do you want to drive?' he'd snap periodically and she'd shake her head and stare at the map again. Better not to look. The map was more interesting than the real thing anyway.

She fixed her eyes on all that green space to the left of the thick blue line they were hurtling along: tiny threads meandering down hillsides, a blue shape like a sleek seal, Haweswater, the long, tapering wedge of Windermere, steamboat written across the middle in red. Incongruously, she pictured tall, black crenellated funnels, massive paddles churning, and Al Jolson on deck in white gloves and a straw hat singing 'Mammy'.

'I wish we could stop off in the Lake District,' she said, hearing the plaintive whine in her voice, raising her eyes and closing them quickly as a red Fiesta swung out in front of them. 'I've never been there either.'

'Haven't you?' He plainly wasn't interested, intent on maintaining six inches between their front bumper and the Fiesta's boot. 'Well you needn't think I'm making any detours today. If I don't get to the guy in Glasgow by five thirty, he'll have shut up shop and gone home. I told you this wasn't going to be a pleasure trip.'

A pleasure steamer. That was it. That was what they called them. The sort where you were helped up a gangplank by a sunburnt sailor in a rough jersey that matched his eyes and you gave him a shy, virginal smile from under one of those droopy sun bonnets with flowers and pink ribbons. After that, you'd stand waving from the deck at the crowd on the jetty; hang over the rail, watching wooded banks slip by, lazy, leisurely, sun on your back, shooting the odd sidelong glance from under your lashes, lashes that were always impossibly long and dark incidentally, at the same sunburnt sailor, now on deck coiling ropes, or whatever sailors did when they were on deck. Something macho and muscular it would be anyhow, that showed off the sinews in their tanned, hairy forearms.

Gerry's forearms were hairy but white, a bluish, unhealthy white below the rolled back folds of his shirt sleeves, the wrist nearest her sporting a flashy gold watch with an expanding strap, the type he drove the length and breadth of the country to sell. He always wore the face turned inwards, so he had to twist his wrist to see the time, making an exaggerated display of it, as though time made more demands on him than on other people. 'God, is that the time?' He was for ever saying that. Really she wondered if the Almighty was the least bit interested.

Twiddling the radio dials, she tried to find something that wasn't a phone-in or frenetic, jarring pop music. All she achieved was the strident crackle of static, a nerve-jangling blur of discordant sound. Gerry pushed her hand away and pressed a tuning knob that brought an earnest, female voice into focus, pleading for the rights of dog-lovers to exercise their pets where they wished.

'Stupid cow,' he muttered and replaced her with another female voice shrieking about needing someone's love and needing it 'bad'.

'Badly, it should be badly, not bad,' Jean pondered listlessly to herself, watching the cars stream past at a round-about. 'I need your love and I need it badly.' Perhaps she should hold forth earnestly on a phone-in about the declining use of adverbs in the English language. It was the kind of thing you heard all the time. Astonishing really that people were so eager to air their tedious opinions to the listening nation. But then she'd spent the last thirty years with Gerry, who was dedicated to the equivalent of muttering 'Stupid cow' and turning her off. It wasn't calculated to inspire assertiveness.

'We're stopping off at Gretna, aren't we?' She felt she needed to keep reminding him. It would be just like him to pretend he'd missed the turning after it was too late.

'We'll stop for a quick snack if we've time,' he conceded grudgingly. 'I don't know what the fuss is about. There's nothing to see. Only a bloody service station.'

'Can't we go and see the blacksmith's where people get married?' she persisted.

'I keep telling you, I've got to be in Glasgow by five thirty. We'll maybe stop off on the way back tomorrow. What's the big deal about Gretna anyway?'

'I've always thought it sounded romantic,' she observed, flatly intoning each syllable of the word, the last one petering out on a sigh as she watched a white transit van racket along in front of them, ladders jutting from the roof, a scrap of red rag flapping.

'Perhaps they're going to Gretna,' she ventured, but the feeble joke was wasted on him. He simply looked blank. 'You know, ladders,' she prompted. 'Isn't that what people are supposed to use when they elope?'

'More likely they're on their way to clean out someone's guttering,' he responded sourly, twisting his wrist to check the time.

She clenched her fists again, pressing her knuckles together in her lap. If I see him look at his watch like that again, she thought, so help me, I'll open the door and jump out. At least that would slow him down a bit, even cause something of a tailback into the bargain. She didn't have the guts to do it of course, but it made her shiver a little inside her shapeless, lambswool cardigan to think how easy it would be to press the door handle, accessible, inviting, just a few inches from her hand, and hurl herself out. It would make a nasty mess. She might even explode on impact, like people who stepped in front of trains. So really, you'd have to be desperate. You'd have to be terribly, terribly desperate.

Stroking absently along the handle with one finger, she watched the changing skyline in the distance, a fold of hills, a solitary church spire, a huddle of barns and farm outbuildings. Miniature black and white cows wandered in a desultory line up a farm track, full udders swaying, in patient defiance of the matchstick man in brown overalls and wellington boots who bullied and chivvied them at the rear. Stupid cows, poor, patient, stupid cows. She turned and watched them until a concrete bridge obscured the distant view and the radio crackled again at the sudden interference.

'Are you listening to this?' Gerry demanded, switching it off anyway. She didn't answer. It had only been background noise after all, as habitual and unnecessary as the barley sugar on her tongue. But without it, the silence was oppressive.

'Where did you say we were staying tonight?' She already knew the answer. The question was as fatuous as the lyrics he'd just switched off, but it was something to say.

'Bed and breakfast place. I've stayed there before. Address is in the glove compartment.'

She opened the flap in front of her and rummaged around. His tie was in there, another empty barley sugar tin and an orange plastic scraper for the windscreen.

'There's no address in here.'

Eyes still on the road, he reached across, pushing her hand aside. 'Of course it's bloody in there.'

He didn't apologise when it wasn't. He was getting more forgetful lately. She'd noticed that. But he wouldn't admit it. It made her feel oddly triumphant though, as if subtly, she was gaining the upper hand.

'We could stay somewhere else,' she suggested. 'We could even drive down as far as Gretna, stay there tonight.'

'You and bloody Gretna! We're staying in Glasgow. I don't need the address. I can remember where the place was.'

I doubt that, she thought, pursing her lips, feeling the residue of barley-sugar stickiness tighten round her mouth like grainy varnish, I doubt that very much. But she said nothing. It wasn't worth an argument.

She didn't know what she'd expected, but it wasn't this. This was the same as every other depressing motorway staging post they'd stopped at, the same featureless carpark bordered with dusty, stunted shrubs, the same overflowing wastebins and bits of spilled rubbish. Even that dog, squatting on the grass to relieve itself, looked very like the one they'd seen doing exactly the same thing a hundred miles back.

'Is this it? You'd think they'd do something a bit different for Gretna Green.'

'Like what for instance? I suppose you were hoping for massed bagpipes playing the wedding march.' He guffawed at his own joke and she noticed how his chin disappeared into the bristly fold of flab round his jawline. Whatever she'd been hoping for, it wasn't this.

'I'm going to have a look in the shop first,' she announced abruptly. 'I'll see you in the cafeteria in a minute.'

The shop was equally disappointing. She knew she should just walk straight out again, but instead she found herself hopefully roving the aisles, fingering lucky horseshoes sprigged with imitation white heather, unfolding souvenir teatowels, gazing speculatively at an array of identical teddy bears on a shelf, with 'Gretna Green Bear' embroidered across their navy jerseys. She lingered in front of the lifeless display for a while, staring back at the disconcerting row of blind, glassy eyes. If she had a grandchild, one of these might do nicely. But you had to have children before you could have grandchildren.

Moving on, she picked up a box of locally produced fudge and smoothed the cellophane flat over the blurred local scene on the box lid. If that was the best they could do with a photograph, then God only knew what the real thing must be like. Half-heartedly, she wandered across to pay.

There was no sign of Gerry in the cafeteria. Assuming he'd gone to the Gents, she queued for a cup of weak, milky coffee and a Chelsea bun. The bun was a long way from Chelsea but it looked fresher than some of the other offerings on the stand, frosted with sugar and studded with a satisfying number of currants.

Chewing her way through these at a table by the window, she kept one eye on the door that led to the toilets. Several men went in and emerged a few minutes later, but still no sign of Gerry. As she tore off another strip of bun and folded it into her mouth, licking the sweetness from her fingers, she wondered idly if he'd been taken ill. She considered the possibility in a detached, objective way, without any trace of alarm, serene and solitary at her round formica table with its view of the carpark and the motorway beyond. The grimy plate-glass window was double-glazed, reducing the clamour of traffic to a distant hum, insulating her, cosy and safe, inside a warm, sugary world where even the sight of the child at the next table failed to inspire the usual pang.

Feet planted comfortably among the debris of squashed

chips and cake crumbs on the floor, she decided to wait a few more minutes before perhaps asking one of the male staff if they'd be kind enough to go in and check. Because it would never surprise her if Gerry were to keel over one day with a heart attack, the state he got himself into sometimes. Meantime, she thought she could probably manage another bun.

It was going to be touch and go. If he hit the rush-hour traffic on the outskirts, he'd never make it. Friday night though. The rush hour would be earlier. With a bit of luck and if this prat in front would get out of the bloody way, he'd manage it.

He braked hard and a round tin rolled forward from under the passenger seat. As he gathered speed, it slid back and jiggled annoyingly against the base of the seat, a monotonous, staccato clatter. It was getting on his nerves. Swearing, he groped with one hand for the empty tin. As he tossed it on to the seat beside him, he noticed a smear of white powder across the grey upholstery and clapped the heel of his palm to his forehead, cursing viciously again. 'Christ! Jean!'

It was her own bloody fault, rabbiting on about Gretna, head full of rubbish, insisting on coming with him. She didn't understand about business, deadlines to meet, missed appointments. That last one had shaken him up, forgetting it like that. Pressure of work, that was all, but the client hadn't been amused. He couldn't afford to repeat that mistake in a hurry, and now he'd have to go back, at least fifty miles, and risk fouling up a second time. He pictured her, ambling across the carpark to the tacky tourist shop at Gretna, backside wobbling in a way he'd long ceased to find attractive, and groaned out loud in frustration.

There was a roundabout ten miles on. He'd have to decide by then.

*   *   *

A car pulled up outside and Jean wiped the crumbs from her mouth and watched it with interest. He was smiling, stretching his arm along the back of the seat, his face close to hers. She turned towards him and wound her arms round his neck and then he was all over her so to speak. Jean couldn't take her eyes off them. Broad daylight, in the middle of a carpark, right in front of the cafeteria.

A girl with a greasy ponytail, lank strands scraped back under a token band of white hat, came and lifted her empty cup and plate, giving the table a cursory wipe.

'It's amazing what some people get up to, isn't it?' she observed cheerfully.

Jean glanced up into the girl's podgy face, at the ripe pimple next to the silver stud in her nose, before turning back avidly to the window.

'It certainly is,' she agreed, distracted for a moment by the sight of the girl's wistful reflection, framed beside her own in the glass.

MAKE THICK MY BLOOD

ALISON MACLEOD

G od I love knives.

How I scared you when I said that. You came in and I was sitting on the floor with a bone-handled letter opener, running its tip over the bare skin of my left forearm. You swore and startled me and it jabbed into the yielding flesh, a small drop of red blood appearing in the middle of all that white. I smeared it away with the flat of the blade. You were shaken and angry, I could see it in the confusion of your eyes. You asked what the hell I was doing and I shook my head, calm and half-smiling, and said I didn't know. Which was the truth.

But you didn't want that. You made me say something else. I love the coolness of the bone, I said, and the smoothness where it's been worn down by so many people holding it. I love the way the metal shines and reflects the light. That's what I love. You were happier then and you put the letter opener back in the drawer and kissed me. I was pleased I could comfort you so much just by telling you such a little bit of the puzzle. I was glad I could make you understand me without understanding myself.

We went to bed and you said you loved me eleven times. I believed you the first time.

* * *

The bread knife was waiting for me when I came down in the morning. Its serrated edge looked like teeth. I cut the bread with it, rationally, but couldn't resist running it over my thigh where the silk encasing it fell away. The metal was cold against my bed-warmed skin. I pressed it to me and little teeth marks appeared. I stopped before it really started to bite. I knew it wasn't time yet.

I took your toast up to you and watched you spread it with butter and marmalade. I licked the knife clean, slowly, watching you not noticing. We talked about the day we were going to have. I watched the taut curves of your body as you dressed and shaved and kissed me goodbye.

You left your penknife on the dressing table.

The first cut is the best, always the best. I do it slowly, watching the flesh gently unfold, opening up to me. Then the blood clouds and softens everything.

Winter sun is struggling to slide through the curtains. I can see my breath hang in the air when I exhale. I feel stingingly alive. I slide the knife down the inside of my leg and admire the silent way it slices through the skin. I love you for keeping it so sharp.

One more. I'll allow myself one more. It sweeps round the smooth curve of my abdomen. I feel soothed and refreshed, invigorated. Enough. The rules say three. I'm feeling good. I shower now that the blood is sticky and rusty brown, I only like the deep red flowing of it. I wash the knife blade too and enjoy restoring its metallic glint.

When you come home, I'd cut myself climbing over a barbed wire fence walking the dog, and I'm kissed and comforted. I can see how happy that makes you, to know that you love me.

You can have treats but then you have to pay for them. It's fair. So I go out. I feel good enough to do it with no more cuts beforehand, yesterday energised me. I go out and feel the world form a layer over my skin, deadening. I try not to breathe too much of it, not to let it in to interfere with the inner resonances of self, the balance.

I fight it but it comes at me, engulfing. It's too much, I remember the rules and their reassuring sonorities but here they seem hollow. I feel myself struggle and drown in outside, in its wave-like advances . . .

But I have the power of knowing what to do, of somewhere to go. The vegetable knife waits for me and I hear the grab and snatch of my breath come easy and calm as I tear away at the confusion, cut it to shreds and everything's so simple. So easy.

But come on, hold on. The rules, remember the rules. Because it's too much and where's all my beautiful control now?

Come on, hold on. I make one final mark, under my left breast, slow and deliberate and we're back to normal now.

My skin cracks with disgorged blood. I shower but it's too much to hide. I tripped with the knives I tell you and I see the shards of doubt flicker through your eyes before you blink them away, smile sad and accepting and we go to bed.

I've woken and there's too much white. Something hurts somewhere, everywhere. The first thing I see is your smile but it looks nervous and sometime around now realisation stabs into me. I'm bandaged. I don't remember . . . I remember the bread knife, and the cleansing, the purity of new blood metallic in my mouth, tasting it, breathing it, light . . .

You ask why. I don't want to say it but I do. It's the rules. You ask too gently who makes the rules. The rules aren't made, they just are. I tell you that. I feel this is breaking them, telling them, wonder how I'll have to pay for that. You want to know more but you can't because I don't, because there isn't anything more. So I can't blame you when you say ignore the rules. Forget them. You say you love me and I know that. You kiss my forehead and make me feel ill. I promise to be good. I promise to be good.

The rules wake me from the dead after too long, oh too long! I've shut them out and filled myself up with outside, but somewhere inside me I've held out through this pollution and waited till it was time. It's time. I've waited so long, now I deserve so much. Everything is suddenly clear. A raw and urgent clarity.

One sweep and the dirt is flowing away. The roof is lifting and I'm seeing the sky. I love the freedom, you catch at me but I'm so alight and alive, you've given me so much but you don't have this to give. Now I can feel who I am and I give myself back to myself. And this time it's final, I understand the rules at last and they and I merge into one ultimate sense, forever.

IN MEMORIAM

REGI CLAIRE

N ow that her mother's dead, Celia has all the time in the world. No more fuzziness at the edges of days when late afternoon would blur into evening and evening into night, then midnight and finally early morning, with those cups of milky tea, bowls of soup and hot water bottles dripping and sloshing over the few remaining gaps in between. From now on she'll sleep undisturbed, ten hours at least, and rip each day from the next in one clean tear.

A bit like yanking off the curtains in here a week ago, Celia thinks and looks up at the empty runner above the lounge window. She'd never taken to their grainy texture, their dirty skin colour. 'Silver sand' was what they'd been called in the catalogue, and her mother had stubbornly insisted on the term: 'Please, Celia, would you mind drawing the "silver sands", it's getting dark,' she'd whisper from the sofa if she wasn't too weak. A couple of nights after the funeral, while answering some letters of condolence, Celia had suddenly heard that voice again, like a slow tremble in the dusk. For once she hadn't hesitated. A few steps and she'd pulled, pulled as hard as she could. The fabric had spoken to her as it came away in her hands, shaking itself free from a decade's dust to cry out at last.

Time, of course, isn't the only thing Celia has in abundance now. There's the money, too. And space, yes, space most of all. Without warning it had exploded around her, expanding indefinitely until she could hardly see the corners of the room she happened to be in, as if the sharp winter sunlight had obliterated them, leaving her in the vastness of a desert. That's when she'd realised she'd better phone up some decorators.

Seven minutes past eleven; the man's late. Celia's eyes have slid away from the runner and are staring out into the street. The ash tree in the garden's waving its pale bare branches at her as if to say, 'Nothing doing, nothing at all'. She pushes up the sash, leans out, willing the van to appear. She hopes the firm's name is emblazoned: 'Stillwell & Biggs, Decorators', spray-painted in colourful lunges to let the whole neighbourhood know that she, Celia Jones, is starting a new life.

She feels elated, and excited, because this is the first time she's ever made a decision that's bound to change things. *Things* as opposed to *ideas*. Things are visible, she believes; ideas and opinions can be hidden away. But now her turn's come. At last she'll be able to mar those creams and salmon pinks, those flaccid greens – the paint will stick, and so will the paste underneath the new wallpaper. Even steaming won't restore the place to its previous state of unholy insipidness. Something will remain, she is sure. And that something will be hers and hers alone.

'Just don't say later I didn't warn you, Miss Jones.' It's five past twelve and the decorator, who had arrived in a van not unlike a hearse (jet black and polished to a gleam, with the firm's name curlicued discreetly in gold on both doors), sounds a little petulant. His professional pride's been hurt over and over, a room at a time, as it were. The woman's slightly off her rocker that's all, he consoles himself, or she wouldn't have clung to that nightmare of a colour scheme. Much too speedy she is, too eager to get it all over and done with in less than an hour, including tea or coffee and biscuits. He's worried. He's been through this kind of thing before: first the I-know-what-I-want rashness of choice, then – with the wallpaper still blistered and the paint still wet – the stunned silence, the murmurs of regret, shrill complaints, and acts of sabotage (sleek and wide-eyed and usually involving pets that always 'just happen to be moulting').

Celia doesn't bother to reply; words of caution no longer have power over her. She reaches for the order form on the coffee table, signs and dates it, her face glazed with obstinacy. Then, bringing out her cheque book, she suddenly relaxes, smiles towards the decorator: 'I'll pay two hundred now, if that's OK. The rest on completion of each room.'

'Suits me,' he nods, careful not to shake his head. While she writes out the cheque, he detaches the 'client's copy' from the form. Her signature's an almost-scrawl: 'Celia Jones', for God's sake! *Psychedelia*, more like! He closes the sample files, locks them in his briefcase with an extra loud snap. Then he brushes the biscuit crumbs off his trousers. A job's a job, after all.

A week from now the room they're in will be purple all over, various shades of purple to be precise. A lighter tone for walls and ceiling; the skirting, cornice, window frames and door surrounds a nuance darker; the shutters and doors darker still, with the inside panels near-black, like madly diminishing perspectives into some private hell.

It's the middle of the night and Celia's awake. She forgot to pull down the blind and cover up the chinks with the red scarf as usual, and now the moonlight's all over her. It's soaked into the bedding on top of her, underneath her, soaked into the folds round her head and feet, along her sides, making the sheets stiff and cold-heavy. She can't move, not even her little finger, just lies there and stares out at the huge frosty disk that's forced itself on her, stolen her sleep. Not a face, and

143

certainly not a friendly one, that's for sure. She can't think clearly because every now and again the disk becomes a gigantic eye that's trying to suck her into its brightness. After a while she begins to feel dizzy, and though she still can't move, it's as if she'd shrunk and was turning round and round inside those hardened sheets. To steady herself, she concentrates on the cloud shadows floating across the disk. But by some incomprehensible trick of the atmosphere the shadows themselves slowly dissolve into a ring of refracted light, a gigantic iris – tawny-orange, red, purple, bluey-green and yellow – to go with the gigantic white eye, which has started sucking again, sucking, sucking her inside . . .

When Celia wakes in the morning, her left hand's clenched into a fist, her knuckles sore and bone-white, as if they'd been clasped round something for hours on end. She sits up, massages her fingers back into place, one at a time. That *something* was less than nothing, a bead of sweat perhaps, dried long since, or a dream she can't even remember.

Breakfast's a rushed affair today because she wants to get on with things before the decorator and his assistant drop off their tools and tins of paint in late afternoon. She's put on her oldest clothes, the pair of 'dove-grey' flares and the 'eau-de-Nil' turtleneck (both presents from her mother, bought by mail-order as 'a surprise' years ago and only ever worn if she'd been reminded). Passing down the narrow hall, Celia pictures the walls in crimson. That's the colour she'd selected yesterday, quite instinctively, without meaning to offend the decorator, who'd ended up making an impassioned stand for 'gentle gardenia' and 'the illusion of spaciousness'. Crimson, after all, is more than a mere colour to her, it's a feeling. It's the flush of anger on her mother's cheeks whenever she'd suspected her of loitering after teaching at the language school, going for a drive maybe or a visit to the cinema, instead of keeping her company. Homecoming *is* crimson for Celia, and always will be.

She pushes open the door to the lounge. Gasps. Reels. Falls to her knees. For the briefest of instants she'd glimpsed a figure draped on the sofa, extending an arm towards her.

What would her students say if they could see her now, so small and helpless, crouching on the floor? Not doubt they're much too busy to spare a thought for her, the advanced group very likely screeching with laughter at Monty Python's 'Dead Parrot Sketch' and all those synonyms for 'death'.

Celia's face feels gritty; her contact lenses itch and bite. She peels off her mother's beige Sunday gloves, soiled now beyond redemption, and pushes back her hair. She'd never have believed a carpet kept so scrupulously clean, vacuumed at least once a week, could produce such a flurry of dust and fluff. The room seems to be swirling with it, to have grown darker, more distinct, as if its ceiling, walls and corners had hauled in the space between them, compressing it, like a snow cloud that's closing in on a winter's day.

She's ripped up a good two-thirds by now, pulling out the carpet staples with a claw hammer. One of them, near the fire-place, had stuck so fast she'd lost her balance and staggered back against the sofa; the hammer had missed her by inches and instead gouged a hole in her mother's favourite silk cushion. Another of her childish whims, Celia thinks, staring down at the floor: a white carpet in a room with a live coal-fire.

Her mother'd had it fitted shortly after Father left them, 'to find his luck elsewhere', as she'd explained. The phrase has lodged in Celia's mind like a precious stone. When she was little, she used to associate it with 'that man' or 'Daddy', picture him mining for gold and diamonds, far away; now that she's grown up and learnt to deal with abstracts she asks herself at times: 'Once you've lost it, whatever *it* is, how do you know where to start looking?'

Celia still remembers the day of her first real date and how nervous she was, so nervous a big lump of coal fell off the scuttle and bounced a smudge-trail across the white carpet, yards beyond the carefully laid-out newspapers. She'd done her best to conceal the stains temporarily – it *was* an emergency, after all – regrouping the armchairs, the coffee table and the standard lamp, scattering a few books on the floor, spine up, as if for further reference. Then, dressed in her purple trouser suit with lipstick and eye shadow to match, her hair combed one last time in front of the hall mirror, she'd reached for the spare set of keys on their hook by the door, just in case.

'Oh, before you're off, Celia dear: I noticed a small mishap in the lounge . . .' Smiling her cleanest smile, her mother had held out a basin of soapy water, a toothbrush and several sheets of blotting paper, pale-blue blotting paper.

'I'm really sorry. I'll sort it when I get back. Promise.'

'This isn't a coalmine, Celia.'

'Honest, I promise.'

'Which only leaves me, doesn't it . . . ?'

She'd been three-quarters of an hour late, and her young man was long gone. Ever since, Celia's hated that bland soggy blotting-paper blue; she never walks to the school now if the sky's that colour, she either drives or takes the bus. On such days she waits for night to come like the spread of a dark cloth.

Celia squeezes her mother's gloves back on, rumbles the furniture over on to the floorboards, and sets to tearing off the rest of the carpet, kicking and rolling it up into a slumped kind of shape. It's too heavy to shift, a leaden weight with none of its former springiness left. She'll be glad to see it carried out of the house to be burnt or dumped in one of those landfill sites.

The floorboards and the dirt gaps running straight and black in between seem to give the lounge direction at last. As if it was free to move now, at any moment might incline slightly towards the ash tree in its patch of wizened grass out front or, especially of an evening, retreat through the next room into the peace of flowerbeds, birds and clothes-lines at the back.

'That should come off easily enough,' the decorator says, sliding his knife sideways under the champagne wallpaper next to the door surround. 'See?' he half-turns to Celia, then tugs sharply and pulls off a strip, exposing a sea-green mural underneath, complete with whorls of blue, yellow and red like tropical fish. He brandishes the paper-strip but Celia's no longer paying any attention. She's gone up to the wall and started tracing the different colours with her fingernail, up, down, left, right, round and round and round.

The decorator's assistant brushes past with a stepladder and some dustsheets. She doesn't seem to notice, and for a moment he watches her finger drawing circles on the bare patch of wall, his eyes hooded from years of guarding against splashes of paint, loose flakes of plaster and wallpaper, and single ladies who want their immaculate flats shredded, then re-padded for no reason that he can see, except perhaps to keep themselves busy, and entertained. With a shrewd, well-rehearsed glance-and-grin towards his boss he says:

'That green colour's nothing special, just ancient paste. You get it in most old houses. You'd be surprised, though, at some of the other things found under wallpaper. Isn't that so, Colin?' Here he forces open his lids, raises his voice a notch, 'Like that time over at the manor house, eh?' The woman's hand doesn't stop, never even slows down; she reminds him of the black cat he had as a boy and how it used to sit behind the closed door, pawing and pawing to be let in.

The decorator, meanwhile, has crossed to the fire-place, knife in fist, and stabbed the wall high up, slicing off another strip, neatly, right down to the skirting. He's decided to play along for a bit, not really to humour his assistant nor to tease the woman either – he's not the teasing sort – but because she annoys him, plain and simple, annoys him standing there, ignoring them like they're a couple of dummies. He looks over his shoulder and calls out, rather loudly, 'No dark secrets here, Rob. Not yet, at any rate . . . !'

Celia's aware, of course, that she's being watched, made fun of, only she couldn't care less. It's just like writing something on the blackboard with one's back to the class. She can do what she wants now, can't she? And if she feels like stroking the wall she'll damn well do it. The surface has a waxy sheen that reminds her of skin almost . . . Such schoolboys' jokes, anyway: do they expect her to be bothered about ghosts and things? About dead mice and rats, wing-cases of beetles stuffed into wall holes?

Abruptly, Celia swivels round to face the two men, who, she notices with a certain teacherly relish, jump into action at once, flapping their dirty white dustsheets over the book-shelves, armchairs, sofa and coffee table, stacking rolls of paper, tools and tins into neatly useless pyramids. She is getting impatient; they can do all this tomorrow, it's half past four now and they promised not to keep her. A gleam of metal catches her eye:

'Excuse me,' she says, and stoops to pick up the stripping knife, its handle faintly warm still, 'may I borrow this?'

She'd laughed out loud at their sheepish, scandalised looks, at the threat in the decorator's voice when he wished her 'a pleasant evening' from the doorstep. Afterwards, like a good girl, she'd put the knife back down because she doesn't really need it, does she? Celia leans her head against the painted coolness of the open lounge door. Her eyes have started to water, she's laughed so much.

'You don't blink enough, that's what's wrong with you,' the optician had told her last week. She'd gone to see him a few days after the funeral, because of the bleary featurelessness she'd begun to experience in the flat. What a sad man he must be to want people to blink all the time, she'd reflected and smiled to cheer him up. In response he'd taken hold of her head, squirting something from a bottle straight into her eyes: 'Come on, Miss Jones. Blink!' And again, his voice split with impatience: ' "Blink!" I said. BLINK! BLINK!'

And now Celia's blinking and blinking and it doesn't help. Not one bit. The room's a liquidy blur and already the walls are receding. The dustsheets are looming larger and brighter, with an unbearable hint of blue leaking from their folds, as if they'd blotted up too much daylight. Celia wants to shut the door and walk away, but there's that cold-heavy weight again all round her, like last night. Blink by blink the clutter of furniture beneath the dustsheets changes shape, its jagged outlines slacken, level out, merge into one single mass, more and more familiar; and although she knows this is impossible she can see it just the same, right in front of her: that oblong object, shrouded.

Celia blinks and blinks. If she blinks long enough, the room will settle down – she's got all night. If she blinks long enough, the furniture won't pretend to be anything but furniture, and she'll be fine. All the time in the world. She'll blink and blink, waiting for the rustle as the sky's turned inside out.

THE EYES OF THE SOUL

MICHEL FABER

T he view from Jeannette's front window was, frankly, shite. Outside lay Rusborough South. There was no Rusborough North, West or East, as far as she knew. Maybe once upon a time, but if so, they must have been demolished long ago, wiped off the map, and replaced with something better.

Jeannette's house was right opposite the local shop, which had its good and bad side. Not the shop itself: that had four bad sides, all of them grey concrete with graffiti on. But having your house right near the shop: the good side was that Jeannette could send Tim out for a carton of milk or a sack of frozen chips and watch him through the window in case he got attacked. The bad side was that the shop was a magnet for the estate's worst violence.

'Look, Mum: police!' Tim would say almost every evening, pointing through the window at the flashing blue lights and the angry commotion just across the road.

'Finish your supper,' she would tell him, but he would keep on watching through the big dirty rectangle of glass. He couldn't really do anything else. The blinds were never drawn on the front window, because as soon as you blocked off the view, ugly though it was, you immediately noticed what a poky little shoebox the sitting room was. Better to see out,

Jeanette had decided, even if what you were seeing was Rusborough South's teenage substance abusers arguing with the law.

'What are police for, Mum?' Tim had asked her once.

'They keep us nice and safe, pet,' she'd replied automatically. But deep down, she had no faith in the boys in blue, or in the zealous busybodies who tried to get her interested in Neighbourhood Watch schemes. It was all just an excuse for coffee mornings where other powerless people just like herself complained about their awful neighbours and then got shirty about who was paying for the biscuits. Positive action, they called it. She much preferred to buy lottery scratch cards, which might at least get her out of Rusborough South if she was lucky.

The one thing that got Jeanette angrier than anything else was window companies. They would ring her up about once a week, telling her they were doing a special promotion on windows just now, and could they maybe send someone round for a free quote. 'I don't know,' she had said the first time. 'Can you just tell me how much you'd charge to replace my front window when kids throw a rock through it?' But the window companies didn't do that sort of thing. They wanted to do the whole house up with security windows, double glazing: serious money. Jeanette didn't have serious money, but still the window companies kept phoning.

'Look, I've told you before,' she would snap at them. 'I'm not interested.'

'Not a problem, not a problem,' they'd assure her. 'We shan't trouble you again.' But a week later, someone else would call, asking her if she'd given any thought to her windows.

Then somebody called in person. A woman with an expensive haircut, dressed like a New Labour politician or a weather girl on the telly. She stood in Jeanette's doorway, clutching a leatherbound folder and what looked like a video remote control. Parked against the kerb behind her was a bright-green van with a huge muscly man at the wheel. The side of the van was marked: OUTLOOK INNOVATIONS, and showed a little picture of a window with trees and mountains beyond it.

'You're not a window company, are you?' said Jeanette.

'No, not really,' said the woman, smiling like a doctor telling you that you're not having a heart attack after all but just a spot of indigestion. 'We offer people an alternative to windows.'

'You're a window company,' affirmed Jeanette irritably, and shut the door in the woman's face. She hated to do this to another human being, but when she'd first moved to Rusborough, some red-faced, panting little kids had come to the door asking if they could please have a drink of water. She'd considered shutting the door in their faces, but let them into the kitchen to have a drink instead. Next day, her house was burgled. Shutting the door in people's faces had got a little easier after that. But the lady with the leatherbound folder popped up at the window and looked awfully embarrassed.

'I'm honestly not selling windows,' she pleaded, her voice flattened pathetically by the grubby pane of glass between her and Jeanette. 'Not what you'd think of as a window, anyway. Couldn't I please have five minutes of your time? I can actually show you what we're offering right here and now.'

Jeanette hesitated, trapped. She should have had the blinds drawn, but she just couldn't bear that. Her eyes and the eyes of the other woman were locked, and all sorts of humdrum intimacies seemed to be flowing between them, like *I'm a woman; you're a woman*, and *I'm a mother; are you a mother, too?* Her shoulders slumping a little in defeat, Jeanette walked back to the door and opened it.

*   *   *

Once allowed into the living room, the saleswoman didn't waste any time.

'What do you think of the view through your window?' she said.

'It's shite,' said Jeanette.

The saleswoman smiled again, and tipped her head slightly to the side, as if to say, *I'd have to agree with you there, but of course I'm too polite to say so.*

'Well,' she purred, 'if you had a choice, what would you be seeing out there?'

'Anything but Rusborough South.'

'Mountains? Valleys? The sea?'

'Listen, when I win the lottery I'll let you know where I move to, how's that?'

The saleswoman seemed to sense she was annoying Jeanette, and, cradling her folder against her immaculate breast, she pointed her remote control thingy towards the window, straight at the man in the van. There was a soft *neep*. The man seemed to get the message, and the van door swung open.

'At Outlook Innovations we like to say, windows are the eyes of the soul,' said the saleswoman, reverently, almost dreamily.

Jeanette considered, for the first time, the possibility that she had let some sort of religious loony into her home.

'That's very deep,' she said. 'Look, my son's going to be home from school soon . . .'

'This won't take a minute,' the saleswoman assured her.

The man was fetching something big out of the back of the van. His overalls were bright green, to match the vehicle, and had OI emblazoned on them. Jeanette thought of skinheads.

Out of the back of the van slid a large dull-grey screen. It looked like an oversized central-heating radiator, but was apparently not as heavy, as the man lifted it by himself without much effort. He carried it across Jeanette's horrible little 'lawn' and lifted it up onto the windowsill, only his massive fingers showing now. Then he shoved the screen right up against the window, with a scrape of metal on prefab something-or-other. It blocked the view snugly, with no more than a millimetre to spare on all sides.

Jeanette laughed nervously. 'You've had me measured, have you?' she said.

'We would never take such a liberty,' demurred the saleswoman, faintly offended. 'I think you'll find that almost every front window on the estate is absolutely identical.'

'I'd wondered about that, actually,' Jeanette sighed.

Slid so securely into place, the screen sealed the room with claustrophobic efficiency, making the electric light seem harsher and yet at the same time more feeble, like the mournful glow inside a chicken coop. Jeanette tried to be well behaved about the way it made her feel, but to her surprise the saleswoman said, 'Awful, isn't it?'

'Pardon?'

'Like a prison, yes?'

'Yeah,' said Jeanette. There were scrabblings going on outside the house, which must be the technician making adjustments.

'If this particular Outlook were installed permanently, the seal would be soundproof, too.'

'Yeah?' said Jeanette. Being boxed in was giving her the heebie-jeebies, and the thought of being shut off from all sound wasn't exactly the thing to cheer her up. She wondered if it was going to be difficult to get this woman to leave.

'Now,' said the saleswoman, 'I'll hand you the control, and you can switch it on.'

'Switch it on?' echoed Jeanette.

'Yes,' said the saleswoman, nodding encouragingly as if to a small child. 'Do go ahead. Feel free.'

Jeanette squinted at the remote, and pressed her thumb on

155

the button marked ON/OFF. Suddenly the screen seemed to vanish from her window, as if it had been whipped away by a gust of wind from nowhere. Sunlight beamed in again through the glass, making Jeanette blink. But it was not the light of Rusborough South. The shop across the road was gone. The dismal streets the colour of used kitty litter were gone. The bus shelter with the poster about saying no to domestic violence was gone.

Instead, the world outside had changed to a scene of startling beauty. The house had seemingly relocated itself right in the middle of a spacious country garden, the sort you might see in a TV documentary about Beatrix Potter or somebody like that. There were trellises with tomatoes growing on them, and rusty watering cans, and little stone paths leading into rosebushes and rickety sheds half lost in thicket. Much love had obviously been poured into the design and the tending of this place, but nature was getting the best of it now, gently but insistently spilling over the borders with lush weeds and wildflowers. At its wildest peripheries the garden merged (at just about the point where the shop ought to be) into a vast sloping meadow that stretched endlessly into the distance. The tall grass of that meadow rippled like great feathery waves in the breeze. An undulating V-formation of white geese, golden in the sunlight, was floating across the sky.

Entranced, Jeanette moved closer to the window, right up to the windowsill. The smudges on the glass were just as they had been for weeks, years maybe. Beyond them, the world really was what it appeared to be, radiant and tranquil. The perspective changed subtly just the way it should, when she turned her head or looked down. Just underneath the window, a discarded slipper had moss growing on it, and flower petals were being scattered by a tiny sparrow. Jeanette pressed her nose against the glass and tried to peek sideways, to see the joins. All she could see was some kind of ivy she didn't have a name for, nuzzling at the edges of the window, dark green with a spot of russet red at the heart of each leaf. Her ear, so close now to the glass, heard the little beak of that sparrow quite clearly, the infinitely subtle rustle of the leaves, the distant honking of the geese.

'It's a video, right?' she said shakily. To keep her awe at bay, she closed her eyes and tried to see the view through her window objectively. She imagined it as a sort of endless re-run of the same film of a country garden, with the same birds flying the same circuit at intervals like in those shop window displays at Christmas, where a mechanised Santa Claus lowered a sack of presents into a chimney endlessly without ever letting it go.

'No, it's not a video,' murmured the saleswoman indulgently.

'Well, some sort of film anyway,' said Jeanette, opening her eyes again. The geese were out of sight now, but the golden light was deepening. 'How long does it go for?'

The saleswoman chuckled, as if a small child had just asked her when the sun would fall back to the ground.

'It goes *forever*,' she said gently. 'It's not any kind of film. It's a real place, and this is what it's like there, right now, at this very moment.'

Jeanette struggled with the idea. The sparrow had jumped on to the windowsill. It was utterly, vividly real. It opened its minuscule mouth and chirped, then shivered its wings, shedding a couple of fluffs.

'You mean . . . I'm looking into somebody else's back yard?' she asked.

'In a way,' said the saleswoman, opening her leatherbound folder and leafing through its waterproofed pages. 'This is a satellite broadcast of . . . let me see . . . the grounds of the Old Priory, in Northward Hill, Rochester. This is what is happening there right now.'

Jeanette became suddenly aware that she was gaping like an

idiot. She closed her mouth and frowned, trying to look cynical and unimpressed.

'Well,' she said, staring out across the meadows. 'There's not very much happening there, is there?'

'That's a matter of opinion, of course,' conceded the saleswoman. 'We do have Outlooks which view on to more . . . *eventful* landscapes. There is the Blue Surge Outlook, which broadcasts the view through the lighthouse at Curlew Point, Cruidlossie, the third stormiest beach in the British Isles. For those who like trains, we have the Great Valley Crossing Outlook, which has three major railways running services past it. For animal lovers, we have the Room To Roam Outlook, viewing on to an organic sheep farm in Wales . . .'

Jeanette was watching her little sparrow hop away across the garden, and the saleswoman's voice was a twitter in the background.

'Mm?' she said. 'Oh well actually, this is . . . fine.'

'It's particularly lovely at night,' added the saleswoman in a soft, beguiling tone. 'Owls come out. They catch mice in the garden.'

'Owls?' echoed Jeanette. She had never seen an owl. She had seen a drunk and bleeding boy pissing in a circle from on top of a parked car, his arc of urine narrowly missing a dozen of his laughing companions. She had never seen an owl.

'How . . . how much does this cost?' she breathed.

There was a pause while the wind blew a few leaves trembling against the window.

'You can buy,' said the saleswoman. 'Or you can rent.' Her eyes twinkled kindly, offering her customer the choice which was no choice.

'How . . . how much per . . . um . . .'

'It works out to a smidgen over fourteen pounds a week,' said the saleswoman. Observing Jeanette swallowing hard, she went on: 'Some people would spend that much on scratch cards, or cigarettes.'

Jeanette cleared her throat.

'Yeah,' she said. Then, desperate for a reason to resist the pull of the beautiful world out there, Jeanette narrowed her eyes and demanded, 'What if some kid throws a brick through it?'

Again the saleswoman opened her leatherbound folder, and held a particular page out for Jeanette's perusal.

'All our Outlooks', she declared, 'are designed and guaranteed to withstand the impact of any residential missile.'

'Full Coke cans?' challenged Jeanette.

'Gunfire at point-blank range, if necessary.'

Jeanette looked at the saleswoman in alarm, wondering if she knew something about the Rusborough gangs that Jeanette didn't.

'We do a lot of business in America,' the saleswoman explained hastily.

Jeanette imagined movie stars and celebrities like Oprah gazing through these wonderful windows. The saleswoman let her imagine, keeping to herself her own more accurate vision of the urban slums of Baltimore and New York, where rows and rows of windows – twenty, thirty, fifty a day – were being plugged up with grey screens of Outlook Innovations.

'Of course, they're the ideal security, too,' she pointed out, as if this were a trifling but comforting afterthought. 'Nothing in the world can get through.'

Knowing deep down she had already given in, Jeanette made one last attempt to appear hard-headed.

'They could still get in through the other windows,' she remarked.

The saleswoman accepted this gracefully with another little tilt of the head. 'Well . . .' she suggested, hugging her folder full of Outlooks to her breast with unostentatious pride. 'One thing at a time.'

Jeanette looked back at the garden, the fields. They were still there. She felt like crying.

While the man outside laboured to fix the screen permanently into place, Jeanette found herself signing a contract, pledging sixty pounds per month to Outlook Innovations Incorporated. She knew she was making the right decision, too, because while the screen was being bolted on to her house, it had to be switched off briefly, and Jeanette missed her garden with a craving so intense it was almost unendurable. There was no doubt in her mind that this was an addiction she would gladly give up smoking for.

An hour later, long after the saleswoman and the green van had driven away, Jeanette was still at the windowsill, gazing out at Northward Hill. Some of the geese were returning, closer to her house this time. They beat their wings lazily, trumpeting their alien contentment.

Suddenly Tim burst into the house, safe and sound and chirpy after another long day at his soul-destroying penitentiary of a school. He skidded to a halt on the dining-room carpet, goggling in amazement at the view through the window. He pointed, unable to speak. Finally, all he could manage was:

'Mummy, what are those birds doing out there?'

Jeanette laughed, dabbing at her eyes with her nicotine-stained fingers.

'I – I don't *know*,' she told her boy. She was feeling utterly lost, but happier than she'd been for years. 'They . . . they just live there, I guess.'

CROSSWORDS

ELIZABETH REEDER

S he left me in silence one morning. I did not hear her go, I
simply noted spaces where before there had been none:
fewer pots in the kitchen, one less toothbrush in the bathroom, entire bookshelves empty. It took three days for the
spaces to accumulate as an ache in my chest.

I planned to buy more books, another toothbrush, eat out,
but I could not forgive her for the space she left beside me in
the bed.

The walls were the only thing which remained as they had
been before: crammed with prints, paintings, framed photographs, a corkboard, hooks for coats and calendars hung on
thin nails. She left the walls as I had meticulously, sometimes
maliciously, created them and on the third day, for the first
time, they looked cluttered and unnecessary.

If she had had her way the walls would have been free of
everything except the basics. A clock here, a light-switch there.
She argued that there were books for pictures, albums for
photographs. Walls were for support. Wherever she was now
she would have broad expanses of bright walls, uncluttered
vistas of floor. And in this openness she would speak my name
not unkindly, but with relief that, with distance, she could
think of me without rage.

*   *   *

Once I came home to find her standing in the middle of the living room with her arms outstretched from her sides. She had pushed the furniture up to hug the walls, rolled and lifted the rug leaving it leaning in a corner. I asked her why she was standing there and she said that from there she could feel the cool draught-filled air flowing over her, beneath her arms like clouds parted by the wings of a plane. She took my hand and led me to the centre of the room, took off my jumper to expose my T-shirted arms and lifted my arms up and out in crucifixion fashion. Her cool fingers, prints on my elbows. Close your eyes, and I did. She stepped back leaving me at the mercy of the space and the draughts. Goosebumps fluttered on the surface of my skin and my heart started to race. I knew at that moment what I was capable of alone. With eyes still shut I sought her out at the edges, enclosed her in my arms. She surrounded me.

When she let me go she was more distant and I found this space, like all spaces, terrifying. I prefer the closeness of cloth, the nearness of breath, the comfort of smells, the decisiveness of words. A space, a physical silence, can mean anything, become anything, and it is this unknown which sends me into a panic. In conversations I have trouble choosing sides (if I go to one side I create a gap on the other). On planes I prefer the middle seat – shoulder to shoulder to shoulder with strangers. The awkward brushes of knees and arms, long-haul alcohol-sleep breath and forced conversations comfort me; they juxtapose the large distance between the belly of the plane and the ground.

At parties I am a true wallflower: arm, hip and shoulder leaning against a wall, knowing at least that to be solid. At home I can never go to bed with any of the boxes on the quick crossword left empty. If I do not know the answers I fill them in randomly or romantically. It used to be a running joke that we shared. She would dare me to leave just one blank, just one box. I could never do it. I would lie in bed thinking about that space where there should be meaning and I would fill it in with a 'b'. Thinking, just let me be.

Metal on stone. If our first meeting had had a sound it would have been metal on stone and then silence.

On the day we met I stood behind her in the small store and could feel the warmth of her body, the strong, large space she took up. I could smell last night's curry on her skin. My dislike of spaces means that in queues I stand too close. This day was no different. She kept moving forward and I kept closing the gap between us. I could feel her bubble of security around her and I wanted to be within it, feel what she felt. She almost became annoyed, but when I smiled at her she mistook envy for desire and I let her. From there I would get too close and she would occasionally get close enough.

It is odd that she is the one who knew how to hold me so tightly that I could stop fighting the need to be enclosed. This beautiful woman hated the closeness of city buildings, could not stand the physical clutter of everyday life, could stay in the flat for hours or days at a time with no TV or radio, enjoying the silence and solitude. Each night she clearly delineated her half of the bed so that her body could be free in sleep. (And I as meticulously crossed over invisible lines, first with breath and then with light fingers and more solid body curving into her own.)

This woman with her large arms did that for me. Her hips and thighs took up the space between my own. When she made love her needs seemed to reverse and then revert back. She would be there for me, legs, arms and thighs pressed and warm and then she would be opening up, moving covers aside to expose us to the cool air and letting that be her freedom. Her touch on me solid and undeniable. Mine on her light, consistent. And if it was night she would hold me until I slept and then she would gently move me over to one side and remove herself to the other. Lying on her back, both arms on top of the duvet, hands spread wide on flannel. It is here, hours later, that I would breathe first, then lift one arm and place my head in the crook between her shoulder-blade and her breast and carefully place my body along the full length of her own. My warmth to hers.

I thought that we had worked it out. Our different needs. We talked about it before we moved in together and tried to make room for her spaces and my objects. A decade passed with only small crossovers, the usual friction and compromise. Near the end though, something else happened. Somehow, like inevitability itself, my need for objects overtook the spaces that she had carefully carved out. In the beginning she said that she did not mind, that she would get space outside, that she could take her car and drive and climb and there would be the vastness that she needed. But her needs seemed to overpower her own will. This was about the time I found her standing in the living room, almost gliding. And when books kept disappearing into boxes and then storage. When knick-knacks became piles in cabinets and our wardrobes became one (less closet space taken up).

Meanwhile I started to hang pictures. An O'Keefe here, a Kahlo there. Pictures of mountains, photo-montages of our families and friends, an antique barometer in the hall, take-out menus taking over the corkboard, a calendar in each room just in case we forgot the day or the year. The walls became my compulsion. If I had had an eating disorder I would have eaten, instead I hung pictures. To make up for what I felt that I could not control I tried to make more spaces on the shelves, dress in black (to give the illusion that I took up less space) but the walls mocked me, had to be filled.

After a bit she started to talk less and less, lusciously

letting the silence creep around the edges of the room. Mysteriously the CD player developed a glitch and would not play, I got it fixed and then the speakers blew. I understood and left them unrepaired. And still I am not sure that we were unhappy. We had moments when we could understand why our lives needed to be like this. Sound to silence, darkness to light, rock to scissors. Her touch still came to me, a need, pressing. However, I started to let her sleep in peace, sometimes sleeping on the couch. Not out of anger but of kindness. Somehow I think that this was the last straw for her.

Soundlessly it approached. Louder, bigger than I could have imagined – she blew. Her body expanded to fill the room; she held her arms straight and stiff by her sides. Fists clenched. Her voice belted out the words at me. I was weak as I faced her.

We spat cross words and put downs; circled each other like prey and predator. The room was filled, electric. I have to admit that it thrilled me: her heat and the fullness of her rage. In the midst of losing the woman I love I was thrilled by the incredible intimacy of our anger.

She recognised it too. Could see it in my eyes reflecting her own. Curiosity, excitement moving in company with furious anger. This stopped her. I had driven her to the intimacy of rage and that made her seethe even more. Her stiff arms released in breath and her chest expanded like a yell once more, and then collapsed in peaceful controlled resignation. She said no more.

I slept on the bed, she on the sofa. In the morning she was gone. She had taken my books, my toothbrush and all of our pots. Wood planks were left bare, reminiscent of Novocain dentists' visits where you emerge with far fewer teeth than when you went in.

*　　*　　*

Eight days later the missing pieces remain as she left them. I still have not forgiven her for the space in our bed.

I find myself following her less closely around the flat. I have stopped setting a place for her at the table. I draw a line down the middle of the bed and am on one half when I drop off, but wake sprawled, criss-crossed over imaginary delineations. I push the furniture to the edges of rooms and stand topless with arms open, palms forward. I stand there and cry. Images of wildness come fast and furious, shocking me and knocking the wind out of my lungs. I know how much further I can go without her and that in our intimacy, my insistence of touch, that she had found herself for the first time protected.

Seventeen days later a letter arrives. Her handwriting. The envelope and sheets are a thick handmade paper with rough edges. One page is tiny, a fragment, the second almost full sized. To fit everything on to the first page her writing is in miniature and tight. She fits years into a very small space.

> spaces love hollow missing bitch bastard
> damn compulsiveifthatwouldmakeyouhappy
> obsessive closeminded pleasestay pleasecomeback
> iamsorry loveyouthismuch biggerthanthat
> youarefreenow iamtoo youfilledspacesinme
> iwillalwaysrememberpleaseremember
> youarepresentnowforeveralongmysleepingbody

The second page has a roughly drawn puzzle on it. It is one of those crosswords that does not have any numbers. This one has no clues either. There is a criss-crossing of boxes, a line for each year we spent together. Twelve to the day.

It takes willpower. I find a frame. I cut out the words and phrases of the letter and glue them to a bright blue background around the indecipherable crossword. I take a calendar off the wall in the living room and, knowing that this one is too important to make up, in its place I hang the empty crossword proudly, kindly. It gives me strength: I remember what passed between us in silence, in the fullness of our rage.

THE DEAD WOMAN
AND THE LOVER

DILYS ROSE

W e've been in the morgue all afternoon and I'm chilled
to the bone but at least – as Nick the cameraman has
reminded me more than once – I can go home at the end of
the night. Nick has also promised that even though I spent
most of the time lying stark naked on a slab, it will all be all
right in the end. In other words, any accidental flashes of pubic
hair will be edited out. I tried keeping my knickers on – a hand
on thigh shot was all that was needed – but no matter where
Nick put his nimble, busy self, a white, elasticated leg band
kept creeping into the frame. There was nothing for it but to
bare all, shut my eyes and try to think about something other
than the fact that a roomful of completely clothed people was
focusing on me.

As well as being minus my clothes, I have a new, short
haircut – for the likeness – which exaggerates the sharpness of
my chin and cheekbones. Under the merciless lighting, I
expect to look hard and haggard as well as dead but what
bothers me more is the business of playing, not a character,
but a real, recently living person. I've been in a number of
historical dramas, breathed some life into loyal or scheming
ladies' maids, feckless or streetwise waifs, a queen or two,
numerous lady pioneers, witches, mistresses, molls and ruina-
tions of famous men.

When someone has been long dead and the details of a life have gone largely unrecorded, my roles have involved more interpretation than imitation. Fictional characters, of course, provide even more scope for input on my part. But no matter how convincingly I might appear to step into another's shoes, acting is a job; I like it but also like to leave it behind. Fraser jokes about bringing Lady Macbeth home one night and Ophelia the next, though I've never played either and I'm too old now to be offered Ophelia.

Occasionally, though, a character will follow me out of the studio or off the set and lurk around the flat, popping up at inconvenient moments like an uninvited guest and snarling up the domestic routine I try to maintain, in spite of unsociable working hours and a man who has enough order at work not to need it at home. But usually when I've cleaned off my make-up and put on my own clothes again, it doesn't take too long to switch back to myself. Today, I don't know; it's the first time I've played a corpse in the reconstruction of an inquest.

Philip's project is a long shot. The facts point to suicide but gut feeling is that even if the husband didn't do the deed, he was guilty, one way or another, of causing his wife's death. A jury is not asked to make a decision on the moral question, only on the actual cause of death. The law may have been upheld but justice – we're all with the sister on this – has not prevailed. If Philip's film succeeds in drawing enough public attention to the dead woman, the case may be reopened, the truth may be revealed. If, if, if.

The dead woman had nothing noteworthy about her except her death and even that, first time round, only merited a couple of column inches. If it hadn't been for her older sister's almost lunatic persistence, the case would have been laid to rest with the minimum of fuss and interest. After all, the husband had an alibi and the suicide note was verified as genuine. But the sister insisted that there was more to it, that something had been missed. On she went, badgering anyone and everyone to consider more than the facts, to look further back than the empty vodka bottle and the cold bathwater to uncover the real cause of death. Which is why, today, I've been earning union rates by taking off my clothes for the camera.

It's been a long day; we're all tired, hungry and cold but nobody is complaining much; even Nick has kept his moans to a minimum. At his suggestion, Fraser, Philip and I have called into a nearby pub with him, a Polish place he recommended, for schnapps and blinis to take the edge off the day. Normally I'd go straight home with Fraser but the warmth and bustle of the cluttered little pub, its odours of cigars and pickled cabbage, are comforting. Nick managed to grab a table near the imitation log fire, over which I'm slowly defrosting my fingers. The schnapps, served in dinky, medicinal-looking shot glasses, is having the same effect on my insides.

Fraser doesn't like my haircut; he prefers women to look soft and yielding. Ever since he arrived at the morgue, he's been quizzing me about my day, the nudity in particular. Was it essential for the purpose of reconstructing the case or just a gratuitous ogle for the crew? It can't be easy imagining your partner's body on view to millions, even if all it's doing is lying on a slab and trying not to shiver. But what's done is done; the day needs to be put to bed. I pull Philip into the conversation with Fraser as a way of slipping out of it.

I've worked with Philip before; as a director, I trust him. He's patient but thorough. As a person, he's an airy individual, who floats in and out of my life like a feather. Fraser doesn't trust Philip but Fraser doesn't trust anyone, not even himself – as he's fond of saying.

I sip my schnapps and rub the numbness out of my hands. Very much a man's pub, Nick's choice, dark wood, tobacco-stained walls plastered with photos – of sporting personalities and greasy old portraits of patriarchs on horseback. The polished gantry is stocked with a wide range of vodka and schnapps. A few solo men perch on stools, nursing their drinks, and one of them, I'm convinced, is Q. We almost met a couple of years ago, at an awards ceremony. We had been seated at neighbouring tables. Neither of us won anything that night but during the envy-laden applause for those who did, we exchanged small, consolatory smiles. It's him, no doubt about it. He's been on the cover of every women's magazine this last year. Leaning against the bar, collar pulled up around his ears he looks as though he too has been in the morgue all afternoon. Either that or he's trying to avoid recognition. Getting on a bit, now, but the careworn look is part of Q's appeal to the countless women who attend cinemas to feast on his narrow, glinting eyes, his squint, lip-curling smile. The film doesn't matter much.

Q, aka The Lover, is running a hand along the smooth surface of the bar and I find myself following the movement of his fingers as if there were nothing else to look at in the room. This is what he does, what he's become famous for doing. Give him the part of a stubble-chinned ne'er-do-well, or clean-shaven, sensitive soul, it makes little difference to his fans. What they see is his hand caressing a table, running a fingernail along the grain of the wood. Q can – and does – make a block of wood look cherished: when he wipes his boots on a mat, sinks into an armchair, opens the latch of a window, women long to be that doormat, armchair or window latch.

On screen Q has, of course, fondled other items. He's unhooked basques and bodices, raised petticoats, slid hands beneath ballgowns and miniskirts. He has sighed and moaned, closed his eyes or kept them open in rosy, backlit interiors and grainy back alleys but it's not for the sex scenes themselves that women flock to the Roxy, the Rio, the Odeon. It's Q's attention to inanimate objects that draws women in their droves. He has practised all his subtle, clandestine stroking of everyday household fixtures, choreographed the spiralling index finger, dragging nail, the sweep of his palm, he has perfected the gestures of desire. He's done his homework.

But it's not only suggestive gestures which have encouraged such drooling adulation. Q's voice, sweet and dark, can be tasted. It can whisper words of passion, confess to terrible secrets or utter something as banal as *I'm looking for employment* and a breathless, female sigh will ripple through an auditorium. To be honest, Q could recite a page of the telephone directory and create the same effect.

The schnapps is going to my head. We ordered our blinis ages ago but no sign of them so far. Drinking on an empty stomach's never a good idea. The dead woman drank herself to death. Or drowned. Or both. But whatever the body expired from, the spirit had already had the life squeezed out of it. Does Fraser have the same capacity for cruelty as the dead woman's husband? Or Nick, or Philip? This isn't a rational thought, I know, just a nasty black flicker in my head.

As I'm the only one of us who's come close to meeting Q before, Fraser has been nagging me to ask him over. Like many men, of either persuasion, he claims not to understand what women see in Q. However, Fraser's addiction to success tends to outweigh personal taste; he consumes it like other people eat pizza, and can sound knowledgeable about productions he's never seen. Sitting next to me, stroking his trim little beard and looking as fresh as he did when we left the flat this morning, I realise that, though we've been together for five years, there are huge areas of Fraser's life that I know very little about. His work and the people he knows through it are usually dispensed with in the time it takes to remove his jacket and switch on the TV. Computing isn't the easiest subject for small-talk but I have tried. Fraser just doesn't give much away.

Q doesn't look as if he wants company, or, for that matter, if he'd be much fun. Gloomy and preoccupied, he's faithful to the dark, brooding persona his fans can't get enough of. He's never been one for comedy.

Fraser: I think Q looks lonely.

Nick: If I were him, I'd be bored by now. I can never bear more than half a drink in my own company.

Philip: Drinking alone begins as a bid for independence but turns into an exercise in loneliness.

Nick: You don't go to a bar to be alone, do you?

Fraser: Maybe he's waiting for someone.

Nick: Looks like the someone's kept him waiting long enough.

Me: All right!

Q is staring into the middle distance and scrupulously avoiding eye contact with anyone. My choice is to shout or touch. As I detest raising my voice unless I'm being paid for it, I reach over and tap the shoulder of his soft, mole-brown coat. Close-up, in the flesh, Q has plenty of plain, ordinary angles as well as the familiar photogenic ones. Being short, I have an intimate view of his nostrils which are no more appealing than anyone else's.

He seems pleased enough that I came over to speak to him though he doesn't remember me from the time we almost met and I misquote the title of his latest film. Our conversation begins with the usual – are you working, what are you working on now, what are you working on next? against a wall of background noise; glasses being thrust into scalding water, the bleeping till, a fruit machine vomiting coins. Q's voice arcs through the racket, a soft curve of sound swings towards me until I notice a platter of blinis on its way to the table and Fraser beckoning impatiently.

Once the introductions are done – Q is obliged to do a lot of manly hand-shaking – we dig into the food. The blinis are fresh and hot and reassuringly stodgy. I'm half-way through my second before I realise how hungry I am. And still, in spite of more schnapps, chittering.

Fraser: She's had a hard day.

Fraser claps me heartily on the back, like a dog. Q nods. His lips crinkle in my direction.

Nick: Haven't we all. God, I want to go back to making commercials; something wholesome, like breakfast cereal or vitamin supplements, or gardening tools. No, not gardening tools. What am I saying? The last time I did gardening tools, the clapper loader fell off a ladder and impaled herself on a hedge clipper.

Already Nick is talking too loud.

Nick: You like this place?
Q: It's handy.
Nick: Right! So you live nearby?
Q: Not far away.
Nick: Whereabouts? This is home territory, man.
Q: I try not to publicise my address.
Nick: Quite right, too. Keep the fans at bay. Protect your privacy.
Q: It's not that . . .
Nick: He's just being modest, isn't he? I bet he can't walk down the street without some obsessed female stalking him. By the way, this woman we've been working on had most of your films on video.

Q: I have to go.

Nick: You've only just sat down! You're not supersti-
        tious are you? Let me buy you a drink. I haven't
        even bought you a drink.

Q: My wife . . .

Nick: Say no more. Half an hour late and the wife goes
        spare. Do I remember that shit. Used to drive me
        bonkers, having to account for every minute as if I
        were under contract. Glad to say, I'm no longer
        accountable.

Nick's cheeks are flushed – from the schnapps or the fire – and
his eyes are worryingly bright. It's not quite a year since his
wife left him for a quiet but punctual librarian.

Q: My wife . . . needs me. And I need her.

Since we left the pub, I haven't stopped shivering. On the tube
we perched stiffly on our seats, intent on the Somali family
across the aisle; stoic, impassive parents and sleepy children
who pressed their pretty heads against the dirty upholstery.
Fraser is annoyed; with Q, maybe, for rushing off so quickly or
Nick for prompting Q's departure, or me for having a star to
myself for five minutes, I don't know but I don't like the way
he's crashing about in the kitchen looking for something else
to eat and cracking open another beer. If he'd just come right
out with what's bugging him instead of transmitting his bad
mood through the floorboards . . .

My head hurts; nothing drastic, just a dull kind of hungover
throbbing. The steam from the bath I'm running has fogged
up the mirror so I can't see whether or not my new hairstyle is
an improvement. My neck feels naked, exposed. Though I'm
alone and the bathroom door is locked, I can't shake off the
sensation that there's someone behind me . . .

The dead woman must have felt like that almost all the time. She must have looked over her shoulders for years, quaking at the sound of her husband's footsteps. A small, weaselish man, fast and vicious. His explosive rages left her shaking for days at a time. The bathroom, with its puny snib, was her refuge, hot water and vodka her comforters. The husband had to break the lock to discover her body but – according to the sister – breaking things was something he was good at. The bathwater was cold, the vodka bottle empty. The husband summoned the police immediately, leaving the submerged corpse of his wife fingerprint-free for the law to deal with. Her damp, farewell note – *I'm so sorry, Marguerite* – was on the shelf, under the tooth mug. I wipe the mirror with my hand and see a tired, shorn woman fading as more steam adheres to the surface of the cold glass. I turn off the taps and slide down into the hot, comforting water and do what countless women do; close my eyes and think of Q, backlit, mouthing seductive, rehearsed words.

LIFE DRAWING

LINDA CRACKNELL

I got the job without even taking my clothes off. It never occurred to me there'd be an interview. I imagined you'd get your kit off and give the whole staff a twirl, like a stage audition, them looking on with thumbs and forefingers on chins, clipboards even. And then they'd hold up score-cards, Eurovision-song-contest style.

I answered Trevor's questions.

– No, never done it before; there's a first time for everything!

– I guess it's just a job . . . and I quite like a college atmosphere. Reminds me of being at school.

– Actually I've never tried keeping still for that long. But I'm very patient, and I think a lot – won't get bored.

– I don't think I know anyone here, no.

And the bearded eyes studied me, not undressing me, but trying to see my motivation for a difficult job with crap money.

I have my reasons. Perhaps it was the wording of the ad, the small word 'life' that attracted me when the paper fell open on the public library desk: 'Models wanted for life drawing. Male and female. £5 per hour.' And what I didn't tell Trevor; a job where I didn't need to speak. OK I'd be naked, there'd be people looking at me, but they wouldn't need to know me.

*　　*　　*

179

'It's the *pose* you're after' says Trevor to his class, 'forget light and shade, look at the angle of the arms, the twists here. Amazing what the body can do.' And he points at a part of me as if I'm not in it. I become a machine and that suits me fine.

To start with the students exist to me as a semicircular presence of boards, easels, and paint-splattered jeans. I can tell without looking at their faces that they frown and purse their lips. The room is heavy with concentration. Theirs and mine. You just hear the scratch of pencil or charcoal, the shuffle of feet as Trevor approaches and they make way for his superior eye, his chat.

'How's it going?'

'So-so . . . I'm having a bit of trouble with x,y or z/I think x has gone a bit y.'

'OK. Try using marks like these . . .' and he's away, re-shaping what they've done, imposing his view on their work. The students grunt, acquiesce, thank him.

And then it's the break and I un-rack myself. I go behind the screen to put on my robe. Can't bear the intimacy of putting clothes *on* in public! Then the hard part – to drink coffee, co-exist as a human in the same room as the students. They're happy to ignore me; they gather around each other's work, chat, bang in and out through the swing-door for loos, coffee, whatever.

When they go out there's a chance to find out what they see when they look at me; how they interpret me. I vary. In some drawings I look too thin, in some too muscular, in others fatter than I would like. Mostly I have no face. There are angles, form, the suggestion of the pattern on the drape behind, but no face. They cannot read me. Thank God. Five minutes shrinks to seconds and we're called back by a clap of Trevor's hands. It's a relief to become a machine again.

The studio is quiet when I arrive each morning. Trevor's there, taking small gout-steps around the studio with his nose in a mug, the white beard collecting coffee droplets. His gut pushes against the fisherman's smock, the belly pockets bulging with pencils, paintbrushes, cigarettes.

'Ah, morning, supermodel' he says when he sees me.

I have no name.

There's a different pose each day. Today it's the couch. It might sound comfy but how would you like it? One buttock clinging to the edge of the couch and the other in fresh air supported by an outstretched leg, the upper body thrust back on to cushions, arms folded above my head. I try to wear a relaxed expression on my face. God knows why.

If I look downwards along my body in this pose, I can see the parting effect of gravity on my breasts, the rise of a not so flat belly and the knee and ankle of the curled leg. The ankle looks so far away, it hardly belongs to me. The dome of ankle bone points at the ceiling. My strange ankle bones. 'Ankle and elbow joints like nipples,' he always said. He lies on his back on the old Indian rug we used to have, with my foot flat in the palm of his hand, as it dangles from my chair. Laughter throws him backwards. Regaining control, his head rises, the eyes return to the foot and its protruding ankle bone, and he shakes his head and smiles.

'Could you put your right foot back a bit?' A student's voice cuts into my thoughts. 'That's it.'

Sorry – that guy on the floor was distracting me. I wrote him a long letter actually. Six months after and I wasn't going to think of him anymore. I told him about my fresh start, told him he was a bastard for leaving me, but that I was going to be OK. I even put it in an envelope, then looked at it, wondering what to do with it. What was the address now? I left it inside my writing pad for a few days in the drawer, then I took it out and burnt it. That was my real new start. There's a small cough nearby and I realise my head is levering backwards, pulled by the tightening neck muscles. I empty my head, relax.

As the days go on, I become more aware of the students, look at them obliquely when they don't realise. I look at their drawings too, but only when they leave the room. You pick it up. I heard some students in the cafeteria complaining about one of the other models, who visited them all during the coffee breaks, squatting down, still naked, 'dangling all his bits on the floor'. They don't want intrusion either.

I don't know their names. I only learnt Nick's because of Trevor getting agitated with him.

'C'mon Nick, man, let's get the feeling for the form going. Fuck all the detail. Here, give me your pencil. B1? Use something softer for Christ's sake.' And after a few minutes I hear long lead lines being stroked on to Nick's paper. 'Get the feeling for the whole body.' Out of the corner of my eye, I see him hand the pencil to Nick. Then he goes on to the next student.

Despite the tuft of goatee, Nick looks young. He's tall and gangly, one of the few students who work standing up, cocking his head to appraise his work with one leg crossed over the other. He reminds me of a cricket.

I make a particular point of looking at Nick's drawing when he leaves the room. From a distance you can tell where Trevor's pencil has been; length and fluidity. The hard long line of the outstretched leg, the other knee foreshortened, curled on to a different plane, the weight of the upper body pressed back. All expressed with a few simple lines. Yes, the pose *felt* like that. I have to move closer to see Nick's work. I see what Trevor means. The faint lines of detail confuse the eye against the sheer spaces of the naked form. The strangest thing is that my face has features worked into it. The eyes stare directly at the viewer; the face is in pain. The forehead puckers; the lips are full and sour. Why was he drawing it? This was defeating the point of the exercise. And though my eyes stare back at me now, I know damn well I never looked in his direction once.

There's a slight shuffle behind me and Nick looks down at me, smiling and pulling at his goatee, the other hand folded on the elbow.

'It's a good pose,' he says.

I pause before I answer, making him wait, wanting to stay in control, give him access to less. 'Fancy swapping?'

And as he laughs, I move on to the next easel, pulling the robe tighter about me.

When I go back to the pose, I feel exposed.

The next day the studio welcomes me with the now familiar rush of turpentine and coffee up my nose. And a new pose. I'm to stand, holding the arms of a chair, leaning into it with my back to some of the class. Trevor says it'll be hard going, I can rest every half hour. I release my hair from its clip so it curtains my face as I stretch forward. The semi-circle of eyes clamp me, start their analysis. I make myself a machine again. The tilt of the upper body in space reminds me of diving. Just a little more forward motion and it would be a tumble towards the big studio window, with its release into a suburban cul-de-sac.

Windows. When the police came, they sat on the sofa, helmets in laps, and I sat on the moss-green velour armchair opposite. The armchair was arranged to give a view through the French windows on to the lawn. It was the first thing that came into my head when they told me; how am I going to mow the lawn? That was his job. The pull start has always been too difficult for me, too stiff.

Back at the studio window, a woman crosses the cul-de-sac with a shopping bag. She stalks down the hill. Even from here I can tell she's frowning, her body says it, with her coat whipping up around her legs in the wind.

My eyes drift to the car park immediately below. A man leans into the passenger seat of a grey car. I can only see his back, but I know it's him; the greying hair shaved up the back of the neck and the wide beige shirt that I gave him two birthdays ago tucked into straight jeans. Suede boots. He backs out of the car carrying a box and kicks the door shut. I'm ready to rush down the stairs, shake him by the shoulders, scream at him, 'But I thought you were dead. They told me you were dead.' But as he turns towards the building, I see that the buttons are wrong. On the shirt. Dark rather than pale. And the face is too thin; too old; too unkind. My body prickles in fury – tricked again.

'Need a break, supermodel?' And although I'm aware that my arms are trembling and my neck in spasm, I think I'm still in the pose.

'No. I can hold it a bit longer.'

I pick out the dialogue between Trevor and Nick with relief.

'Better, Nick, better . . . much more feel for the overall form, a real sense of movement here. See if you can loosen it up even more. Try these sweeps here.'

During the break, I stretch my arms above my head, circle my head to free the shoulder muscles. I walk around the room to look at the drawings. The proportion of leg to arm has obviously been a problem. The drawings are mostly ugly and I resist the urge to laugh. Nick's drawing stops me. This time there's no face. The drawing is dynamic, more purposeful than the others. The lines are bold, smudged charcoal. He's captured something. The angle of the back and limbs, especially something about the head, suggests a pull upwards. The drawing conveys the pull of shock; a transition out of composure; the spirit in a tangle with the body. I look around the room for Nick but he's not here. How did he dare? I leave the studio for the toilet.

By lunchtime I've recovered and am in the cafeteria dropping bits of cress out of a sandwich into the *Daily Mail*.

'Mind if I join you?' Nick plonks himself down opposite me, a plate of sausages and chips in front of him, all goatee and sloping shoulders. His hands are petite on the knife and fork. He sees me looking.

'Concentration makes me hungry – it's my main meal; don't eat much at night.' He loads his fork and then his mouth with chips and ketchup, still chewing when he speaks. 'Trevor says life drawing's important because the naked body's the thing we all recognise most. We react to a live human presence.'

'Oh really.' I ignore the question mark in his voice.

'Yeah, like it's something really fundamental we're looking for? "To be naked is to be oneself, without disguise," said . . .' he looks around for inspiration and then smiles, '. . . some-one!'

'More mystical than a lump of middle-aged human flesh, then?'

'I just wondered how it felt for you, being the focus for all our learning, our . . . discipline. All of us trying to get the greatest insight into human life by studying you.'

I look at him steadily; I have to stake out some fundamental ground here, but he carries on.

'I guess when I look at you with a pencil in my hand I'm looking for what's going on underneath.'

'It's a job. I earn £5 an hour. And no one asks me difficult questions.'

Tomato ketchup slides off the fork in front of his mouth and drips on to the front of his check shirt. He wipes at it with a forefinger and sucks it.

'I guess it'll be a bit of extra for you – on top of your husband's salary?'

I nod, then catch my head. 'No!' Caught out by wanting to forget again. I don't really have to explain, do I? We fall silent for a moment.

'Your drawings . . .' He looks up from his chips, perhaps happy to be drawn back to the subject. 'Well, maybe you should just be getting the mechanics right. You know, forget all this meaning of life stuff and, well, learn to draw?'

He doesn't respond. It's hard to tell if he even hears.

'What's your name anyway? I guess you're not really called "supermodel"?'

After lunch it's the same pose and there's no curtain of hair that can hide what my body seems to reveal. I am more naked than I've ever felt before. The scratch of each pencil illustrates my pain, outlines my anger. My hands grip the arms of the chair, force me through the minutes and hours to five o'clock.

I get dressed behind the screen. Slowly. I hear the studio empty, measured by the bang of the swing door with the rubber damper missing, the retreat of footsteps and voices up the corridor. I hear the studio fall quiet as the last one leaves.

His board on the easel is empty – he's taken the drawing down. But it doesn't take me long to find his portfolio, leaning against the wall behind where he works. I lay it flat on the floor, kneel down to undo the neatly tied ribbons and unfold the flaps. And there I am. I'm in date order, still acrid with the fixative spray they use to stop the charcoal smudging off. I lay each of the drawings flat on the floor and stand up to look at them. Two of them mock me, display my history to the spectator. Where could I end up? Perhaps framed at a posh exhibition or on the sitting-room wall for his friends and family to admire.

I'm careful with the others – replacing them, still in date order, re-tying the bows. Then I pick up the one with the face. My fingernails shiver on the chalk-feel of the surface. The paper is tough and strong, resistant between my hands. The tear goes diagonally, separating upper and lower torso. But it's not enough; the face still stares back at me. I tear again and again until the pieces are so small they cease to offend. The second drawing is easy, my arms flex confidently until there's a frayed pile at my feet. My hands are black and some of it is probably smeared on my face. I feel triumph and relief.

The swing door bangs, and Trevor is there, looking at me. Then he's standing next to me, looking at the floor by my feet. Without turning, he cups a hand over the top of my shoulder.

'Are you OK, supermodel?'

I feel the salt-heaviness rise at the back of my throat, and the novelty of tears on my face.

WHAT COLOURS MEAN

RON BUTLIN

A t first, every day was the same and afterwards I'd fall into bed exhausted. An hour later I'd be jackknifed out of sleep, ready to scream the house down.

Screaming's a therapeutic 'plus', no doubt, but not a real option at three in the morning. So I lay and held my breath, it seemed like, between strokes of the church bell forcing me another quarter of an hour closer to getting up, getting dressed and starting the day after you were killed all over again. Every chime and echo gave the darkness a few seconds' weight – like a paving-stone, let's say, where I could rest before taking the next slow-motion step towards daylight. At 3 a.m. there'd be fifteen paving-stones still to go – I'd be wide awake and dead beat on every one of them. Washing-cleaning-cooking-laundry-shopping-teaching-preparing-marking-the boys' tears-the boys' tantrums-chaos. It was when I was going out of my mind one long night at the end of that first week that I thought of a plan to bring the chaos to an end.

The following afternoon as each boy straggled back in from school I met him at the front porch, then stood him against the wall to be measured: William, 3 feet 10 inches; Michael, 4 feet 2 inches; Frank, 4 feet 4 inches. That done, and with the through-doors wide open, I marched them in turn the length of the house (93 feet there and back), and timed them.

I insisted they maintained a straight line and a steady pace throughout. At first they thought it a great laugh and chased each other up and down the hall as if it was some kind of race. I soon put them right. Once they understood how painstakingly I'd done the calculations, they respected my seriousness of purpose. William, as fair-haired and sweet-tempered as yourself, proved the most biddable and kept to his prescribed rate of 3.25 mph with metronomic regularity; because of his tendency to be easily distracted, Michael needed shouted at; Frank, threatening adolescence in a couple of years, managed his set rate (3.75 mph) only when I paced alongside him, blowing my whistle every few steps.

That first night together twelve years ago, I never slept either; nor did you. We kissed, undressed, made love, talked, made love again, then, all at once it was time for the breakfast tea and toast. A whole night gone with nothing to show for it but your steamed-up windows – and me in love! Until then I'd thought love was a woman's country where men wandered in and out on limited-stay visas, sightseeing and collecting souvenirs, but never quite managing to settle. That one night changed everything. A kind of soft-focus madness began: I turned up at your flat the following evening with yellow roses, 'to match your hair'. Having trimmed them to fit, you put them in a vase: 'I can look at them and think of you when you're not here.' Not there? My idea was that from then on I lived in your heart . . .

The days that followed were dream-days when I sat blissful in a roomful of eight-year-old dinosaurs and pterodactyls without even trying to nail them to their seats. Benign from the heart outwards, I left them free to roam among the desks, like so many anarchic miracles come back from before the Ice Age screeching and swooping with life. A man in love, set down in the mayhem of pre-history. Oblivious to the ravages of fifty million years' evolution happening around me, I'd appear to be cutting out paper-dinosaurs and pasting them down in the Dinosaur Checklist when really I'd be imagining your arms around me, tasting your skin, feeling your tongue against mine.

I'm still a man in love, so why can't I do that now? Why is there nothing or, even less than nothing – only your absence?

Now that we have no car we've regressed back to public transport. Unfortunately, the boys' bus goes one way and mine the opposite. Hence every morning's frantic rush. Hence my plan. Measurements and calculations completed, it swung into action the following morning and worked like a treat: the previous night's dishes still in the sink, the previous three days' unwashed laundry still on the floor, I was running late when I got them lined up at the door – three paratroopers ready for the big drop – and set them off at the necessary intervals. By going separately they didn't interfere with each other's progress and so kept more or less to time. That was the plan. Three perfect days followed. Then came the fourth. The bins put out, the shopping list discovered, I was running even later when I locked up the house and marched myself to my bus-stop. It was when I'd sat down in my seat and we were passing their stop that I glanced out the window. They were still there. Next second, I'd jumped to my feet, rang the emergency bell, explained to the driver and was off the bus before the end of the street. I returned to where the three of them stood in a neat line, satchels on their backs, grins on their faces, William clutching his gym kit in a Tesco bag. He smirked up at me:

'It was early.'

The other two held their sides and howled with laughter. But not for long.

The next bus wasn't for another hour. I'd have to phone their school, then phone my own. Teaching cover would have to be arranged, timetables altered. I walked them home ready to start all over again.

That evening I wrote to the bus company. My first letter of complaint ever. I told them I'd done everything possible on my side: I'd timed the boys, timetabled their separate mornings up to the moment each of them arrived at the stop – only to find the Eastern City Bus Company hadn't done its part, the driver in particular. I pitched it strong, presented my case and the attendant circumstances with reasonable fairness. Afterwards I made a special trip to the post box at the street corner.

Every so often since then, it seems someone hits the PAUSE button and the momentum I've managed to build up is abruptly stopped. I have to grab the edge of the table or the back of a chair to steady myself. Then the button's released and everything returns to normal. If the boys notice anything they never say.

Exactly a month to the day after you were killed I decided it was high time the boys and I wrote a joint-letter to the bus company as my previous ones had gone unanswered. During lunch I explained how important this was; we had to demonstrate to the owners that their duty lay in their drivers' strict adherence to their own timetable. There could be no excuses. Each of us would tell his own story in his own words, explaining how the bus's leaving too soon that morning had affected his life. William, for example, had missed gym and that was the day they were picking the under-nines football team; I had arranged to take a class to the museum . . .

Having cleared away the dishes we would sit at the dining table, each with a piece of paper and a pen. Stick to the facts I told them, but stress the personal. William, as the youngest, was to be allowed a set of coloured crayons should he wish to illustrate what he'd written.

For a moment before going in the room to join them I paused outside. A pleasing, busy sound was coming to me through the door: the rustling of papers, the scraping of someone's chair, whispers as the boys discussed what they were planning to write. It was a good moment.

I pushed open the door and went in. Three faces were staring up at me. Trusting, hopeful faces. Another good moment.

I gave out the pens and paper and was about to go over some final instructions, then give them an opportunity to ask any last questions when, from over at the window, I became aware of an agitation on the outside of the glass. A small bird was beating its wings trying to get in. At once, I crossed the room and pulled the curtains shut. There had to be no distraction from the task at hand. I returned to the doorway, clicked on the light then gave a slight cough to indicate we were ready to begin.

'Right, boys: top right-hand corner: our address and the date – the nineteenth of the second nineteen ninety eight.'

Frank finished this first, then Michael. The three of us waited in silence for William to blot his way to the last digit and put his tongue back in his mouth. Then we continued.

'Left-hand side, on the line below the date line. Write: "Dear Sir", capital D, capital S.'

The clattering and drumming of the wings seemed more frantic than ever, but I was glad to note the boys paid no attention. Their three faces – Frank's first, then Michael's and, nearly a whole minute later, William's – were eventually raised from the paper.

'A good start means the job will go well.' I smiled. 'Now, when you're ready, in your own time and your own words, continue your letter.'

Three heads bent down and three pens were poised to begin. Before a word was written the boys had immediately moved into exam-mode, shielding their work from each other so there could be no chance of copying. It was a pleasure to witness such commitment, such enthusiasm. I'd wait until things were well and truly started, then begin my own letter. The bird must have flown away. Within seconds a calmness had settled over the room; and I was almost smiling when I took up my pen.

We might have gone swimming that day, or played football, or gone for a bicycle ride, or stayed at home. Or anything. Instead –

I'd been accelerating past the Fairmilehead sliproad when I began waxing teacherly about the mystery trip I'd thought up that morning. No one else knew where we were going. The whole thing was my idea.

Mine alone.

The boys were in the back seat performing low-volume animal impersonations to pass the time; you were sitting next to me. You wanted to join in with them but had just asked me for a clue about where we were going, so as not to have me feel left out.

'Not far from Edinburgh. It's a kind of farm, but only for the one thing – there'll be hundreds and thousands of them though.' To tease you, I added: 'They migrate here from Spain, from Mexico even.'

You were looking so puzzled I couldn't resist one final clue: 'They fly all the way, but you'd never believe it.'

Out of the corner of my eye I could see you were half-laughing. You must have been humouring me all along because a moment later you smiled:

Fragments of glass had risen in a broken-coloured shower that for a split-second seemed to hang motionless in front of me. Your voice had come from beside me, from the point of impact:

'Butterflies?'

From behind came the boys' screaming.

This letter was going to be the best yet. Polite, but a real stinger. I leant forward to begin. Then stopped. My sheet was already half-covered with writing. How had that happened? I looked up again: the curtains were standing open once more. William was now the only other person still at the table, the only other person still in the room even. What the hell was going on? He was looking at me, his face a smear of red and blue ink and tears.

'They're outside, you told them to go outside,' he blubbered.

I'd told them?

'Have they finished their letters?'

Without meaning to I'd shouted at him. He rushed from the room. I heard the back door slam.

I began reading what was in front of me. A mess. A furious scrawl of obscenities. Was that handwriting really mine? Here and there the paper had been ripped.

I leant on the table to pull myself to my feet. None of the boys had managed to get anywhere near finished. A few lines, nothing more. Well, they could finish them later. I smoothed out the sheets and started stacking them, mine at the bottom, then Frank's, then Michael's; William's I placed on top. He'd not written a single word – it was a drawing of three small stick-boys and their stick-man of a father chasing after a bus as it disappeared towards the edge of the paper. I was about to scrunch it into a ball when a detail caught my eye: he'd made the driver a woman. A woman with long yellow hair.

It's nearly midnight. I've returned to the dining-room to pull the curtains as I always do last thing; and I've just noticed a hairline of refracted light running across one of the panes. The left-hand window-pane's cracked. Surely that bird beating its wings couldn't have broken the glass? I would have heard it at the time, wouldn't I?

But there it is. I stare at the laceration of reds, greens and dusk-blues as if it might mean something. But what can colours mean?

I want to pull the curtains closed.

I want to turn and leave the room.

To shut the door behind me. To lock it.

Colours: gradually unfolding and, with the very slightest quiver of unsettledness, beginning to lift themselves free from the glass –

Layer upon layer of invisibly-spun lightness and fragility –

Thickening, hardening, shutting out the long night ahead, the church bell and exhaustion – The very last word spoken before all the days and years to come.

THE PRACTICALITY OF MAGNOLIA

RAYMOND SOLTYSEK

B y the time Isobel discovered that the boy sleeping in her upstairs bedroom was wanted for attempted murder, it was too late to turn back. And anyway, he was co-operative and quiet and, provided he didn't realise that she knew, he'd no reason to turn against her.

She suspected something even before he arrived, since she'd watched him as he came down the road from the west. That led past a couple of holiday homes, a few caravans, the cottages of the Fitzgibbons and old Sandy Macdonald, and ended at the automated lighthouse. It puzzled her that anyone wearing shabby training shoes and hooded sweatshirt should come from that direction late on a late summer Wednesday looking for bed and breakfast for a few days, for there was nowhere from which to come.

'Could Ah have a bath?' he'd asked, edgy, his head turned down. 'Ah huvny had a good wash furra wee while – been on the road, like. Ah widnae want to dirty yir clean sheets.'

'Of course,' she'd said. 'When you've finished, put your clothes in the laundry basket in the bathroom and I'll wash them. You're very welcome to join me for supper if you like. Just toast and butter.'

'Aye, that'd be great. Ta.'

He had eaten hungrily but civilly, and asked if she had a

newspaper, but she never bought them because they were filled with terrible happenings, and he'd smiled and nodded and agreed. She had to apologise too for not having a television – she found them noisy, she said, and after James died, well . . . But the boy didn't seem too bored listening to Radio 4 with her, and he had gone to bed early without asking about public houses nearby, not that there was one.

She slept badly that first night, though not because of the boy, since she felt safe enough with her door bolted and the telephone moved beside her bed: besides, no one had responded to her 'Vacancies' sign all summer, so she certainly couldn't be choosy. She listened to the unfamiliar creaks of the floorboards, imagined the regularity of his breathing, thought she heard him cry out, once, around three. When light came up, when the magpies began to swirl around the eaves, encouraging their last shrieking chick to fly, she was still awake.

'When can Ah come back the night?' he'd asked after breakfast. He sounded childish, reluctant to raise the question at all, looking for an 'Och don't bother,' from her. Not that she had children herself, but she'd trained as a primary school teacher before marrying James. Knew their ways.

'You don't have to stay away if you don't want to,' she'd said. 'Go for a walk, over the hill, if you feel like it. There's some nice lochans up there, and you get a lovely view of the bay from the top. Just come back whenever you need to.'

He seemed grateful, went up the hill and returned in the afternoon. 'It's great up there,' he said, flushed, and told her about bullets he'd found, hundreds and hundreds of them. From the war, she said, the whole area was evacuated, used to practise D-Day. The bullets were quite safe, though. He'd hung out her washing, made his bed, hoovered upstairs, then sat at the bottom of the garden with a pot of tea. She watched him fall asleep in the sunlight, the shadows of beech leaves flickering over his face. Almost hairless, sunken sockets dark. His chin fell on to his scrawny chest.

'Eh, see yir grass. Ah'll cut it for ye,' he offered when she brought him sandwiches – no extra, because he'd been so helpful, she said. 'Ah'd like tae stay, furra cuppla weeks mibbe. Ah huvnae much money but. Thought mibbe Ah could dae a few jobs. Pay ma way, like.'

She made her mind up then, seeing the possibilities in an instant. 'I do have something that needs done,' she said, and took him to the garage, behind James' Volvo, where she'd neatly stacked the tins.

'I'd like the rooms painted,' she said. 'It's been years since they were done. We had decorators in. My husband liked magnolia, you see. Because it goes with anything.'

'Right,' he said. 'A wee freshen up?'

'Well, a bit more than that,' and she pulled the cans of paint out one by one. 'I got these delivered. Awfully difficult to get up here.'

He weighed them in his hands, brushing dust from lids. Coral Blush. Dusty Jade. Sienna and Golden Amber, gloss and satin and colourwash. Tins and tins of Brilliant White, Diamond White, Sparkling White. And then rollers and brushes and brand new stepladders, gleaming steel.

He pulled a face at the Mulberry Crush emulsion. 'Is it no a bit much?'

'It is a bit daft, I suppose. All these colours. The local man who does the painting and decorating would think I was gone in the head. Eccentric old Sassenach, he'd say, and I've been here forty years.' He was shaking his head. 'I wonder if you would? Just as much as you can while you stay.'

It would take weeks, he said, but he had nowhere to go if she didn't mind: no, she wouldn't, and he'd have all his meals there and he needn't pay for his bed though she couldn't promise to pay him any more. That was fine by him, very generous of her, his hand seeming as frail and thin as hers when they shook on the deal.

He started the morning she found out, driving in the Volvo to Acharacle for extra bread and tea and vegetables, listening to the radio station from Glasgow. A girl, lying *gravely ill in hospital*, battered, police searching for her boyfriend, *Charles McCausley, twenty-one*, a perfect description, even of his clothes. *May be desperate. Do not approach.*

'A lodger, you say, Mrs McCandlish?'

'Yes, Mrs Farmer. An American girl. Walking round Scotland. Very brave of her, if you ask me.'

'Foolish I'd say. You hear terrible things with these serial killers on the loose everywhere. Is she staying long?'

'She might. But she's very quiet. I don't think you'll be seeing much of her around here,' and she packed the car quickly to be off home.

The ceiling gleamed white. *Snow White.* He'd masked along the cornicing, the edge crisp and neat against the dullness of the old magnolia, and he was sitting at the table drinking tea.

'Just while it dries a bit, like,' he said, flinching as she pushed her way past the hallstand, the telephone table and the old blanket box he'd moved into the kitchen.

'Of course,' she said, 'don't be silly. You're allowed a rest you know,' and she cut him some fruit cake she made for visitors and watched the muscles in his neck uncoil. 'Take all the time you need.'

The next day, Isobel visited her sister-in-law in Tobermory. They spoke of James – what a good man he'd been – and Agnes' husband Archie, senile and hostile in an old folks' home run by an English couple, more incomers, and about the young American woman staying with Isobel. So very helpful.

Then the Volvo wouldn't start to catch the last boat back to Kilchoan.

She telephoned five times before he picked up the receiver.

'Hullo,' he said, his voice strange, as if on a starting block.

'Hello, it's Mrs McCandlish,' she replied, and wasn't surprised by the rush of relief she heard. 'I'm afraid I've missed the last boat. I won't be back until the morning. Can you manage on your own?'

'Aye. Ah'll just get on wi it. Is that all right?'

'Yes, fine.'

'Listen,' he said, 'just leave it till later. Ah'll have it done by the afternoon. It'll be a surprise tae see it finished.'

'Okay then,' she said, absurdly flattered.

She got home after five and stepped into a hallway that was orange, deep, burned, smoky orange, and the wood even darker, almost toffee.

'Ah had tae gie it two coats: it's a really deep colour,' and she gasped and gaped and felt she was wrapped in a warm blanket.

'It's wonderful,' she said, and his head came up, pleased and cocky.

'Huv Ah done a good job?'

'Just – wonderful.'

She found herself cooking real food again, shepherd's pie, and proposed he paint the bedroom next. She would sleep in the sitting room, and would he mind doing something a bit special for her? He'd first asked what, and sounded dubious when she showed him the heavy greaseproof paper and suggested stencils. 'It wullnae work,' he said three times – but she ferreted out a craft knife from James' old toolbox and showed him how.

* * *

He was sullen, put out for a day, but the work overtook his mood and he gave her a flower frieze only a whisper darker than the lavender of the walls. She set the room out just right, the cream lace bed linen the best she had, the woodwork and furniture polished rich and sensuous. She read for a while in bed, her attention constantly drawn to the flowers and the walls, and when she slept she dreamed of a man for the first time ever, though she couldn't remember who he was or what he looked like when she woke.

She insisted he take two days off, but he showed no sign of going anywhere or doing anything, simply pacing up and down the beach before breakfast and sunbathing in the secluded back garden in the afternoon. He stripped off his T-shirt and she saw that he wasn't scrawny or frail, but taut and tightly corded across his shoulders and down his arms, and she wondered how often he held and how often he hit the girl. Once he did exercises, push ups and sit ups. She watched his muscles tense and slacken, the sweat glistening and pouring down his back, the tattoo of a dragon, blue and red and green, flex and stretch on his shoulder blade, and she felt ashamed, a stupid old woman.

The kitchen was next, sunshine and cornflower blue, and when it was finished Isobel made lemon tea and a special meal for them, something foreign that astounded Mrs Farmer.

'Well, Mrs McCandlish, I've never known you to want capsicums before. Is it something fancy you're cooking for your young American friend?'

'Yes it is.' Isobel scanned the notices behind Mrs Farmer's head. A ceilidh at the Salen hall. Local watercolours by that strange Dutch woman.

'It's her birthday, you know.'

'Oh I see.' A face appeared behind the shop keeper's. A photograph. 'It's quite a while she's staying, is it not?'

HAVE YOU SEEN THIS MAN?

'I suppose so.'

MAY BE HIDING ALONG WEST COAST.

'Still, that's good news for you. It's not often you get such a client even during the season. It's funny we never see her around though.'

STOLEN BOAT.

'Och, she's very quiet. She reads a lot.' She took the whole twelve, red and orange and yellow and green, their skins waxy and breathtaking. At home she put them in a blue bowl in the centre of the kitchen table and thought they were better than flowers.

'Will you be wanting to leave soon?' she asked.

'Naw,' he said, then urgently, 'how, d'ye want me tae go?'

'No, no, you're doing an excellent job. I'm delighted. It's just – I thought you might have to be moving on.' She'd wanted to say it might be safer.

'Ah'm okay.' He scratched his forearm, red strips flaring under the tanned skin. 'Ah want tae finish the job.'

The upstairs bedroom became deep terracotta, the room which James had used as a study mulberry, both ceilinged in dazzling white, one more outrageous than the other. She loved them both, she said. He painted the stairwell blue, the insides of cupboards white, the utility room at the back of the kitchen bright green. One by one he picked them off, and all that was left was the sitting room. They sat there, looking at the last of the magnolia walls, listening to a comedy quiz show, which he said he was beginning to enjoy.

'Ah'll strip the paint aff the fireplace if ye like,' he said. 'Ye've goat the strippers in the garage, and some varnish. It'll take a few extra days mind.'

'Do you think it's worth it?'

'Aw aye. It'll look great. 'Sides, might as well. Out wi the auld, in wi the new, eh?'

'Yes,' she said. 'We'll just clear away the mantelpiece.'

She fetched a cardboard box from the cupboard under the stairs, began to pack the accumulated paraphernalia of a long life: photographs of their parents, James in Navy uniform, her on her wedding day, always looked like Deanna Durbin his uncle Angus said. He dusted each quickly as she passed it to him. Candlesticks. Two china dolls. A tiny silver-plated box. Her fingers shook and it slipped between them, smacking loudly off the hearth rail. The top flew open and something small and light flicked across the room under her chair.

'Ah'll get it,' he said.

'It's all right, I'll do it.' She brushed past him and was on her knees, her hand exploring the tight space beneath the chair.

'Is it valuable? Looked like a pearl.'

'No, nothing like that.' She felt her fingertip scrape against it, and she stretched a little farther, dragging it towards her. 'It's nothing, just an old reminder of James.' It disappeared into her apron pocket. 'I forgot I even had it.'

It took him the best part of a week, brushing on chemicals that blistered when they splashed on to his skin. Careless, he said, and she made him wash his hands in warm soapy water and gave him plasters and rubber gloves when he went back to work.

When the fireplace was finished, she did admit it was worth the effort, the wood deep and dark and lustrous. She ran her fingers over it. 'Yer photies'll look good up there now, eh?'

'They'll look tremendous. Thank you. For all you've done.'

'Aye well. Ah'm getting to stay here, amn't Ah? So it's nuthin.'

'Don't be silly. It's become very important to me. Until you started, I didn't realise how important it was.'

He shuffled, too embarrassed to comprehend an old woman's feelings. 'Ye don't say much about yer husband. Whit he was like and stuff.'

'Oh, he was a man. A bit like you I suppose.'

'Aye? Whit way?'

'Just some of the things he did.' She gathered up their tea cups to take them to the kitchen. 'Perhaps when you've done the sitting room we should make a start on the *outside* of the house. What about Sugar Pink?' she said, and they laughed at the image. He made a joke about her house being like the Forth Rail Bridge and how he would have to start all over again, and though she knew that wouldn't happen she said it was a good idea.

He took time over the last of the painting, not deliberately but perhaps unconsciously. Hardly surprising really. He left each coat of emulsion for a full day to dry, and then the same with the gloss, and he filled holes and cracks and sanded to get a perfect finish. She saw little of the room, the dust sheets and ladders making it difficult – even dangerous – to push through the door, but she had the sense of subaqueous jade light mellowing and pouring out into the orange hall.

'How are you getting on?' she called. He'd been nervy, moving in a funny, jerky way all morning, so she guessed it was almost completed. 'Shall I put some tea on?'

'Naw, no yet. Ah'm nearly done. Mibbe another twenty minutes.'

Nearly done. Twenty minutes.

She quietly unplugged the telephone from the hall, took it to her bedroom and connected it to the socket by her bed. The policeman in Mallaig was very helpful, very polite, and it wasn't at all unusual that Isobel hadn't realised who her lodger was until now.

'You know,' she said, 'I even told Mrs Farmer at the shop it was a girl staying with me. I thought it would sound scandalous. Whatever will she think now?'

The sergeant laughed. 'Don't you worry about that. Just try not to alarm him. We've a car out now that can be with you in about half an hour.'

She sat on the edge of the bed, gathering herself, trembling slightly with the power of what she'd done. She smoothed her hair, her apron, felt the sharp little bump in the pocket, and took out the tooth. A young woman's tooth.

What bother she'd had, searching the floor of the hotel room the morning after their wedding night, keeping it from James all these years hidden in the lining of the little silver box. She held it up to the light. It was perfect, no decay, no fillings, far too healthy, good roots. Her jaw had ached for weeks after he'd done it. She ran her fingernail over the enamel, pale, translucent.

Off-white.

She suspended it momentarily over the waste-paper basket, then dropped it in and took the telephone back to the hall table to wait.

The boy went meekly when the huge policemen came for him. 'Don't worry,' they said when they'd locked him in the car, 'he'll never find out it was you. The report will just say "An Informant".' Someone would be round later for a statement, and she'd been very brave, and Isobel saw their eyes pulled over her shoulder to the colours within and noted the scratch of a head, a slight curl of the lip.

Not to everyone's taste.

Thank you, thank you very much for everything, she told them, and she closed the door softly but firmly on the men.

ACCOMPLICE

ALISON GROVE

'Nothing's changed, has it?' I fling the words cheerily over my shoulder into the silent room.

Even the shop fronts look the same from up here, although they must have changed hands a few times. I have to concede that the scene has curled a little at the edges, like an old photograph. There are drifts of litter now to blunt the harsh concrete angles, and squatting bollards keep traffic out of the Estate's awkward recesses. But people are scuttling by just as they always did, recoiling from the same old biting wind.

I shiver, although the room is thick with accumulated heat. Surely I've changed more than the view. I need to confirm my separation from this place, and I'm already totting up the minimum number of days I'll have to stay. I'm afraid that my flimsily constructed bridge to freedom might collapse before I re-cross it.

I twitch back the net curtain and a dead fly falls on to the window sill. It lands on its back with a light patter, legs dried and crumpled close to its belly. It has lived, died and decayed here.

'Give that a run over with a wee damp cloth,' Gran always used to say when wholesale fumigation was what she had in mind.

Or else she'd hand me the feather duster and suggest a 'wee flick-about'. When I thought I'd finished, she always discovered some secret reservoir of grime above the picture rail, or at the back of a shelf.

'Filthy! Can ye no' dae a thing wi'out me standin' over ye?' Her spread fingers, darkened with dirt, stabbed the air as though she were casting an evil spell.

'Did that slattern no' teach ye anythin'?'

At first I tried hard to answer Gran's stream of baffling questions. It seemed necessary to explain our life to her, as though she were a tourist or a maker of documentaries. But I didn't have the answers to satisfy her. She was far too angry. She dealt out her rage almost equally between me and the Geranium Woman.

Day after day I scraped the Hoover aimlessly about Gran's flat.

'No point unless we're actually wading in muck,' Mum would have murmured comfortably. At home we only bothered to vacuum if a pot plant happened to tip and scatter soil across the rug, or if the Boston fern had been disturbed into another moult. Then we would hear that satisfying patter of dirt against the metal tube. The noise was encouraging. It gave us a sense of achievement.

Gran vacuumed every day. Her carpets were threadbare from the punishing routine. Without a gritty tattoo to guide me, I couldn't tell which bits I'd already covered. Gran knew though, swooping into corners and under chairs, picking up infinitesimal specks between thumb and forefinger and holding them accusingly under my nose. Wordlessly, she uncoiled the flex and switched the machine back on. I sidestepped this way and that like a boxer, until in exasperation she sent me out on some errand. The roar of her industry trailed me like a bloodhound out on to the landing.

*   *   *

'I'm off out to the shops now Gran. What would you like for your tea?'

She ignores me as usual, pretending to be asleep. My relentless and solitary cheer is even beginning to get on my own nerves. But it keeps a lid on the sour stink of my real feelings. She knew I wouldn't be able to ignore such a letter. Disappointment and shame gripped me with equal force when I arrived to discover her not quite as large as life, but definitely not as shrunken as death.

But I've made all the arrangements now with the nursing home, and I'm counting the hours until I can return to the friendly rummage of my tiny room, and to the urgency of work.

The return ticket in its laminated wallet takes up too much room in my handbag, but I like to feel it there, to scrabble around it for my keys and purse. Home and work seem to need such careful maintenance. I'm afraid they'll take on a temp if I'm away too long. And I must be on-hand in case the landlady tries to re-let my room, or my plants begin to die from neglect.

It was always a relief to escape from the flat. I roamed the public spaces of Gran's block, but was too afraid to explore the alleys and walkways criss-crossing the Estate.

English besom! Stuck-up bliddy Sassenach. Strange words and twisted vowels chased me in cruel circles, until I found myself cornered in some rancid dead-end. My school coat became scarred with grey concrete scuffs, and they plucked at it, mimicking my despised accent. Some would have been my cousins, too afraid of Gran to really hurt me, but what they knew about me made them powerful enemies.

Here the past was as bitterly lived as the present. Those who had grown hard and inflexible propelling the wheels of heavy industry watched in disbelief as jobs and young trickled

South. The mine had closed, its cottages torn down to make way for the tall blocks and mean alleys that formed the new estates. Structures began to crumble and stain even before the men who built them were laid off and forced to take up residence. Boundaries blurred and were forgotten, merging with neighbouring sprawls, homogenising until the local bus routes led only to Sauchiehall Street, and everywhere was Glasgow.

The communal resentment was such that Gran was always having to explain to people about me.

'I'll no have anyone say I didnae dae the right thing by her, the thankless besom. But I cannae say I'm pleased about it.'

And she tugged me along up the stairs so that we wouldn't have to share an awkward stillness while the lift creaked up through the core of the building.

I loved the lift, but was forbidden to ride in it on my own. Gran said it was too noisy, adding pointedly, 'We old folk dinnae like tae be disturbed,' as though she belonged to a club of cubicled geriatrics nodding beside their electric bars, and starting awake angrily as the lift clattered by their thin walls.

Sometimes, if the lift didn't smell too bad, and Gran was out, I battered the door and walls with my feet, so that the clang of metal resounded up and down the shaft.

That was in the beginning, when I was still secure from recent cherishing. After joining Gran in her war against the Geranium Woman, I was too frightened to get into the lift on my own. I was terrified of meeting her, of having the doors clang shut on us like the lid of a coffin. And afterwards, even over the stink of urine, the lift seemed to smell of geraniums.

At ground level it's easier to see how things have changed round here. Scabby kids with transparent skin and desperate eyes flit like fleas about the ankles of the concrete blocks, and I've seen the syringes lying in stairwells. Perhaps I should feel nervous walking about on my own. But I'm no longer connected to this place. Cloaked in anonymity, I feel untouchable.

I find myself inside the greengrocer's. At the ragged edge of his plastic lawn he has arranged a row of potted geraniums. Ignored by his customers, they have been left to shrivel and fade in the window. Before I know it, he's wrapping one in coloured paper, and I'm digging in my purse. I can sense he's trying to place me – smart clothes, skin still fresh and eyes bright, rich enough to squander coins on dying plants. But I'm careful not to speak, conducting the transaction with gestures and murmured thanks.

Whenever I was on watch for the Geranium Woman, I climbed up to the top of Gran's block, a stitch knotting in my side by the time I reached the balcony.

Once, forcing my eyes open against the high-flying wind, I thought I saw Mum in the street below. Her sandy hair waved about her head and brushed the shoulders of her winter coat. Running down the stairs to catch up with her, I collided with Gran. Though the set of her face warned against it, the words spilled out of my mouth, 'She's come for me! Let me go and meet her. Let me go!'

Gran squeezed my arm fiercely enough to raise a cluster of blue circles, and hissed into my ear, 'It's no' her. She'll no' come for ye here. And I'll no' have ye chasin' into the street like a maniac.'

I shouted and struggled, daring in the depths of my misery to defy Gran. Hot tears washed my face, purging me of childish dreams. I knew then that Mum was never coming back.

Gran pushed me back up the stairs, her voice stiff with bitterness.

'Your mother's away down There – where she wants tae be . . . recovering.'

'Dying!' cried the deep lines in Gran's face and a loud voice in my head.

My fingers brush against the leaves as I finish arranging the geranium on Gran's bedside table, and the room is suddenly pervaded by the sharp odour of the disturbance. Gran sniffs and lifts an eyelid. She frowns and I feel the same thrilling terror as a child who teases a fierce dog, knowing it is securely chained.

She pretends not to notice me, and turns her face back up to the ceiling. Her flesh already seems to be sinking away into the cavities of her skull, and I can't help giving the geranium another little shake before leaving the room.

'She's gone out. I just saw her,' I reported breathlessly.

'Of course she's gone. It's Tuesday – flower arranging at the Community,' snapped Gran, the corners of her mouth drooping with distaste.

Disappointment hunched over me. This was the only time of day I was likely to wriggle close to Gran, and I had already said the wrong thing.

'Dinnae stand there like a knotless thread,' she ordered. 'Put on the kettle.'

Gran already had two pans bubbling on the stove, ready for the daily offensive. I lifted the piece of a drainpipe that stood convenient and sinister beside the larder, and took up my post. I put on Gran's oven gloves and held the pipe so that it swung over the balcony like a huge elephant's trunk. The opening was misshapen and blistered, deformed by the passage of so many gallons of boiling water. It grinned up at me like the mouth of a leper. The kitchenette grew cloudy with steam, and my eyes watered as Gran tipped cupfuls of bleach into the pans of water.

'Doubling the dose today,' she muttered.

I held the pipe steady while Gran emptied the kettle and the pans down on to the geraniums crowding the balcony below. I trailed it backwards and forwards along the ledge, hoping she would notice how thorough I was. This was always the happiest moment of the day.

Once I asked her what was wrong with geraniums. Pursing her lips so that it looked as though a thread had been drawn through them, she said, 'They smell like cats' doings.'

I thought it was funny how much worse they always smelt after their daily dose of bleach and boiling water. It was awesome to imagine the skill of the Geranium Woman, who had kept her plants alive for so long. Whenever I walked along the street, I looked up at the gash of colour between the balconies and knew that Gran was losing the war. Sometimes I caught a glimpse of the white permed head of the Geranium Woman herself, nodding over her charges like a heavy bloom.

At tea time Gran almost genial. The empty bleach bottle had been rammed upside-down into the kitchen bin so that its rear stuck out in a sad undignified salute. There would be no more afternoons helping Gran, nothing left to draw us together.

A door slammed downstairs and Gran's mouth tightened into a small triumphant bud. The movement dislodged a crumb clinging to her lip, and I was ashamed of the thrill I felt as it dropped on to the carpet. I imagined the Geranium Woman stepping out on to her balcony, her nostrils stinging with chlorine and the unhappy scent of distressed geranium. The broad leaves, heavy with cooling poisoned water, would be yellowing already.

'I don't want any more,' I choked, pushing away my bread and butter.

'There'll be no scones until you eat what's in front of you.'

I dared to shrug, but Gran only muttered thickly about 'pernickety English ways', and clattered the plates together.

*   *   *

213

'Would you like your teeth in?' I call, my voice lifting into that unnaturally hearty register that nurses sometimes use. I don't expect a reply.

I load the tray with milky tea and shop-bought scones. Pressing such food into Gran's inert frame seems pointless, but I don't know what else to do. The doctor has felt her pulse and sounded her chest without curiosity. His diagnosis is vague, his manner indifferent, and he has offered no advice on how to look after Gran. In fact, I'm not sure if he's even noticed me. People seem to be dying in Gran's block all the time, so he'll be accustomed to the gaudy presence of close relatives, strangers in his patients' homes.

With her dressing gown clasped to her throat, Gran watched the ambulance arrive, not even switching on the kettle until she saw the stretcher emerge from the street door. She stood at the window, her neck red with excitement, relaying the drama to me in trembling detail.

But I was busy with my own private images of the Geranium Woman's final hours, struggling in agony under our poisonous deluge, mad with grief. I watched Gran suck tea into the slit of her mouth, and felt my soul curl with shame.

The landing below throbbed with the funk of terrified geraniums. They were carried out pot by pot, brushing the door of the Geranium Woman's flat with despairing leaves. As they were packed into the lift, petals sprang from their heads like tears or drops of blood.

Her flat should have been identical to Gran's, but the passage seemed to wind away into a vast green hinterland. Removal men sweated to and fro, plucked from all sides by fronds and spikes and trailing creepers.

A whiff of bleach reached me from the pot of dead soil propping open the front door. It sent me stumbling up the stairs to the top floor, where I hid sobbing all afternoon. I realised I could no longer remember the names of any of Mum's plants.

I decide to make Gran's teeth available anyway. I discover them floating in a dusty plastic tub on the bathroom shelf. A slight film has settled over the surface, and I wonder whether I should have changed the water daily, as if I were looking after a goldfish. Part of me wishes that Gran would put them back in and fill out her puckered mouth.

I fetch a jug and dribble water over the parched soil around the geranium. Gran turns on her pillow, wrinkling her nose and pursing her lips. The geranium drinks thirstily, swelling its shrivelled leaves and sweating out its acrid scent.

The street moves beyond the window like a silent film, and I wonder if Gran will be installed by the weekend. I could be back at work on Monday.

There is a sudden crash, and I try to compose my features into a cheery shape before turning round. There will be milky tea everywhere, and I'll have to change the bed and scrub the carpet to get rid of the smell.

But I'm surprised to discover Gran still propped in place, calmly sipping her tea. Pale colour tinges her grey complexion, and her plastic teeth clink faintly against the rim of her cup. She is wearing an odd expression, almost like a smile.

I move around the foot of the bed as though circling a snake, and a familiar smell gusts into my nostrils. The briefly revived geranium lies dying on the carpet, roots trailing through the thin pile and scattering soil over the valance.

'Thought there must be a cat in here!' says Gran, sucking her teeth, challenging me.

'You'll have to behave yourself in that nursing home,' I reply evenly, dropping down to clear up the mess.

But Gran makes a face that is even more like a smile, revealing quite a slice of shiny pink gum.

'I'll no' be going now,' she says.

'What?' I can feel my smiling mask disintegrate.

'I gave them a wee 'phone while you were out. Told them to gi' ma place to some puir soul wi' nae family tae take care o' them.'

'But they'll take you off the list. You'll never get a place.' Panic lifts my voice. I'm down on my knees, scraping up crumbs of earth, caught like a fly in a web. My fragile bridge collapses, and freedom fades like a receding dream.

Gran pushes her finger towards the clods of soil on the bedside table.

'Try a wee drop o' bleach on a damp cloth.'

Shaded beneath drooping flags of skin, her eyes have faded to watery pools, so that I can't see past my own horrified reflection.

AN INVISIBLE MAN

BRIAN MCCABE

Sometimes on dark winter mornings he watched them before the doors were opened: pressing their hands and faces against the glass, a plague of moths wanting in to the light. But you couldn't look at them like that, as an invading swarm. To do the job, you had to get in among them, make yourself invisible. You had to blend in, pretend to be one of them, but you also had to observe them, you had to see the hand slipping the 'Game Boy' into the sleeve. Kids wore such loose clothes nowadays, baggy jeans and jogging tops two sizes too big for them. It was the fashion, but it meant they could hide their plunder easily. You had to watch the well-dressed gentlemen as well – the Crombie and the briefcase could conceal a fortune in luxury items. When it came down to it, you were a spy.

He was in the Food Hall and they were rushing around him. He picked up a wire basket and strolled through the vege-tables, doing his best to look interested in a packet of Con-tinental Salad, washed and ready to use. It was easy to stop taking anything in and let the shopping and the shoplifting happen around you, a blur, an organism, an animal called The Public. The Public was all over the shop: poking its nose into everything; trying on the clean new underwear; squirting the testers on its chin, on its wrists, behind its ears; wriggling its fingers into the gloves; squeezing its warm, damp feet into stiff, new shoes; tinkering with the computers; thumbing the avocados.

He was watching a grey-haired lady dressed in a sagging blue raincoat, probably in her sixties, doing exactly that. The clear blue eyes, magnified by thick lenses, looked permanently shocked. A disappointed mouth, darkened by a plum-coloured lipstick, floundered in a tight net of wrinkles. There was something in her movements that was very tense, yet she moved slowly, as if she had been stunned by some very bad news.

She put down the avocados – three of them, packaged in polythene – as if she'd just realised what they were and that she didn't need them. He followed her as she made her way to the express pay-point and took her place in the queue. He stacked his empty basket and waited on the other side of the cash-points, impersonating a bewildered husband waiting for the wife he'd lost sight of. He watched her counting her coins from a small black purse. The transaction seemed to fluster her, as if she might not have enough money to pay for the few things she'd bought. A tin of lentil soup. An individual chicken pie. One solitary tomato. Maybe she did need the avocados – or something else.

The pay-point wasn't the obvious place to catch shoplifters, so they used it. It was like declaring something when you went through customs, in the hope that the real contraband would go unnoticed. Or offering a small sin at confession, hoping that it would distract God from his ferocious omniscience. An amateur tactic. It was easy to catch someone with a conscience, someone who wanted to be caught.

He ambled behind her to the escalator down to Kitchen and Garden. When she came off the escalator, she waited at the bottom, as if not sure where to find what she was looking for. He moved away from her to the saucepans and busied himself opening up a three-tiered vegetable steamer, then he put the lid back on hastily to follow her to the gardening equipment. She moved past the lawn-mowers and the sprinklers until she came to a display of seed packets.

It wasn't often that you had this kind of intuition about somebody and it turned out to be right, but as soon as he saw her looking at the seeds, he was certain she was going to steal them. He moved closer to her, picked up a watering can and weighed it in his hand, as if this was somehow a way of testing it, then he saw her dropping packet after packet into the bag. He followed her to the door and outside, then he put his hand on her shoulder. When she turned round he showed her his i.d. Already she was shaking visibly. Her red-veined cheeks had taken on a hectic colour and tears loomed behind her out-raged blue eyes . . .

'Please,' she said, 'arrest me. Before I do something worse.'

He took her back inside and they made the long journey to the top of the store in silence. For the last leg of it he took her through Fabrics – wondering if they might be taken for a couple, a sad old couple shopping together in silence – and up the back staircase so that he wouldn't have to march her through Admin.

It was depressing to unlock the door of his cubby-hole, switch the light on and see the table barely big enough to hold his kettle and his tea things, the one upright chair, the barred window looking out on a fire-escape and the wall-mounted telephone. He asked her to take the packets of seeds out of her bag and put them on the table. She did so, and the sight of the packets, with their gaudy coloured photographs of flowers, made her clench her hand into a fist.

He told her to take a seat while he called security, but when he turned away from her she let out a thin wail that made him recoil from the phone. She had both her temples between her hands, as if afraid her head might explode. She let out another shrill wail. It ripped out of her like something wild kept prisoner for years. It seemed to make the room shrink around them.

'Now now, no noise please,' he said, like a dentist who'd just drilled into a nerve. He cursed himself inwardly for bringing her here alone – he should have collected a security guard on the way. Now he was on his own with her in the cubby-hole and she was wailing. If the people in Admin heard, it might be open to all sorts of interpretation. His job was under threat as it was, what with the security guards and the new surveillance cameras.

She wailed again – a raw outpouring of anger and loss. Christ, he had to get her out of here. He stooped over her and reached out to take one of her hands away from her head, then he thought better of touching her at all. His hand hovered over her as he spoke:

'Look, you don't seem like a habitual shoplifter . . .'

She blurted out that she'd never stolen anything in her life before, but it was hard to make out the words because she was sobbing and coughing at the same time, her meagre body shuddering as if an invisible man had taken her by the shoulders and was shaking her violently.

'I'm sure it was just absent-mindedness. You intended to pay for these.' He motioned with a hand to the scattered packets of seeds on the table, but she was having none of it:

'No, I stole them. I don't even like gardening.' The words came out in spurts between her coughs and sobs but there was no stopping her now that she'd started: 'It's overgrown, weeds everywhere. It was him who did it. He was mad about his garden. He spent all his time, morning till night, out in all bloody weathers.'

Relieved that she was talking rather than wailing, he let her talk. Her husband had been obsessed with his garden. It had been his way of getting away – from her, from everyone and everything. He'd withdrawn from the world into his flowering shrubs and geraniums. She hardly saw him, and when he'd died all there was left of him was his garden. Now the weeds were taking over. When she'd seen the seed packets, with their pictures of dahlias and pansies and rhododendrons . . . It made a kind of sense. Why had she stolen them rather than pay for them? He should have known better than to ask. He got the whole story of her financial hardship now that she was on her own, including the cost of the funeral. It was an expensive business, dying.

When she'd finished, she fished a small white handkerchief from her coat pocket to wipe the tears from her eyes. It was the way she did this that reminded him of his mother, the way she had to move her glasses out of the way to get the handkerchief to her eyes. He told her to go home. She looked up at him in surprise, then clutched the handles of her bag, realising she should get out while the going was good. When she stood up her blue eyes were alert with curiosity.

'Why are you doing this?'

'I don't know.'

He had made thieves of so many people. But this one reminded him of his mother. He absolved her with a wave of his hand. Still she made a fuss of thanking him, reaching up to touch his collar. When she'd gone, he noticed the crumpled handkerchief on the floor and bent down to pick it up.

He had stepped into the lift and pressed the button for the ground floor before he realised that the lights weren't working. The doors hissed together and he was alarmed to be shut inside a box of night. He crossed himself without thinking, although he hadn't done so for years. He heard the machinery of the lift working – a slight gasp of the hydraulics he'd never noticed before – then he began to descend slowly through the darkness. He imagined that the lift was his coffin and he was descending into the earth. Then he wondered why they didn't bury people upright, what with cemetery space being at a premium. When his mother had died, hadn't he had to take out a personal loan to cover the funeral and the cost of the plot? As the woman had said, it was an expensive business.

The lift came to a halt, the doors slid apart, but no one was waiting to get in. He looked out at Lingerie. From the crowd of people shambling around the counters rose a line of perfect legs sheathed in stockings and tights, their toes pointing at the roof. Above them the elegant models stood on their plinths, dressed in camisoles and negligées, averting their eyeless faces like disdainful idols.

Some of the creations in there were unbelievable. They were designed to tempt men, so it made sense to put them on the same floor as Menswear. He'd apprehended one man, about his own age, respectable in his choice of casual wear, greying at the sides and balding on top, trying to cram an expensive Gossard scarlet basque into his inside pocket. He'd wanted to buy it – for his wife, he'd said at first, then had admitted later, when he'd got him in the cubby-hole, that it was for his mistress – but he'd felt too embarrassed to take it to a pay-point and hand it over to be wrapped. He'd begged him to let him off – poor man, in his Yves Saint Laurent polo shirt. Maybe not so poor: he'd probably get off with a small fine or an admonishment, and although he was in his fifties, he had a mistress – one who would wear a scarlet basque.

The doors hissed together and he was shut in with the darkness again. She hadn't wanted to be cremated, in case the soul turned out to be located in the hypothalamus, or some other part of the body. She'd had some funny notions that way. She'd believed in an afterlife, having been brought up a good Catholic, but in her later life – maybe because of him, because he'd turned his back on the priesthood – she'd stopped caring what form the afterlife might take. Heaven or reincarnation – she'd settle for either. In the hospice, she had accepted the services of the priest, the vicar and the visiting humanist, keeping her options open. If there had been a rabbi and a Buddhist coming round, she would have signed up with them too. With more eagerness, maybe, because they would be new to her, and she had always believed in anything she didn't know about, as if the very fact that she hadn't heard of it gave it credence, so complete was her humility.

There was the gasp of the hydraulics as the lift was released and he felt himself sinking again. It all seemed to take much longer in the dark.

He had watched her body shrink into itself like a withering fruit, but she'd gone on smiling, determined to keep up appearances. He remembered the last demented thing she had said to him as she lay there, scandalised by her own condition, about her bedside locker being bugged, about the other patients and their visitors being spies. Then she'd urged him to eat the fruit in the bowl.

'Have a banana, son,' she'd said, then died.

He remembered the moment when the faint pressure of her hand on his had faded away completely, leaving a dead hand there with no touch left in it.

None of it had made any sense to him then, but it did now as he was lowered slowly through the darkness. She'd died in public, in a ward full of strangers. They weren't involved with her death, but they were watching it. She was right – they were spies. And her bedside locker, with its fruit and its flowers and its cards bearing tactfully optimistic messages – in a way it had been bugged.

He hadn't eaten the fruit, but maybe he should have. She had wanted him to, but he'd remembered reading, at the Seminary, about the sin-eaters, the people in ancient times who were hired at funerals to eat beside the corpse and so take upon themselves the sins of the deceased.

If they buried people upright the graves would have to be deeper, of course, but they'd take up less horizontal space, which was what you were paying for, in the end. At the same time, the thought of people being buried in a standing position was ridiculous. It made him think of the dead standing in a queue, waiting to be served. They had chosen, and now they would have to pay the price. Think of the inscriptions: 'He was, and still is, a fine, upstanding citizen.'

He could hear a Tannoyed announcement passing from under his feet to above his head – where was he? Surely he'd reach the ground floor soon. Or maybe he'd gone past the ground floor and he was on his way back down to the Food Hall. The motion of the lift began to make him feel queasy, as if he'd lost control of his own movements and was part of the workings of the store. He felt as if he had been eaten and was now being slowly digested by a huge machine.

The lift came to a halt at last, but the doors didn't open. Where was he? Without the illuminated numbers above the door, it was hard to tell. In a dark lift, you could be anywhere. You could be in the confessional, except that there was no one to confess to. All you had was yourself. He felt the sweat trickle from his scalp and took the crumpled handkerchief from his pocket, but instead of dabbing his brow he brought it to his lips. It tasted faintly of salt. Then he felt himself begin to travel upwards through the darkness, like a slow missile launched into the night, or a soul departing the body.

THE WARNING

FRANK KUPPNER

A worried Mrs Clarke left the confessional box and looked round the large church uncertainly. It was virtually empty. That was one of the reasons why she liked to visit so early in the morning. The walk was good for you, and you didn't build up resentment by having to wait your turn for confession in a long queue of sinners. There was little risk involved. Usually two or three of the priests could be relied on to be in their boxes at that time of day; and Father Norman, whom she had particularly wanted to see, was nearly always among them. No doubt it was merely to ensure that penance would be on offer for any sinner who, after the events of the previous night, might need it in a hurry. But at this time of day no one ever seemed to be in very much of a hurry. Certainly no one was in a hurry on this particular morning. She hesitated on the marble floor outside the door, shadowed by a pillar. Then she made her mind up. She turned decisively and went back into the confessional.

– Hello, Father. It's only me. Agnes who just left. I'm sorry to say I'm right back again.

– Oh, hello. Did you forget something? Are there no others waiting?

– No; nobody. The fact is, there's something still troubling me.

– Is there? Well now, what might this be? Is it something you didn't confess to?

– No, I don't think it's that. Not quite that anyway. I don't think it's anything sinful. At least, I'm not sure. There seems to be so much changing nowadays.

– Not a bit of it. New strands are always being developed, Mrs Clarke, that's all. None of it is really new. It can't be. Not even the newly minted coins. No. So, what exactly is the problem?

– That's just it, Father. It's a bit of a problem. Advise me, Father, would you? About ghosts. What is the Church's position on ghosts?

– Well, we're very keen on at least one of them. I think you'll find that that much hasn't changed. But a lot would depend, I suppose, on what sort of a ghost it is that you're talking about.

– I mean the usual sort. What other sort is there?

– What sort of ghost is the usual sort, Agnes? Tell me. Describe it. If it helps, I can tell you that you're by no means the first to talk of such things in here. Have you seen a ghost in the church, is that it?

– Oh no! Why – is there a ghost in the church?

– I hardly think so myself; but some people have claimed to see one. We can't entirely rule it out, or something like it. Of course, it can't be anything pagan or malign, but we ourselves have a longstanding tradition of visions and visitations.

– What sort of things are seen? (asked Agnes, her interest somewhat piqued).

– Oh, the usual things, I dare say; but never mind them. It tends to be Joseph, I believe. No. The question is what is troubling you? What brings you back in here? You've come this far, you might as well go on right to the end of it.

– Yes. Well it's this. I can't work out whether I'm being

226

uniquely privileged, Father, or whether in fact I am just going off my head.

– Well, that's a genuine old dilemma and no mistake. Some of our finest minds have had much the same problem.

– Oh, I'm not at all claiming to be one of our finest minds, Father. Or anything near it come to that. The fact is I used to just laugh at the mention of such things. I used to have no time for them at all in fact. To tell you the simple God's truth, I once had a friend, Jean Murphy as was – I hope you don't know her – and she used to live directly opposite the church. And she said she had more than once seen lights swaying about and odd shadows passing late at night when nothing should have been happening. She's from Connemara. That's what she said anyway.

– Well, what's so odd about that? They would very likely have been preparations for whatever was going to be done in the church in the morning.

– Which is exactly what I said to her, Father. In almost exactly those words. She told me she had thought of that *of course*, and it looked to her to be something quite different although she wouldn't say quite what. She always liked her air of mystery, did Jean. She said I would be welcome to come along some time; she said she would phone me up whenever it was going on if I liked and I could come along and see for myself what sort of rehearsal it was.

– Hmm. And did you phone up and go along?

– No, I did not. I had better things to do with my time. Sleep, for one thing. As if I was going to go running round there at three in the morning or whatever it was on the off chance of seeing a couple of weird shadows swaying about. It was ridiculous. We fell out over it, in fact. I even mentioned her wig, which I had always sworn to myself I would never do. Which makes what happened a couple of nights ago all the stranger.

– All right then. Why not just forget about Mrs Murphy and her wig and you tell me what happened a couple of nights ago?

– Well, I'd like to but the thing is I don't know. Not for sure. That's why I wanted to have a word about it with you first.

– I'm getting a little confused here, Mrs Clarke. You saw a ghost, or you think you did. Is that it?

– I don't know, Father. Ever since my late husband died – do you remember him?

– Yes, a little. He didn't often come into the church, did he?

– No. He was a Marxist, Father. He had his own sort of holy book with pictures of Marx and Engels and Stalin in it. He came in at Christmas sometimes for the singing and that was about that. Better than nothing, I suppose. But I'm glad you remember him. He was as stubborn as a mule, but he meant well and I don't think he ever harmed anybody in his life. Not even when he ought to have done, if you don't mind my saying so.

– Yes, I remember him quite well. He was a fine-looking man.

– I often told him he would have made a fine-looking priest, Father.

– Good heavens! How many of us can claim as much?

– In fact, I told him once he would make a fine-looking Pope, if you'll forgive me saying so. He said a Cardinal would do him fine. Anything like that would get you off my back he said to me, talking about me, meaning because the clergy don't marry, though he was only joking of course. I still dream of him. In fact, I still dream of him a lot.

– That's only to be expected, Mrs Clarke.

– I didn't at first, but I do now. I'm always dreaming of him. In fact, that's why I'm here. Or thinking of him, you know? And sometimes it gets quite hard to tell which is which.

– One moment. Is it your late husband you want to see me about?

– Yes. Or something very like him. You know that way that you're not sure whether you're awake or asleep?

– It usually sorts itself out one way or another soon enough, does it not?

– Most of the time, Father. Most of the time. But perhaps not always.

– You dreamt of your husband?

– He appeared to me, yes.

– In a dream?

– I was in bed and it was early morning and all that.

– And you dreamt of him, is that not right?

– I dare say it is, Father. I dare say it is. I suppose that's really all there was to it. The only thing that still worries me is – well, I've dreamed about him often enough. I know what that's like. But this one was particularly vivid. Also there are one or two things about him that I have no wish at all to describe accurately, if you don't mind. No, the thing is this. I was wondering in fact, Father, whether it might not have been a vision. That's the thing I wanted to ask you. I thought maybe you could tell me that.

– Could tell you what?

– What the difference is exactly between a vision and a dream.

– Oh, right; I see. Well, as far as I remember, Mrs Clarke, the main difference, or one of them, is that when you have a vision you're awake. Unlike when you're dreaming.

– Yes, but I've been thinking about it, Father, and my feeling is that I was awake when I saw him that morning.

– Hmm. What did you think at the time?

Mrs Clarke paused for the briefest of moments before answering.

– Well, if I was sleeping I would hardly have known I was sleeping, would I?

– I dare say not, Mrs Clarke. Were you sleeping?

– I don't know. It was early in the morning. I think I certainly thought I had already woken up for the day.

– And had you?

– I don't know. I was thinking that if you could tell me what was possible and what wasn't then I would know what might have happened and what actually couldn't have done. Does that make sense?

– Yes, I would say it made perfect sense, Mrs Clarke. Well; tell me about your husband. Did he do anything? Did he say anything? Can you describe it to me?

– Well, he just said one or two personal things, and then he said he had come back to me with an important message.

– Those were his actual words, were they?

– Well, that was certainly what I think I heard.

– He had come back with a message for you?

– Yes.

– Did he say where he had come back *from*?

– No. But I got the impression he wasn't too happy about it. I deliberately didn't press him. Actually, it never even occurred to me.

– This becomes more than a little alarming, Mrs Clarke. And can you tell me what the message was? Did he leave one?

– Yes, he did.

– Can you tell me what it was?

– I think I have to, Father. He said he had come back for a moment as he happened to know for a fact that you are the Devil.

– A devil?

– I'm fairly sure he said *the* Devil, Father. I was struck by that even at the time. He mentioned you by name.

– By name? He knew my name? And what did you think of that? Did you believe him?

– Father, would I be here at all if I had believed him? I just want to know what I'm supposed to do and what it might mean, if it means anything at all. It shook me up quite a bit, Father.

– I can well imagine it might. I can't say it leaves me completely untouched either, Mrs Clarke, to be quite honest. I've had a few ripe things said about me in this parish I dare say since I came here some years ago, but this is the first time I've been identified as the Prince of Darkness. As far as I'm aware. God knows what they are saying about me behind my back. Did he say anything else? Not that that wasn't enough in itself, mind you.

– Well, actually, Father, he told me to go along and confront you with it. Not that that's why I'm here, of course not. But he said you would reply by using a mysterious phrase that would convince me right away that that is who you were.

– What phrase?

– What phrase? I don't know. Something about money. He didn't mention it clearly. I got the definite impression it was too ghastly to utter in full. But he left me with the feeling that I would recognise it all the same when I heard it – which, now I think of it, is not very flattering to me, is it?

– Not flattering to you? How do you think *I* feel? What else did he do? Who else did he choose to blast while he was on the premises?

– Well, that's just it. Do you think he really *was* on the premises?

– If I really thought that, he would be hearing very promptly from the lawyers, I can tell you that. What a nerve! What you had here, very obviously, is a most peculiar dream. A most peculiar dream. Even as a dream, of course, it must have some sort of significance to it, though I have no idea what that might be, and I shudder even to think of it. Don't you think it was a dream? Wouldn't you *prefer* it was a dream, rather than a vision?

– I suppose so, Father; now you mention it.

– If that were the sort of thing a vision is, I'm glad I'm spared them, that's all I can say. The mind can play tricks, Mrs Clarke. The waking state and the sleeping state can sometimes seem to overlap. Need I say more? My advice to you is just try to ignore it. Ignore it. We all have strange dreams. I have strange dreams myself sometimes, in fact.

– Do you, Father? Do you mind if I ask what they're about?

– Oh, they're absurd more than anything else. They're not worth a moment of our attention. I don't remember them anyway. Put it all behind you and get on with real life, that's my advice to you.

– Do these dreams involve people you used to know?

– What else could they involve? But I think we've had enough about dreams to last us for a long while.

– I suppose in the back of my mind there's the thought of what I ought to do if he comes back.

– Comes back? You talk as if he had really turned up! Comes back from where, had you thought of that? If he comes back, tie him up and ring for me. I'll be round in very short order indeed to confront him, don't you worry about that. Anyway, I can see there's someone else outside there, waiting his turn. So. Go away and think about what I've said to you. You'll very likely find that this matter clears itself up on its own. Strange things happen. Behave dutifully and put your trust in God and no harm can possibly come to you in the end. God bless you. Now go.

– I'm sorry to have taken up so much of your time, Father.

– Not at all. That is what I am here for.

– Father, I haven't offended you, have I? I do very much hope I haven't offended you.

– Not at all. Not at all. It has all been most entertaining, to say the least. If he ever does come back, do let me know. But for the moment let us just try to get by as best we can without him, shall we? I think that would be the best thing for all concerned.

He repeated a departing blessing over her, and soon Mrs Clarke was once again in the aisle outside. To her surprise, she saw there was no one else there waiting to get in to the confessional. Perhaps whoever it was had gone away; or perhaps the priest had made a mistake; or perhaps he had simply wanted to get rid of her. Who, she wondered, could blame him for that?

She made her way over to a bank of candles, put her money in the slot, picked one up and lit it. She placed it in its holder, gazing mesmerised at its peculiarly intense glow, trying to think for what cause she might be lighting it, something which could be better than the mere cause of lighting a candle in a somewhat gloomy interior for the delight of the act itself. Then she turned and began to walk to the side-door of the church.

As she did so, she saw a figure come in through the main entrance and go over in the direction of Father Norman's confessional. It was another priest. Then she saw that it was Father Norman himself. But how could it be? Surely he would not have had time to leave his place, go outside, and now come back in again? Hardly; unless he had run silently in and out. And why would he do that, even if he could?

For a few moments the two of them were quite close. Mrs Clarke knew it was wrong to raise her voice in such a sacred place, and she had no desire to mark herself out; but when they were at their nearest point she none the less found herself calling: 'Father Norman, is that you?' Quickly, without stopping, the priest turned his head towards her. He frowned and was obviously somewhat angered at such a breach in protocol. He waved his hand to indicate their sacred surroundings and angrily muttered something before disappearing off towards and into the confessional box. Mrs Clarke had not been able to make out quite what it was he had said. Even so, she had a vague sense that she had heard it said before. The more she thought about it, the more certain of this she became. She hesitated for a while beside the door, uncertain what to do next.

THE OLDEST
WOMAN IN SCOTLAND

JACKIE KAY

The oldest woman in Scotland still bakes. The day she stops baking she will stop being the oldest woman in Scotland. She bakes even although none of the other people living in her sheltered housing scheme, The Beeches, ever has her round to their house. But they always come to her house. Ring the bell and shout, Are you in? Are you in? knowing full well she is never out. Knowing that all her groceries are bought for her by her youngest daughter Elsie, who is seventy-two. Oh they all come and fair gobble up her baking. Her light sponge, her currant buns, her rock cakes. Into their old crumbling mouths, the crumbling cake goes. Some of them have not the wherewithal to wipe their old mouths and are quite capable of having crumbs stuck to their chin the whole length of an afternoon. Just as the old swines are perfectly at ease sitting about the place, until the oldest woman in Scotland has to boot them out. To do that, she has to stand up and go to the door. For they won't take a hint. She has to stand up, go to the door, yank it open and say, Is it not about time you were home? Oh the old articles can't take anything subtle.

No one will ever think of taking their plate through to the kitchen to help the oldest woman in Scotland. Nor of giving the plates a wee wash. She has to stand by the sink, at her age, a hundred and six, and rinse them under the cold tap. Never the hot. She has never had a lazy day, nor a long lie in her life. The idea of having a long lie upsets her. What would anybody want with lazing around in their bed for half the morning, whilst the sun just goes up and up and up? How could anyone bear to lie about in their old bedclothes reeking of sweat and God knows what? It is strange to her this idea of the long lie. Do they dream when they have these long lies? Do they just sink in and out of terrible dreams? Oh, it makes her dizzy just to contemplate it. And of course it just hides pure idleness, for people that weren't brought up to know the meaning of hard work.

The reason the oldest woman in Scotland is the oldest woman in Scotland is all down to hard work. Give hard work its due. If it hadn't been for the fact that as a young woman she walked all the way from Lochgelly to Alloa to thon sheep dye place and then all the way back – three hours' walking a day, never mind the work, and the awful dye on her fingers; if it hadn't been for washing the backs of seven miners and their moleskins – and this in the days before the washing machine; if it hadn't been for the constant nose to the grindstone of the sewing, the cooking, the cleaning, the oldest woman in Scotland would not be where she is today. And although modest to the end of her hem-stitch, on her long wide skirt, she will admit that for her age, she is looking good. An awful lot better than some of them that are twenty years younger. True enough: the fine blush that used to appear on her cheeks willingly now has to be put on with a bit of rouge powder. All the real colour has finally drained out of her cheeks. It went when she became one hundred, the same year that she gave up her pipe at night. The eyes are drooping and dropping and heavy now, there's no getting away from it. And the teeth are not her own, have not been her own for years now; so long, in fact, that if real teeth were to suddenly smile in her mouth, she'd be alarmed, frightened. There's a comfort in these odd flat false teeth. The way she can move them around, the clucking sound she can make with them, if she wants another noise in her house; the way she can just get rid of them altogether at night and watch them float like wee sharks in the glass beside her. You couldn't do that with the real ones. You couldn't just haul them out when they annoyed you. But her hair is all there and not as thin as Jessie Harvey's or Ruby Baxter's or Nell MacIntosh's. Yesterday, the oldest woman noticed that not only is Nell MacIntosh's hair thinning, but bald patches gleam like secrets underneath the thin straggly hairs. Poor Nell. And her only eighty-five, too. A youngster compared with the oldest woman in Scotland. A skittery jittery youngster.

But look at her hair. She's got to admit that her hair does not look like the hair of a woman who is one hundred and six years old. It is pure white, where it used to be blonde, but it is thick, and it still has a bit of a bounce in it. If you work hard all your life, your scalp will respond. Your scalp will not get dandruff or alopecia, or dry hair. If you work hard and look after yourself and eat the right foods, you'll keep your hair; you'll not end up being one of those bald, hard-faced Scottish women that go about the place buying bargains. For years she's known this secret to health. Hard work. Aye. There's many that will shirk from hard work, including ones in her own family. But she's no shirker. The shirkers always fall down with mysterious illnesses, the like of which she has never heard. Diseases, she's quite sure, the lazy folk have gone about the place inventing.

The oldest woman in Scotland has had the flu four times in her life. Piles after she gave birth – big black soor plooms. A bit of arthritis in her back, but not, thank God, in her hands. Mild angina pains. Now that she is cracking on towards the new millennium, towards devolution and the new Scottish parliament, towards all these new computers, and new ways of talking about sex, the oldest woman in Scotland would like to see the basics acknowledged – hard work, very little alcohol, no long lies.

In her day you were never told anything about sex. Not a word. The words they use these days, the oldest woman in Scotland scandalises herself, Oh God's trousers! The words they use. The things they do! She never knew anything about any of it. You just lay there in the dark mostly. When Edward VIII abdicated, the oldest woman in Scotland was in bed with her husband, she had what she now realises was her first and only orgasm. It shook her about like the only shortbread in a tin. A great big wha-hay inside her. The man's clipped voice on the wireless going on behind her: 'I can no longer perform my duties without the help and support of the woman I love.' That was what, 1936? She was forty-six. It never happened again, that wha-hay.

Outside the house of number eight, The Beeches, is a blue plaque which states: *Here lives the oldest woman in Scotland*. It is of considerable worry to her what will happen to this plaque when she goes. Will they give it to the next oldest woman in Scotland? Or will they change the wording and put, 'Here *lived* the oldest woman in Scotland.' Of course she'd have a preference for the second choice.

This morning she is up early at 7 a.m. It is her birthday. She is one hundred and seven. Another year in, she says to herself and shakes her head back and forth, a bit of a wobbly shake. Well, there's one thing for certain: the oldest woman in Scotland is not getting any younger. What kind of day is it? It takes her a while to pull back the curtains: she has to move them along bit by bit by bit. A good five minutes. Once, she would have given them a sharp tug and the sky would have suddenly appeared. It is drizzly, wouldn't you just know it. Not a day for going out. Yet out she must go today. For her daughter is holding a little party for her. She shuffles into her bathroom and washes her face with cold water. (The secret to her good skin.) She gets herself dressed, which takes a tedious amount of time. Pulling on her drawers, her tights, her vests, her blouse. The buttons are nigh near impossible now. They slip out of her soft thumbs and she's got to try again and again to manage the blighters. Today she'll wear her purple cardigan, people have admired her in that. And some pearls around her neck. A dab of rouge and a bit of lipstick. She's vain still and she knows she is vain.

She's not feeling like going out today. She doesn't go out hardly at all now, and when she does the bite of the air just about knocks her for six. It fairly snaps at you, the air, like a bad tempered auld dug. She puts her scarf on, manages to tie the knot under her chin. Her neck is wrinkled now. There's no point denying it. She's all ready now for the granddaughter, who has come up from England for the occasion with her English-talking son and daughter, to collect her in her snazzy metallic blue car.

The oldest woman in Scotland's daughter does not bake, even though she was well taught. Hold the sieve high in the air. Crumble the butter and flour between your fingers. Beat and beat until the top of your arm hurts. 'Does it hurt? No? Well, you're no done yet.' Today on the oldest's one hundred and seventh birthday, she knows she must face a shop-bought cake with too hard icing; and she knows that she must try and find it within herself to smile.

'Smile, Great Gran! Say cheese!' shouts her youngest great grandchild in that English voice. She smiles a wee thin smile along her lips, not letting her teeth show. She doesn't like toothy smiles or grins that make her look gormless. She may be one hundred and seven but she still has her dignity to consider. She is not going to wreck things now by leaving a picture for posterity, her sitting on that sofa with her son-in-law, daughter, grandchildren and great grandchildren, smiling like some daft old loony. 'Come on, Gran, you can do better than that! Everybody shout *sizzling sausages*!' In the name of God. 'Sizzling sausages!' they all shout loud enough to break the inner tube of the oldest woman in Scotland's ear.

The table is laid with bits and pieces and everybody's done their best, true enough. But there's no home baking. And the tablecloth is paper! Paper with big flowers painted on it. 'Do you like my table?' her youngest daughter says, 'Flower of Scotland'. Her son-in-law bursts into loud Glaswegian song: 'Oh Flower of Scotland, When will I see your like again,' his mouth full of food. How did her youngest most attractive daughter end up with that uncouth man? The very sight of her son-in-law still makes the oldest woman in Scotland stick out her chin, even though he is seventy-six and she is one hundred and seven. She notices he's the only one that's not bought her a wee gift. 'Open your presents, Great Gran,' they're shouting. So she opens them. Chocolates. She'll have two of them a night with the telly till they're all done. A new nightie. What's she wanting with nighties, she's got plenty. A new cardigan; what's she wanting with cardies, she's got plenty. A bottle of Grand Marnier. Well she can have a wee nip of that in the drawn-in nights.

The daughter is out of breath from all the effort of the wee party as if it had been any work when it's all shop-bought. 'Are you alright, Mum?' she says, waiting for the oldest woman in Scotland to pay her a compliment. Well she will not be forced into compliments. 'Aye, fine, fine,' she says and sups the tea that is far too weak. Suddenly someone shouts for speeches and her great grandson stands up on a chair and says: 'We are gathered here today to celebrate the birthday of our great grandmother, who also happens to be the oldest woman in Scotland. We wish her health and we are proud to have her in our family. Each birthday, she gets a card from the Queen. But the Queen doesn't love her like we do.' The speech moves the oldest woman in Scotland and a few tears come out the corners of her eyes. It would have been perfect if only the great grandson didn't have an English accent like Edward VIII. She had to keep saying to her daughter, 'What's that he's saying?' and it just about spoilt it for her. It's an awful shame when families move away to England and lose their good Scottish tongues. The young boy doesn't even ken who Rabbie Burns was. It's a shame the oldest woman in Scotland could do without – a great grandson that's never tasted a haggis.

They look a queer family anyway all lined up on the couch for the camera. There's her youngest, her favourite daughter, Elsie, who has still got braw skin like her mother used to, a natural bloom in her cheeks; there's her scruffy son-in-law with his hair falling in every direction and the shirt of a dead friend on his back; there's her overweight black granddaughter with her bonny face and her dark eyes and her long dangling earrings; there's the great grandson – black as the Earl of Hell's waistcoat, with such tight curls on his head and his English voice; and there's the great granddaughter with her long loose black curly hair and her cheeky wee smile. Every new homehelp that comes to the oldest woman in Scotland's sheltered house, says, 'Oooh who's that you're with?' And once when she replied, 'My grandchildren and great grandchildren,' this particularly gormless girl says to her, 'How did that happen?'

'How did what happen?' the oldest woman in Scotland practically shouted at the homehelp.

'Well, they're black, aren't they?'

'My daughter adopted them,' the oldest woman in Scotland said, trying for the right note in her voice. 'What a nice thing to do,' the homehelp said and busied herself with the dusting. 'They've got good skin like me,' the oldest woman in Scotland said, sensing an insult somewhere.

As she gets older, the insults become more sneaky and clever and she has to be on her toes, sharp as a tack to pick them up. People think just because she's old they can get anything past her. 'Why don't we open your chocolates now, Great Gran?' the English boy pipes up. 'You will not! These are for my lonely nights with the TV on. The rest of the world's got company, so I'll have my chocolates.' Her daughter does the strange breathing again.

'What's the matter with you?' the oldest woman in Scotland swings round and faces her daughter. 'You're all red in the face.'

'Don't start, Mum,' says Elsie, pleading as if she was just a young lassie.

Oh if she could just take a swipe at her, a good hard swipe across her face. 'Start what? It's no me that's starting anything.'

'He's only being friendly,' says the granddaughter.

'It's your birthday, Mum. Don't spoil your birthday,' says Elsie.

The rest of the oldest woman in Scotland's large family are not talking to her and are therefore not present at her one hundred and seventh birthday party. 'Do you know I haven't heard from our Billy for over thirty years? Do you know that time that I was at our Robert's funeral, Peggy just plain ignored me, pretended she didn't see me? That was at the funeral of our own brother! We know what she was after though. Hobnobbing with those others, looking for favours.'

'What are you talking about, Great Gran?' the English granddaughter asks.

'None of your business!' the oldest woman in Scotland replies. 'Children these days expect answers and it's not right. We never expected to be answered in our day you know,' she says.

'Mum!' Elsie says. 'Please, it's your birthday.'

'That family of mine,' the oldest woman in Scotland continues.

'Mum!' Elsie interrupts her. 'They are all dead. You are the last surviving member of the family, though you were the eldest of ten!'

'That family of mine,' continued the oldest woman in Scotland, completely ignoring her daughter's entreaties, 'will send me to an early grave.'

'An early grave?' her daughter says. 'An early grave?'

ABOUT THE AUTHORS

Tom Bryan was born in Canada in 1950, and has long been resident in Scotland. He lives in Wester Ross. A widely published poet and fiction-writer, his work has appeared in leading Scottish magazines and anthologies, and has been broadcast on Radio 4 and Radio Scotland.

Ron Butlin was born in Edinburgh, and was brought up in Hightae near Dumfries. He has been a full-time writer for many years, winning several Scottish Arts Council Book Awards. His work has been translated into over ten languages. He now lives in Edinburgh.

Andrew Byrd was born in Blackpool in 1969. He has lived in Edinburgh since 1994.

Regi Claire grew up in Switzerland and now lives in Edinburgh with her husband and their dog. Her first collection of stories, *Inside–Outside*, is due out this year.

Linda Cracknell was born in Holland and came to live in Scotland via Surrey, Devon and Tanzania. Currently she lives in Highland Perthshire, where she works for an environmental charity.

Morgan Downie enjoyed an Anglo-Orcadian upbringing before finally graduating as a Scottish man. The centre of his world is his daughter, but in his spare time he dreams of making beautiful books.

Bill Duncan was born in Fife in 1953 and lives in Dundee. He has had his non-fiction, poetry and fiction published in a range of magazines and books north and south of the border.

Michel Faber is Dutch by birth. He grew up in Australia and has lived for the past six years in the Scottish Highlands, where he writes stories and the occasional novel.

Mark Fleming was born in Edinburgh in 1962. His fiction has appeared in *The Big Issue*, *Cutting Teeth*, *Flamingo Scottish Short Stories*, and *The Picador Book of Contemporary Scottish Fiction*.

Alison Grove lives with her husband and two small children, and works part time at a hotel. What time she has left is devoted to writing.

Kathryn Heyman grew up in Australia where she worked as an actor and playwright. She has lived in Scotland since 1994 and has published one novel, *The Breaking*. Her second novel, *With Your Hands on the Wheel*, is to be published in June 1999 by Phoenix House.

Jules Horne was born and raised in Hawick. He had a tough start in life thanks to XX chromosomes and child labour as an envelope-to-greeting-card clipper in the family firm. He is currently a broadcaster for a Swiss radio station.

Jackie Kay's first novel, *Trumpet*, will be published by Picador this August. She lives in Manchester with her son.

Frank Kuppner was born in Glasgow in 1951, and is a poet, novelist and journalist. He won the 1995 McVitie's Writer of the Year Award with his book *Something Very Like Murder*.

Gordon Legge was brought up in Grangemouth and now lives in Edinburgh. He has three novels published and a collection of short stories.

Jacqueline Ley is a former college lecturer and recent graduate of the M. Litt. Creative Writing course at St. Andrews University. She is currently writing her second novel.

Brian McCabe grew up in Bonnyrigg and Falkirk. He studied Philosophy and English Literature at Edinburgh University. He has lived as a freelance writer since 1980.

Fiona MacInnes was born and now lives in Stromness, Orkney. She was a former islands councillor but is now mothering, crofting, writing and painting.

Morag MacInnes was born in Stromness, Orkney. She now lives in Lincoln, and is completing a novel about Hudson's Bay.

About the Authors

Alison MacLeod is currently taking a year out before starting a Law degree at Edinburgh University. She lives at home with her parents and two brothers.

David Nicol now lives in Aberdeen, where he is writing a novel. He stopped planting trees some time ago, and received a Scottish Arts Council Writer's bursary in 1997.

John Pacione was born in Dundee and currently lives in London. He has previously had stories published in *Panurge* and *Stand*.

Elizabeth Reeder was born in Chicago, but now lives in Glasgow. She works for a feminist organisation and believes in the diversity and accessibility of writing.

Cynthia Rogerson is a Californian who has been living in Ross-shire on and off for twenty years. She has four children. She has previously been published in various Scottish literary magazines.

Dilys Rose is the author of *Madame Doubtfire's Dilemma* and *Our Lady of the Pickpockets*. Her forthcoming third collection of short stories is called *War Dolls*. She is currently completing a stage play, *Learning the Paso Doble*, and a novel.

Alexander McCall Smith is Professor of Medical Law at the University of Edinburgh. He is married, with two children. His forthcoming novel, set in Botswana, *The No 1 Ladies' Detective Agency*, is to be published by Polygon this year.

Raymond Soltysek was born in 1958. He lives in Paisley. He began writing in 1992 after joining the Paisley Writers' Group. His short stories have been published in various anthologies and Scottish literary magazines.

Ruth Thomas was born in Kent in 1967. Her first collection of short stories, *Sea Monster Tattoo*, was published in 1997. She was shortlisted for the Saltire First Book Award (1997) and shortlisted for the Mail on Sunday/John Llewelyn Rhys Prize for Fiction (1997). She is currently working on a second collection and a novel.